The Janice Brown Series
MYSTERY AT THE
RED WHITE
& BLUE

SASSY SUE ABBOTT

World Castle Publishing, LLC
Pensacola, Florida
Copyright © Sassy Sue Abbott 2018
Paperback ISBN: 9781629899190
eBook ISBN: 9781629899206
First Edition World Castle Publishing, LLC, May 14, 2018
http://www.worldcastlepublishing.com
Licensing Notes
Cover: Karen Fuller
Editor: Lisa Petrocelli

Table of Contents

CHARACTER LIST

WASHINGTON DC

JANICE BROWN — a perky consulting dietitian, grew up in Florida on the Ranch at Bay Branch near Illahaw, Florida. She escaped with Charlie to Russia when he is shot and where the US Embassy issued a new passport in the name of Bonnie Watkins, Captain of the US Army. Her folks call her EJ, but her given name is Elsa Janine Brown. Leaving dead bodies on the kitchen floor outside Moscow, she's been tasked with organizing a veteran's outpatient diet clinic outside of DC. Charlie coordinates a professional decorator to arrange Bonnie's DC apartment. Janice could become addicted to the VIP treatment. What possible trouble could a group of ladies armed with photographs to assemble family memory scrapbooks, and quilters cause in their after-hours use of the diet clinic facilities?

CARRIE CUNNINGHAM — A US Army dietitian working on her master's degree and Janice's co-worker and assistant. Janice discovered she also works for Frank.

CHARLIE SMITH — Janice's sexy boyfriend she'd met over coffee when catching a red-eye flight. He dumped her at a B&B near Key West. Janice hadn't seen him in ten years until he was shot. There is some confusion on Charlie's day job. Over coffee he said he worked for a construction company. Recently he said he worked with the government alphabet agencies, now with USDA which was to be a cushy job before retirement. Janice moved to DC to rekindle their explosive relationship.

CONSTANCE REYNOLDS — Dr. Reynold's was one of Janice's favorite professors for classes in Dietetics and Nutrition at her Mississippi Alum. Later in graduate school she was her major professor and they correspond frequently. Colleges require courses in many areas related to food, which is the heart of health and nutrition.

DAN RUDOLPH O'CONNEL — Devil Doc to most. He joins the Red, White and Blue Veteran's Center as the in-house medic.

SARGENT MAJOR DOBBS — His duties are to convert an abandoned strip mall to an outpatient diet clinic and babysit the girlfriend of one of his Vietnam buddies. Definitely not a challenging assignment for a man with service stripes the length of his sleeve, or so he thought.

FRANK WARDE — Frank and Charlie have been friends since Vietnam. Frank runs everything.

JOANNE WAINWRIGHT — Janice's sorority sister in Mississippi. They continue to stay close when Janice (now using the name Bonnie) moves to DC.

RANDY — One of Frank's biker crew, a forensics specialist with an engineering degree. He washed out of the SEAL's because he couldn't gain weight. When he lost a bet, he was assigned to be Janice's assistant. He doesn't mind; he's exploring a possible relationship with Carrie, Janice's co-worker.

SUE LI — Sue Li fell in love with Brian Timmerman and Ron Jones from their days at a college beach house in California. She works for her uncle, Mr. Tao in his Chinese and US brothels.

She helped Brian and Ron obtain jobs in the CIA. Will their plot eliminate Mr. Tao to gain their lives together?

THE RANCH AT BAY BRANCH

EDWARD JOHN BROWN — Janice's dad, a cattleman and citrus grower, and a man with a mysterious military past of his own. He has the same initials as Janice, "EJ." Everyone calls him John.

EVA BELLE BROWN — Janice's mom, a classic Southern lady and a wonderful baker. Her apple nut cake is to die for. She and Edward John Brown, Janice's dad, meet Janice in London to explore family secrets after a tour of the French battlefields and uncover key information vital to national security.

LONDON

TREVOR AUGUSTINE and **ANGUS BUTTERWICK** — Janice's tour guides when she joins her parents in England to locate missing family history from WWI and assists Janice in solving a major security breech.

ELIZABETH ADDISON — Raised in Featherlawn, England, and spent the summers across the pasture to the Ranch at Bay Branch in Illahaw, Florida. When Anderson Brown, John's uncle, was drafted into the US Army during WWI, he married Elizabeth, his childhood sweetheart, in the stately church on the hill in the English countryside.

CHAPTER ONE

The web seats on the C-130 were gnawing into her fanny. Janice hated those web seats. She'd departed Moscow in the dark leaving dead bodies on the kitchen floor of the general's chateau in the Russian countryside. Only two hours, two torturous hours before touchdown in Germany. Maybe she could grab a nod or two. If she was sleeping, nobody could talk to her. Hearing wasn't an issue since the plane was deafening. She couldn't hear anything with or without earplugs. Her nose twitched at the smell of the insides of military cargo planes heavy from diesel fuel and the warm, earthy scent of wooden pallets sliding across metal ridges on the airplane floor. Why did Army green tarps have the sickening acid odor?

Two weeks before, she'd arrived in Kamchatka using a forged Russian passport, but on military flights her new military ID card was everything she needed. She'd used her birth name while they were getting Charlie out of the country. Had she known the circumstances, maybe she would have reconsidered, but she didn't have multiple identities like members of Charlie's and Frank's teams. Use of her birth name concerned the US Embassy in Moscow and they insisted she operate with an alias—Captain

Bonnie Watkins—for the trip home. She chuckled as she'd used aliases her entire life. The birth name on her birth certificate was Elsa Janine Brown. Her family called her EJ, which worked well until she went to college in Mississippi, where *refined* women weren't called by initials. The school reluctantly enrolled her as Janice, which she preferred anyway. Using an alias was for the safety of Charlie; but also, the other men on his team. *"If they find you, they've found Charlie and the rest of us,"* she was warned. Frank revealed Charlie was still on someone's radar. But at least she and Charlie were going to be in the same city, even in the same building. She was willing to try again with Charlie. She was looking forward to sharing time with him, but he had broken her heart when he'd left her stranded in Key West ten years before.

For each flight on the way to DC, she was listed on the military passenger manifest under different names. Each of her travel outfits had appropriate rank, unit insignias, and dog tags, and were packaged in individual Army camo bags inside a larger travel bag—an experimental design with a waterproof lining to hold service boots in a special compartment. Where Frank found combat boots, shined to perfection, well broken in, and in her size, she doubted he would ever tell her. However, the green jumpsuit for the first hop was embarrassingly snug. She guessed she could accept it as a compliment the team believed she was so slim and petite. But to wear the flight suit she wiggled, held her breath, and stood extra tall to close the zipper. She'd have to starve forever if this was to be her military wardrobe. Hurray for the extraordinary military standards for double-stitched seams and thread as tough as steel cables to hold the uniform together.

The jumpsuit contained zippered pockets at her thighs and ankles to hold personal identification and a newly issued Bonnie Watkins passport. The bulky field jacket hid the tightness of the jumpsuit. Her mother, the model of Southern etiquette, would have fussed the jumpsuit "touched her skin," and right now she felt her skin and fabric were practically one.

Charlie had given her a few lessons on whom to salute and how. He was adamant: no makeup, don't be friendly, avoid eye contact. "Look out the window, read a field manual, don't look at anyone! And, heaven forbid with your Southern accent, speak as little as possible." She tried to act serious. Charlie said Gustoff had sent her a message, "Avoid leaving fingerprints." She liked Gustoff, maybe because he lived in Dutch Harbor where she had worked as a public health nutritionist. But he was an expert on leaving no fingerprints and trained her in concealment techniques while working together in the galley on the Russian cruise liner during their escape from Alaska to Russia.

Charlie and Frank rehearsed common questions and appropriate responses she might encounter as she processed in and out of Air Force bases in Germany and Fairbanks. She laughed at the names chosen for her travel aliases: first, Major Greene, then Sgt. White. She was to use her own name of Brown for the flight from Alaska to DC. In theory, if anyone remembered her travel names, the hope was they'd be confused as to the color of her name. For each persona, included were a selection of pocket items described as "stuff" — ticket stubs, gum wrappers, family pictures. If someone did link her to an earlier travel alias, she had the right stuff in her pockets to deny their claim and to confirm the current identity.

At the hotel in Moscow she practiced her denial response in the bathroom mirror. "No, I'm Cindy Greene. You must have me confused with someone else. Many people have told me I have one of those generic Midwestern faces." She hoped the situation didn't arise, but regardless, once on the plane she rehearsed the spiel in her mind. If she didn't talk to anyone, hopefully she could travel unnoticed.

Her curly locks were out of control despite attempts to tuck them under the uniform cap. Gone was her long auburn hair she usually twisted and pinned. The flyaway floozy style gave her the appearance of an insignificant nerd-queen, a caricature of a major from a quartermaster unit, clearly nonthreatening. But more importantly, someone no one would likely notice. Bonnie smiled looking at the gigantic Army-issue gloves for the ride to Germany. At least her hands would be warm and the gloves would minimize fingerprints.

When the plane arrived in Germany, she dashed to the restroom and changed. For the following segment she was Sgt. White from a supply unit headed to Fort Wainwright outside of Fairbanks. Name tags, rank insignias, and unit patches were changed for the second flight. The uniform was the Army's classic tailored skirt and jacket and polished low heels. She supposed the jacket was regulation until she found a note telling her to put the other passports in the pockets in the lining along the side seams. With a glob or two of hair gel to tame her wild hair, and a pair of military-issue, clunky black-rimmed reading glasses, optimistically no one would recognize her in different attire. She hung the regulation leather purse over her shoulder, pushed her shoulders back, and walked swiftly to catch her flight.

Charlie proposed living in DC would aid the transition to her new identity as Bonnie Watkins, a captain in the US Army and was flattered when she was offered a position with the State Department. She didn't know how arrangements were made but was impressed. With the State Department assignment, she would continue in her profession as a consulting nutritionist, and would be working with embassy personnel worldwide to create special menus and provide diet information for diplomatic personnel and visiting dignitaries. It sounded benign enough and was certainly a departure from her niche specializing in compiling hospital inspection paperwork.

She wasn't sure what Charlie did. In Moscow, he said he worked for the government. It seemed as if everyone around them worked for the government. Her sorority sister and college roommate, JoAnne, went to work for the FBI after graduation and had recently transferred to the CIA. Charlie's friend Miller, JoAnne's husband, still worked for the FBI. Charlie had transferred to USDA a few months before he was shot in Mexico, but details concerning his job before the recent promotion were sketchy. From clues in hush-hush conversations she could tell he did something mysterious. Military people seemed to be near to assist. And there was a group of men who were friends of Charlie and Frank that they'd met in Vietnam.

Frank lived somewhere in the Florida Everglades; well, at least he said he had a post office box in Ochopee. He was a member of the motorcycle gang who helped shuttle Charlie to Russia. She'd even met Frank's wife, Bonnie, at the strip club when she was trying to keep Charlie off the grid after his injuries. She wondered if Bonnie was her actual name, or if it was also an alias like her own. Frank was bulky and formidable, both mentally and physically. His appearance changed, she guessed based on the assignment. When she met him in Daytona, he was in Levis and leather with wild gray hair pulled into a ponytail and a graying beard. In Colorado they changed clothes and he appeared to be a weekend hunter dressed in foliage-patterned camo and a corduroy vest. She'd seen him go without sleep for days when he and his crew retrieved her. It was a drive of controlled frenzy from Daytona to Bellingham under his direction.

She'd met a number of men who worked with Frank and Charlie. Gustoff hid them in abandoned WWII tunnels when they were in Dutch Harbor, and had bought their escape from Alaska on a Russian cruise liner to meet Charlie's friends in

Russia. To everyone's surprise Gustoff and the ship's captain served together in the Russian Army. There was Roger, a lanky cowboy type, who called her "ma'am" when he applied for work as a tomato grower where she ran the loading dock for a friend of her dad's, later to realize on the way to Russia that Roger also worked for Frank and Charlie. Unbeknownst to her, Charlie had sent him to run interference when he discovered she ran a packing house in a rowdy neighborhood.

In Russia the former motorcycle gang, each a member of Charlie's crew, transformed into college professors or business travelers, clean-shaven and dressed in a wardrobe of tortoiseshell-rimmed glasses, tweed jackets, or cardigans. Charlie said Randy would meet her plane when he arrived in DC. She'd met him for a few minutes when they took Charlie to a clinic in Daytona Beach, and again when he ran the com center at the Russian chateau, but events were chaotic and she didn't have time to visit. He was one of the tallest among the crew. Surely, she would recognize him at the airport.

She was still uncertain how she felt when she discovered Charlie was watching her from arm's length. Was it his love for her, or did he keep an eye on her purely to deal with his own guilt after he abandoned her near Key West? She wondered if his friends would have taken the trouble to find her if he hadn't been shot. She was in love with Charlie and had been since those few hours they spent together over coffee waiting for a midnight flight. She wanted to try again; it was worth the gamble. Charlie seemed to agree and had even found her an apartment in his same building. Her heart wasn't ready to move under his roof.

Months before the trip to Russia with Charlie there'd been a handful of crazy projects. There was a trip to China to investigate a shipment of Florida organically grown grapefruit contaminated with fruit flies, and recently a contract at the spa in Georgia. The pay was respectable, and her consulting business was actually making a profit enough to hire a coworker and assistant, Carrie Cunningham. Later she discovered that Carrie was also one of Frank's team and reported to Roger.

Charlie and some of his friends were in their luxurious suite at the Moscow hotel when stacks of official papers arrived for her to sign to complete the name change. The atmosphere was playful, she remembered, such a contrast to the group's usual mission-driven demeanor. There was champagne, salutes, and plates of cold sliced salmon and bowls of caviar in chipped ice, two of her favorites, and a stacked cart of delightful delicacies for the group. For dessert, a white coconut-covered cake with almond custard between the layers was served, also one of her favorites. Sometime during the morning, Charlie whispered, "Do you love me?" Of course, she responded, "Yes, I do!" It was a perfect day. After the crowd left, she and Charlie raided the bar, giggled, and made love deep into the night.

A day or two later Charlie left and packages began to arrive with uniforms and a detailed schedule of the military flights for the trip to DC. She pondered if wearing a military uniform would be considered disrespectful by some, but Charlie convinced her it was the best strategy to travel home, courtesy of bureaucratic military paperwork. *What a twist of fate*, she reflected. She'd applied for a coveted Army dietetic internship to complete the mandatory year of hands-on training in nutrition after college to obtain credentials as a dietitian, but was told she was above their age limit. What an honor to be serving as a dietitian in the Army Medical Corp, even if it was a cover assignment for the State Department. Charlie and Frank knew she'd be seriously disappointed if at least occasionally they didn't find her a nutrition project or two.

The plane took a sudden bump and brought her thoughts

back to the trip from Russia to Florida.

Once wheels-down in Alaska at Fort Wainwright, she caught a cab to the Fairbanks Mall to purchase clothes to fly to DC. Shopping, she was at the mercy of the store displays: two pairs of dark twill cargo slacks, a plaid flannel shirt in dark blues and blacks, and a soft white wrinkle-proof tailored shirt to wear underneath the flannel. She grabbed a few extra shirts and non-military underwear to carry in a newly purchased backpack. She paid cash.

The guys had planned for possible contingencies, even a soft bag to stow used costumes to mail in a prepaid box to a post office near Tampa. She removed identification tags and unit insignias and mailed them separately via Express Mail to a post office box in a town near Pensacola, another rural town listed solely on local county maps, addresses Frank insisted she memorize. After having her hair colored at the mall beauty shop, she decided the pixie cut wasn't too terrible. The style was mainstream compared to the biker bleached-blonde from the Russian trip. She had the last appointment of the evening and took a cab to the Fairbanks airport.

A ticket was waiting at the counter for Janice Brown, arranged by her assistant, Carrie, probably with the oversight of Frank's team. She had to practice changing identities. Charlie told her in time it would be second nature. Janice arrived minutes before the plane began boarding at ten o'clock, allowing minimal time to be observed by fellow travelers. It was challenging to tell the time during Alaska summers. At midnight the summer Alaska sky was bright, identical to midday. She glanced at headlines on the newsstand, "CIA Field Director Missing." She recognized the picture. It was Brian Timmerman, the man she'd killed in the kitchen at the Russian chateau. She fought off the urge to wretch thinking of the awful events.

15

Commercial travel was luxurious compared to military planes. Alaska Airlines had the reputation of elegance matched by the spectacular Alaskan landscape viewed from the plane windows. Her assigned seat was in the first row by the door and the window. She was traveling on the Alaska milk-run with stops in Barrow, Kotzebue, and Nome to retrieve cruise line passengers on day tours on their return to the Lower-48. Stops were made in Anchorage, Juneau, and Seattle. In Seattle she'd boarded a plane for a direct flight into DC. If anyone recognized her, the cover story was she had been working in a remote Alaska village on a nutrition project. The story would explain her absence. Calls to her office south of Orlando had been routed to Frank in the DC field office. Carrie used the same story to gracefully turn down projects pitched to the nutrition consulting firm while she was away.

Her seatmate was a muscular, clean-cut young man wearing a baggy dark green Carhartt hunting jacket. His tan cap advertised the Alaska Fishing Lodge on Kodiak Island.

"I've stayed at the lodge in Kodiak. The silver salmon run was fantastic! I filled three coolers with fish filets, and I'm terrible at fishing. The views from the lodge were spectacular in fall color, with splashes of golden birch trees among emerald Sitka spruce scattered along a rocky beach. Did you catch anything?"

He nodded and smiled.

After working the summer at the produce packing house, she was asked to organize a seminar at a Kodiak Island lodge for a group of produce buyers during the fall silver salmon runs, expenses paid by several Florida tomato growers. She couldn't turn down a trip to Alaska.

As her seatmate was stowing his gear, his jacket bulged slightly for her to notice a shoulder harness and the butt of a handgun slung under his arm. It could have been a coincidence.

Maybe she was overly optimistic, but she hoped the hat was Charlie's way of sending her a message, identifying her seatmate as one of his crew, a sky marshal, or both.

Janice grabbed a romance novel from her backpack and prepared for the long flight to DC. The romantic novel purchased at the mall brought thoughts of Charlie. She wasn't sure how she felt about Charlie's knowledge of her life during his years of disappearance. She dated a few men here and there. She wrongly believed if she found someone else she would forget him, but no one could replace Charlie and how he made her body melt with a kiss or the soft touch of his hand on her shoulder, in and out of bed. She knew nothing of Charlie's life. Were there other romances for him? Probably. When you love someone, are those details really significant?

She buried her face in the pages of her book to shield her from other passengers, per Frank's instructions, and didn't notice a young, slender Asian lady who boarded in Anchorage. When the lady exited at Seattle, the woman looked straight at her. Maybe it was the lack of sleep or a tad of paranoia, but the dark almond eyes of her cold and hateful stare gave her a chill.

On final approach to DC, she woke to find her book on the floor and a glass of iced coffee with cream on her tray. Normally she could force a smile in support of pilot humor, but when he announced it was a chilly 104-degrees in the nation's capital, she wished for the crispness of the brisk 65-degree summer weather she'd left in Alaska. She couldn't wait to find a bed. After catnapping and too much coffee for three days, she was beginning to feel jumpy. Sleeping on the late-night flights departing Anchorage was always a challenge.

CHAPTER TWO

Sue Li must have played Ron's message on her answering machine a hundred times. She lay on the bed naked listening to the message again and again. She'd brought the tape cartridge with her when she returned to DC after working at her uncle's import/export produce business, Sun'Luk Produce, located on the China coast. Oh, how she missed Ron. The message was bad news. She didn't care; she simply wanted to hear his voice. It reminded her of the days the three of them had made love and formulated secret plans to be together forever. On another tape she played an earlier message from Timmerman, "If Brown takes a plane, we can locate her. We have friends at the Chinese airlines. Can't wait to see you. Love you. Miss you!"

He had been right. She had flown to the West Coast and watched Brown catch the flight from Anchorage to Seattle. She couldn't wait to be in bed with Timmerman and Ron. She hated they were apart. Mr. Tao, her uncle, had arranged for her to meet them as a favor to a friend who worked for the government. At first it was the fantasy of freedom living in California and being able to have her own apartment even if she knew her uncle's guards had her under constant surveillance. Her uncle was

18

generous with funding to buy whatever Timmerman and Ron wanted, be it unlimited drugs or sex. The three of them spent a fantastic six years together during college and graduate school in Long Beach. She couldn't imagine her life without them.

Now her biggest problem was how to kill Janice Brown to please her uncle. Everything had gone wrong. When Janice was invited to work at the spa, Ron planned to use her as bait if Charlie eluded Timmerman's trap in Mexico to kill him. Timmerman was one of the students assigned to investigate Janice Brown and to build a profile of her when Charlie taught at Langley. They were to document her favorite foods, her schedule, even who she was sleeping with. Carelessly, Charlie arranged to intersect her travel before she dropped out of sight. The students assumed it was an amorous interest, but Timmerman later questioned if she was one of his deep assets. When Charlie survived the attack in Mexico, he couldn't have anticipated that Miller would call Janice. Looking back, Janice attended several parties at Miller's house.

Mr. Tao warned Timmerman and Ron Jones of Charlie's friendship with Miller who worked for the FBI and the agency's long reaches within the United States. It was unfortunate they couldn't have killed her at the spa, but there were too many civilians and government types present when Charlie was brought in for surgery, according to Timmerman.

Even with the support of Timmerman's agents embedded in the Georgia Highway Patrol, Janice Brown disappeared with Charlie Smith. Later, she and Charlie Smith stayed at a Russian hotel, which was another disaster. Last time he'd heard from Timmerman he was staging an attack on some general's chateau. Maybe Timmerman had taken care of both of them. Few knew of the operations Timmerman and Ron coordinated for Mr. Tao. Timmerman was also the link between Tao and the CIA. When

Timmerman was in deep cover, she wished he'd call her, but knew from past assignments he'd call her when he could. Oh, how she missed them both.

She had to turn this project around. She knew her uncle was unhappy. Even if she was Mr. Tao's biological niece, she knew he would show no mercy if she failed.

CHAPTER THREE

With her seat by the door, Bonnie was the first passenger off the plane in DC. Her row mate was having problems getting his luggage down. She saw a familiar face as she walked toward the curb to catch a local limousine; it was Randy. She remembered Charlie's warning to avoid acknowledging team members, but Randy was walking directly toward her and initiated the conversation. "Dr. Brown? I thought it was you," said Randy in a joyful voice. "I was in your graduate class a couple of years ago."

"I remember you were a fine student, and your contributions in class were thought-provoking. Can't remember your grade, probably earned an A in the class."

"I was top of the class on the tests, but you gave me a B+ because of my absences; I deserved it," he chuckled. Of course, the class didn't exist, and he wasn't a student. She was amazed at her comfort with the spontaneous fictitious interactions with Frank's team. "Are you visiting in DC? Can I drop you off somewhere?" Randy asked as he grabbed her backpack from her shoulder.

She noticed he didn't offer her his name—probably just as well since names changed by day or week.

"Oh, how nice of you! The confusing one-way streets and

roundabouts are frustrating. Here's the address," she said in a staged dither as she dug through her bag to find a blank piece of paper. Charlie made her memorize the address before she left Moscow. She chuckled. The last time she followed directions written on a torn portion of a page, things evolved into a whirlwind trip across two continents with people shooting at her.

Based on Charlie's descriptions, she'd estimated the ride to the condos outside the Virginia suburbs to be an hour. The ride could be longer with the maze of beltways and interstate highways, and the daily quagmire of DC traffic. Charlie said her condo was down the street from his. She had insisted, for now, on having her own apartment. She wasn't quite ready to have her heart broken if Charlie disappeared again.

As soon as they arrived at the car, Randy responded to someone on a radio or walkie-talkie. "Yeah, Mom, found the spaghetti sauce you wanted — yeah, the white kind. I'm bringing garlic toast and a salad for Sunday's dinner. Okay, I'll check with the bakery for a killer dessert, maybe two blueberry cupcakes."

Randy leaned toward her to provide a status report. "We picked up a tail. The tech center confirmed two men in a blue sedan are following us from the airport. Got 'em on three traffic cameras."

"Y'all have access to city traffic cameras?" she asked with a surprised lilt in her voice.

"Well, it's an unofficial system. We've installed our own visual system to track cars coming and going in the direction of the condos. For now, we're heading to an alternate location south of Baltimore. Look for the Interstate 495 exit, will ya?"

"How did you have information I was being followed?"

"Well, we didn't, but if anyone was looking for you, your name would be on somebody's radar the minute your ticket was booked in Alaska on a plane heading for DC. Damn! We hoped we were wrong. We had time to plan for the contingency. We could've arranged other flights to return you home a little sooner, but the extra time gave us opportunities to check passenger lists, and gave those following you time to intersect your flight. Anyway, think of those extra frequent flyer points you've earned," joked Randy. "The bug JoAnne planted in the travel office was helpful. Everyone tracks the money side of accounting. Few are sneaky enough to consider tracking travel destinations…"

"…expect JoAnne," they said in unison, with a nervous laugh.

"She and I were sorority sisters and college roommates. We sleuthed to find who *mistakenly* took someone's clothes out of the dryer. Or the person who was tearing out pages of the decorating magazines in the inspiration room for our class in art and design. Is JoAnne back at work? It seems too soon after delivering twins."

"She planted the bug before she left, and it signals the field office when anyone from the CIA or FBI books a plane ticket. We have an airline computer to monitor flights and passenger lists. I simply cross-referenced your name and location."

She wanted to ask why Randy would be tracking travel by CIA or FBI agents, but she didn't. She figured he was completing his assignment. Charlie and Frank seemed to hold him in high regard. He seemed to be an expert on everything.

"Everyone wants to eliminate loose ends before JoAnne goes back to work. Timmerman was the CIA section chief. He was her new boss."

She knew of Timmerman. She had killed him. He cornered her in front of the refrigerators and pointed a gun at her. He was momentarily distracted when the team was walking toward the kitchen. He raised his gun, but she shot first before he would shoot her or the team. She couldn't erase the memory of his lifeless face on the tiled kitchen floor of General Shirnoffski's remote chateau as blood puddled around his body. She didn't understand why Timmerman wanted to kill her; she assumed it had something to do with her relationship with Charlie.

"There's the exit in half a mile," she abruptly announced. She was still wrestling with the reality she had killed someone; it hadn't been but a few days. She wished the talk concerning Timmerman would end.

"We haven't determined the reach of Timmerman's organization through the CIA, especially in regard to concerns with Chinese politics. Unfortunately, you were using your actual name in Russia, making you the easiest to track," answered Randy.

"Y'all are using me as bait." She blurted out her unguarded thoughts. She wondered what the connection was with the Chinese. She wanted to trust Charlie with her future. He and his crew had kept her safe before.

"Yeah, sorry about that. We were hoping this would be a drill. But unfortunately, you are unquestionably a target, or they're attempting to track Charlie through you. We're assuming it has something to do with the Russian trip, although we can't follow the logic. Honestly, we were surprised when four tickets were booked to intercept your flights—two at Anchorage, and two at Seattle. Before you left Russia, we bought the unsold seats and didn't assign you a seat until flight time. Our guy sat on the isle with you at the window on the first row. You probably didn't notice, but when passengers enter the plane, most naturally look ahead toward the passengers on the side opposite the door before they walk down the aisle. Few people look behind them once they've passed a row. Your seatmate watched the boarding passengers."

"It seemed strange he reached across me a couple of times to open and close the window shade burying me under the sleeve of his coat."

"He was probably trying to hide your face. We had an agent at the boarding gate who took pictures of the passengers. The experimental NavCis software sends pictures practically in real-time. With your cropped hair, and no makeup, you look completely different than the sexy pictures on your passport and driver's license."

She wondered if Randy concluded her recent makeover was less than sexy. Who said when you look like your passport picture it was time to go home? She made a note to avoid future shopping with jet lag. Her mind was drifting. Focus. She quickly recovered. "I felt reassured once I saw the clue on his hat."

"We wagered if you would catch the message."

"Did you win?" She could tell from his smirk he bet against her. "Now I understand why you were assigned to meet me."

"To change the subject," replied Randy as he cleared this throat. "Two groups are tailing you. The car from the parking lot and the four passengers on your flight. Your seatmate identified those at the airport. Another team is following the passengers," explained Randy.

"Look," said Randy, pointing at the two cars ahead of them. "There's our rendezvous car and our diversion car right on schedule."

"What are you eluding to, Randy?"

"We're switching cars at the rest area. Do you have your backpack? One car will follow us and the other will follow our tail. This maneuver is straightforward, but pretty sophisticated. We control the advantage with additional planning time. Anyway, be chatty when you exit the car. Ask where to find a rest room. Ask me to buy you a soda. Once inside the restaurant, remove your plaid jacket. There'll be a lady to exchange it for a floppy hat and colorful sweater. We'll walk through the restaurant and there'll be a car waiting for us on the other side of the building. Our decoy will put on your jacket, and put a tourist hat on your head. She and another agent with my general silhouette will return to our vehicle and continue north. I told them you were wearing a white top."

"Oh, your comments on the white spaghetti sauce? And the two menu items were signaling there were two in the car?" She was still adjusting to living in Charlie's world, his life of espionage. He and his crew took nothing at face value.

"It's a simple code, but it works. It's also adaptable to the surroundings. It doesn't reveal your identification. The conversation sounds pretty benign if someone overhears the discussion. Everyone is always buying something for their mom," replied Randy in a confident instructive tone.

When they entered the restaurant at the rest area, she followed directions, and the maneuver worked exactly as Randy had outlined. They strolled through the restaurant, exited the building, and crawled into the back seat of a shabby light beige station wagon waiting in the parking lot. She snuggled in the back seat between the two shaggy yellow labs. Randy put a cowboy hat on his head and motioned for her to put her head down. The station wagon turned onto the highway heading south toward Virginia. Minutes later at the exit, the family ordered dinner through the burger restaurant's drive-thru. Randy patted the dogs, and they exited the car. A green minivan was waiting filled with commuters reading their newspapers. They gestured for her to sit between two men in the middle row. Someone draped a dark trench coat around her shoulders, and the vehicle continued west on a side road behind the drive-in.

She wasn't sure how long they rode, an hour she guessed. She nodded off once or twice. Twilight was gone; the North Star twinkled against the darkness of flat farmland, but no clues as to the time. She couldn't remember if she had reset her watch after leaving Alaska.

When she woke, Randy was talking on the radio. "Darn, Mom. I thought you decided on one of those two colors. Oh, they didn't have the paint color you wanted? I was hoping to paint the living room this weekend. Okay, I'll check the other hardware store." He tapped the driver on the shoulder, and a few minutes later the van stopped in a Safeway parking lot. The passengers moved from the van to other cars. "Catch you in the morning," he said as if they were simply ending another day.

Randy unlocked the door to a faded red Volkswagen and headed south to Virginia. "We lost the tail. They've given us the green light to transport you home," said Randy.

"What in the conversations told you things were okay?" asked Bonnie.

"Conversations with 'Mom' at the field office relays information buried in benign topics. The two colors of paint bought at the 'hardware store' indicated Frank caught the two tails and they are probably under guard. We call the condos the 'hardware store' which was the signal we could go home."

"Randy, how do y'all inventory the vehicles? And the people?"

"Well," —he paused as if he wasn't going to respond, but reconsidered— "A couple of years ago, Charlie and Frank bought a few independent car repair companies across the country and a junkyard here and there. It's a cash business and gives us options. You've met Charlie, Frank, Gustoff, and a few others, who apparently have been friends since Vietnam. Miller, Roger, and I joined the organization in the last couple of years. We employ a lot of former military, people we've worked with. The pay is decent—all cash."

Viewing familiar DC landmarks in the skyline flooded her

memory of romantic weekends spent with Charlie when they first dated. They toured the museums along the Mall and spent hours walking the grounds and exploring the gardens of the historic homes at Mount Vernon and Monticello. She remembered Charlie rarely spoke of his work. He didn't exactly refuse, but when she asked it seemed he pivoted the focus of the conversation on her. Their relationship started out cloaked in secrets. She hadn't realized it at the time, and guessed it hadn't changed. Now, she wondered if this was a preview of their future together. She remembered Charlie as loving, amusing, and comfortable to spend time with. He was different when they were in Russia. He was distant, although thankfully when they dated years ago he wasn't injured and no one was shooting at them. Maybe it was the situation and totally unrelated to her.

She had dated doctors, accountants, businessmen; they were smart, pleasant, and considerate, but she couldn't imagine them being supportive or even tolerant if her folks needed her back at the ranch. Charlie was comfortable hiking in the woods, hunting wildflowers, or putting out winter hay for baby calves. His hands were rough. She once asked if he was raised on a farm. He barked that he was from Chicago and changed the subject. She wasn't even sure of his birthday, though knew she was younger. In Russia she had found he worked for one of the Washington initialed agencies. It had been a week since Charlie left Moscow and her bed. The red-eye flight from Alaska was taking its toll and she was losing track of Randy's conversation again.

"But something has us worried," he continued. "We've been methodical to shield the relationship between you and Charlie. We must be missing something from the Russian trip. We have to continue the play until — "

She interrupted Randy's scenario. She didn't want to hear the finale. "Oh, I could've imagined how smooth the vehicle exchange went at the rest stop. It was as if I was in a scene in a Broadway play, performing before an audience who didn't realize they'd bought a ticket."

Randy turned to look at her. The ride was quiet. Her mind was blank. She guessed time zones and plane travel were colliding.

Randy entered a gated community, waved at a pudgy security guard, pushed a button on the garage door opener, and pulled into a huge garage. "We put your Jeep in the garage of the office apartment after we inspected it for tracking devices."

"Of course," she said and smirked.

"Welcome home," said Randy. "There are two entrances to the walled garden. You can enter through the door off the garage, but we'll use the street entrance. We found hand-carved wooden doors in abandoned ruins in South America. Come look."

"Oh, Randy, those doors are gorgeous, they must be three or four inches thick!" she exclaimed as her fingers softly touched the warmth of the carved patterns in the wooden panels. She took in her surroundings. "I'm enchanted with the slate floor tile. The walled patio is intimate for an al fresco private dinner under the stars. In the space along the wall, I've instantly decided to create a French espalier with apple and cherry trees and spring bulbs at their feet." Randy's eyes were glazing. "You said 'we found.' Did you help with the building of these apartments?"

"Yeah," said Randy. He blushed. "This complex was one of my designs. I have an engineering degree. What better way to demolish things than to study how they're built?"

"Randy, I am so impressed," she said on autopilot. She didn't intend to ignore Randy's comments of his background, but her attention was on the condo. She nodded her head periodically as he continued to describe the features and she followed him through the rooms. His functional descriptions paled in comparison with her evaluation of the décor that could have appeared on the cover of any New York decorating magazine. She saw a pair of antique French doors leading to a tiled foyer with large rooms off either side of the entry hall. To the left was a cozy room with a velvet upholstered sofa in celadon green and a rug in an Oriental geometric pattern in shades of green and cream centered on dark wood floors. There was a media cabinet and a striking black-lacquered Asian armoire brushed with burgundy accents centered on the back wall. Two halves of a brass plate became the focal point of the room when the doors of the cabinet were closed. "Oh, look Randy! You brought my grandmother's baby grand piano! It's perfect! It echoes the ebony finish on the antique Oriental chest."

"Your folks insisted it be added to the moving van as a surprise."

Her eyes were getting moist. She quickly refocused when she realized the room lacked chairs and end tables to place a cup of coffee, a convenient excuse to explore famous flea markets in Massachusetts, Virginia, or Pennsylvania, to excavate the perfect additions. Ceiling height pocket doors were behind the piano. Later she'd have to discover where they led.

Randy simply smiled.

To the right of the hall was the kitchen which had pocket doors leading to a huge dining room. She could imagine entertaining using the seamless access between the two spaces. The kitchen would be bathed in morning sunshine with windows overlooking the walled patio by the garage. She looked forward to taking advantage of the sunny spot to nibble a morning treat. While she wondered briefly about groceries in the house, she noticed the Queen Anne dining table and Chippendale chairs covered in a botanical print which anchored the room. She had seen the chairs before and the botanical print fabric, but couldn't remember where. The natural green colors were duplicated in the floor-to-ceiling drapes in a diminutive Oriental geometric print. Potted palms in the corners and centerpieces of white orchids in delicate Oriental tureens gave the rooms a classic tropical attitude, formulas her favorite decorating magazines called "plantation style."

She was overwhelmed when she saw her things from Florida artistically placed in the apartment. Charlie's VIP treatment could be addictive if it came with a decorator. Between graduate school and working in Alaska, her personal collection of furniture was minimal. She'd inherited her grandmother's things, which she loved, and were kept safe at the ranch. In contrast, her traveling belongings could be disassembled and packed in the back of the scrappy farm truck she would drive home after working in Alaska. In the old truck were foldable bookcases, a table with removable legs, a small lamp, and a box of mismatched kitchen items. The only things that matched were a collection of Blue Ridge Mountain plates and cups and saucers featuring hand-drawn wildflowers.

She loved the search through dusty shelves at flea markets, antique stores, and garage sales during her travels. She was amazed to read during WWII that Blue Ridge Mountain Pottery was the largest pottery manufacturer in the US. During the depression the company was the major employer in northeast Tennessee at the Erwin plant. Janice had toured the museum on a college trip to study Southern craftsmanship. Her mind was wandering. Her rusty truck had retired to the ranch. With her savings, thanks to the limited number of shopping malls in most Alaska locations, she upgraded to a four-wheel-drive Jeep, a sexy black Jeep.

There was a steady increase of files and references to tote from contract to contract, taking considerable wall space in her grandmother's house once the contract was completed. In a moment of weakness, she considered thinning out the files, until several contracts invited her back and she needed her notes for background. Besides, Baby Kittie loved sleeping on the stacked boxes for a higher view out the windows. She looked around the apartment. Where were her books?

"Bonnie, there's a hidden stairwell to the second floor from the hall bath tucked in the back of the linen closet-storage room. The main room of the condo can be entered from the hall or from the den through a set of carved Indonesian pocket doors."

"I love the soft color of the doors. The combination with the celadon couch and Chinese antiques are peaceful and serene!"

"It took six coats of paint called 'warm eggshell.' Behind the bath there's a massive fireplace. We covered a wall of windows with oversized freestanding mahogany plantation shutters framing the patio windows for ultimate privacy. Behind the shutters is a wide patio and lap pool."

Janice instantly loved the heavy nubby silk drapes in colors reminding her of the tropical beach sand at Key West. "The patio is delightful. The design is subdued with an understated ambiance. Maybe it's the subtle ground lighting?" she said.

"The decorator suggested the simple stone bench to span the length of the patio, and adding the narrow lap pool. She flew in the large shallow concrete bowls we used for the sculptured Chinese maples at each end of the pool. She offered to purchase ancient bonsai trees, but I told her it was beyond our budget. Some of the team brought their clipper skills and created the bonsai effect using two maples we bought at the garden store."

Mahogany slats lined the walls at both ends of the patio and were laden with hanging clay pots of ferns, white orchids, along with candles in hurricane shades that created a romantic atmosphere. "Smell the sweetness of creeping thyme planted between the giant three-by-three concrete tiles under out feet?

Isn't it lovely? Randy, when did you have time to pull the details together? Who lit the patio candles?"

"They're fake candles. A switch in the hall lights the candles, also turns on the fireplace," Randy answered.

She rested on a cozy couch facing an outdoor fireplace, imagining an intimate evening where she and Charlie could gaze at the stars and each other. She wanted to be supportive of Randy's achievements and could tell how proud he was of the project. "Randy, the condo is fabulous!" However, her thoughts were imagining making love with Charlie in her freshly decorated apartment.

"Come on, we'll look at the bedrooms."

She tried to stifle a giggle. Surely, he couldn't read her mind?

A wide staircase from the living room led upstairs to the two huge bedroom suites. Suddenly she saw the bookcases on the mezzanine wall facing the vaulted fireplace room below. "Randy. These bookcases are an answer to prayer. Did you build them? For the first time there's enough room for my books and reference materials. And you even included a reading nook with a cushy chair and lamp for me and Baby Kittie. Who did the decorating? Everything is exquisite!"

"Well, our shop constructed the bookcases, but one of Frank's companies sent a team of decorators to organize your things. Carrie from your office arrived in time to select the kitchen and your office furniture. My guys were here to supervise the contractors to maintain security. We scanned for bugs before and after the crews left each day, even when they went to lunch."

Randy stood in the doorway as she found the charming set of *Matryoshka*, Russian nesting dolls, in shades of cream and gold. "These are gorgeous!" she shrieked. "And they match Grandmother's antique French provincial bedroom furniture." Now she understood why Charlie wouldn't let her buy the wooden dolls when they toured the shops in the historic section of Moscow. She loved him.

"I was given specific instructions to coordinate the Russian nesting dolls with your bedroom furniture. Our movers in Florida described the pieces via telephone," replied Randy. "Our crew in Russia did the shopping. Your dad told us of the room at your grandmother's farmhouse stacked with boxes of your books."

She grinned. Her dad fussed she should organize her books.

She was enthralled with the elegant simplicity of the décor. Grandmother's drum-top table had been transformed into a nightstand with a stunning floor-length jacquard drape in cream and taupe. The bed linens were layered in soothing colors of pale sea-foam, ivory, and muted celadon reminiscent of seagrass-covered sand dunes of a narrow island south of Tallahassee where she and Charlie had met once or twice. She imagined sharing the room bathed in candlelight and the soft pastels of early morning with Charlie. She hoped he would be captivated. An Oriental floral print in blues and gray sage covered two wingback chairs by the windows and complimented colors in the English botanical prints of hummingbirds perched on orchids painted by Gould and his wife Elizabeth in the mid-1800s. She'd found the prints years ago in a quaint and dusty antique store near the Everglades on a weekend trip with Charlie. She brightened to have artwork from her travels in South Florida and Alaska used in the intimate spaces of the two upstairs bedroom suites.

"I live in the building across the compound." His voice took on a shy timbre. "Can I ask you a question? Do you know if Carrie is dating anyone?"

In light of the warnings to compartmentalize friendships and forget recent events, Randy's question was totally unexpected. "Well, she's quite private. I heard the guestroom at our Orlando office condo stayed full with her military cohorts. I couldn't say if they were visiting her or visiting the attractions. Why don't you ask her? Maybe we could grill hamburgers one evening." Suddenly she felt as if she was the dorm mom. She wondered if Randy knew Carrie reported to Roger, another one of Charlie's key confidants.

She smiled at how Roger orchestrated her to hire Carrie. She believed she was the one who'd found Carrie Cunningham as an office assistant after her nutrition consulting business took off. Carrie was an ideal match—a dietitian on military leave working on her MBA at the University of Central Florida to quality for the captain's promotion list. She was a tall, sandy-blonde basketball player from Kansas. Janice had prospective employees sit in the front office and did a portion of the interview on the phone. Carrie probably considered her crazy, but Janice wanted to hear how she sounded on the phone and how she would respond when clients called, since few clients ever came to the office. The work offered a modest salary and a place to live, a heavenly deal for a graduate student. Thinking back, it was strange when one applicant didn't show and another cancelled at the last minute. To be honest, her focus was on organizing paperwork for an emergency project at Fort Ord. She hired Carrie on the spot and left a few hours later on a late-night flight.

Looking back, she suspected Roger or Frank or even Charlie was behind the Fort Ord commander's adamant demands for a full-scale food service inspection with the post closure scheduled in less than a month. She didn't question. The military had its own system and were quite generous with the contracts. Once she'd been told Carrie worked for Roger, it was logical Roger orchestrated Carrie being hired as her assistant, and manipulated Carrie's transfer to Walter Reed Medical Center after she accepted an assignment in DC. She was relieved Carrie would be close by. From Randy's questions, if she was to ponder, Randy would volunteer to assist Carrie in finding permanent living quarters. She smiled. She was a romantic and freely admitted it.

"Randy, I adore the neutral beach tones chosen for the great room downstairs. I'm a secret beach bunny, if you hadn't guessed. The colors of beach sands and driftwood blend well with the colors in the prints of Chesapeake Bay. The decorating has a subtle suggestion of the beach. And you used my Oriental glass floats in a shallow wooden basket placed on a padded bench in front of the wide fireplace with a long bench hearth. I collected the delicate handblown floats on the sandy black volcanic beaches near Unalaska/Dutch Harbor. I guess it's okay if I tell you?"

"Glad you love it. Carrie helped with the designs. She proposed the industrial stove and glass-fronted refrigerator. We unearthed them at a dusty restaurant supply store," bragged Randy. "We proposed the aged appliances made the apartment appear you'd lived here for a while."

She was amazed at Randy's involvement in the decorating project and his keen eye for detail. "Y'all did a super job! And so quickly!"

Randy was describing the floor supports and the security system. She quit listening when she found a note from Carrie:

Janice. Assisted Randy with the office setup. Stopped by your folks and hijacked Baby Kittie. She was such a flirt waving at the truck drivers from atop her carrier. Carrie

The note was written to *Janice*. Carrie hadn't been informed of her Bonnie identity. But her immediate concern was to find her kitty. "Baby Kittie, Baby Kittie!" she called. Her kitty had to be in the apartment somewhere. She hadn't escaped when they'd opened the door. Half the bowl of cat tidbits was gone, and there was her favorite kitty box with the eight-inch sides. "Randy, we have to find Baby Kittie!" mandated Bonnie.

"Let's hunt through your apartment first. When we built the

apartment complex, I linked the basements in each wing and connected the wings through underground tunnels. If we don't find her in here, we'll explore the secret passageways."

The search of the six rooms took only minutes. No kitty.

She hadn't immediately noticed as Randy was giving the apartment tour, but the apartment layout had been built by someone with an eye for security. Little could be seen from the front door. Even if anyone could breach the four-inch thick wooden doors, the bathroom with hidden staircase behind the massive fireplace blocked the view of the inside of the house and would thwart an assault coming from the patio or the front door. Thoughts of where to hide if someone shot at her again gave her chills.

Randy opened a downstairs closet and showed her space to hang coats and hats. "Behind the clothes rack is a pocket door opening onto a concealed staircase. The stairs also connect the closets in the upstairs master bedrooms to the basement tunnel. No kitty. Okay, let's try the kitchen tunnel. Could she have opened the cabinet door?"

"You haven't met Baby Kittie, have you, Randy? If cat nibbles are involved, then yes!"

Randy opened the cabinet doors beneath a gray marble counter. She watched Randy's telescopic legs collapse to peer inside the lower cabinet. "See the saucepan with a lid?" She nodded. "The gloves are stored in there. Before you move the panels against the wall, grab a pair and you won't leave prints. It'll reduce the work if we ever have to print these areas. Plus, the gloves prevent oil and grease on your fingers from staining the paint which would divulge the panel's location. Oh, it's open. Your kitty could have escaped through these panels. Care to do a little exploring?"

"Sure, let's go!" She followed. They crawled on hands and

knees, snaking through the opening, a three by three-foot space behind the panel. For someone who wanted nothing but a hot shower and a comfy bed, she suddenly found a second wind. She had to find Baby Kittie. She wiggled through the cabinets and emerged in the adjacent apartment; a mirrored layout to hers, but decorated in a subtle patriotic theme using red and blue Oriental platters on the kitchen wall. Couches in the living room were in a military blue accented with pillows in an abstract red and white poppies fabric.

"The apartment is vacant."

"Baby Kittie. Come here, you little punkin," she called to her tortoiseshell calico. Randy looked at her as if she was from outer space. Obviously, he wasn't a cat person. Still no kitty.

"I hadn't planned for you to visit Charlie's apartment, but we've looked everywhere else," said Randy. "Remember there's a sliding panel in the back of the broom closet. Charlie uses it to walk through the basement. Obviously, Baby Kittie didn't travel through the basement. If we can find her we may be able to deduce her path."

She giggled at the mental image of Charlie's muscular six-foot frame squeezing through the kitchen cabinet panels. His kitchen looked akin to a dated display at the hardware store including sales labels and dust. Charlie's apartment was paneled with honey-stained tongue-and-groove pine. Classic leather furniture faced the massive river rock fireplace and a huge muted red, white, and blue Persian rug. A chunky library table was stacked with books. One wall was covered with televisions. She recognized Charlie's reading glasses lying on a porcelain Oriental garden seat at arm's length from a well-loved leather recliner. Baby Kittie's black and gold calico head burst from under a cat-hair-covered sweater, some of her clothes transported in Charlie's luggage from Russia. Baby Kittie had been there longer than a few hours. The kitty box and plate of nibbles confirmed it. The smell of Charlie's cologne filled her heart as she collapsed in his chair.

Baby Kittie jumped on her lap and rubbed her hand to have her ears scratched. "How did you travel here, you rascal?" she pretended to fuss. She placed Baby Kittie on the floor, and the four-footed fur ball disappeared behind the books in Charlie's bookcase.

CHAPTER FOUR

"Frank," how did the transfer go?" Charlie was on a secure phone from somewhere in the Middle East.

"Montana made it to Fairbanks with no problems, but she was tagged on the flight from Anchorage, and again in Seattle. Another group was waiting in DC and she was tailed leaving Reagan International. We've missed something, Charlie. She arrived late in the afternoon, dead tired, but not complaining. Carrie enrolled her in the staff orientation at Walter Reed Thursday or Friday."

"Are we going to have the outpatient clinic finished in time?"

"You would ask. I was hoping for Friday, but we're behind schedule and still have a long punch list before we'll pass the building inspections. It'll be at least the first of the week. Walter Reed is grateful to accept a fully paid clinic site with no maintenance costs. We were able to have Carrie assigned there along with two other dietitians. Once the phones were installed, we sent word through the veteran's organizations to book appointments. We're also hiring them as volunteers. Randy is conducting interviews tomorrow. We're excited to unload a piece of property that was going nowhere. It'll be an advantageous write-off for the property division."

"How's the security?"

"We contacted retired MPs from the DC bases to be security guards, but have to rotate them. Montana is an uncanny observer and would recognize them in a minute if we stationed regular military police folks there. We'll figure out something. How are things in your direction?"

"Same ole, same ole."

"Gotcha. Between Randy and his crew, things are handled here. If things go retrograde, you will be the first call."

CHAPTER FIVE

"Couldn't catch her," Randy yelled through the cabinets. "Kitty Houdini ran from behind the bookcase on Charlie's shared wall across the room in the vacant apartment to the bookcase on the wall shared with your apartment. Close the panels when you come through the kitchen cabinets. She should be back at your place by now. She won't reveal your escape routes using the special cat tunnels."

Janice squeezed back into her apartment through two cabinet passages, stood and straightened her clothes, "Randy, Carrie hasn't been informed of my 'Bonnie' identity. Who else may have seen her note? She also mentioned she organized my consulting office. You mentioned I can enter the office without going outside? Where are my files?"

"The files are in storage, I'll deliver them in a couple of days. You must be tired," offered Randy.

She shook her head. "Of course not, I'm wide awake, ready to go. I've only traveled for four days," she blurted out. "Sorry, Randy, I didn't mean to be snarky. Tell me more about the office."

"We converted the last apartment into a working space for your professional activities. It has a separate street entrance and three parking spaces to receive clients. There's a narrow spiral staircase connecting the closets upstairs to the basement. It's an emergency exit, but you can access the office through the basement in case of a snowstorm.

"Baby Kittie, do you have a map of the exits?"

"Meoww!"

"What's on the schedule for tomorrow?"

"Frank has given you the day off. Wednesday and Thursday, or maybe it's Thursday and Friday, you are to attend orientation in DC at Walter Reed. On Monday he wants you to report to a veteran's outpatient diet clinic located in a renovated strip mall near here. Carrie has also been assigned there. Sometime you should visit the State Department to meet the section heads. We haven't decided if we are handling the transportation, or will let you ride the Metro into DC. They're pleased to have a dietitian to support the embassy staff. Your uniforms are upstairs in the closet with appropriate rank and badges. The jackets have been designed to hold your passports and other essential papers. We're still discussing whether to issue you a weapon."

"You actually think weapons are necessary at the diet office? The gun will confirm I'm the diet police for sure! Should I wear the gun in a thigh or shoulder harness?" Janice asked as she held her hand behind her head and stood in a glamour pose.

"Be serious. If we have to do a rapid extraction, you should be armed. I'll find you an ankle holster."

"Randy, now for the most crucial issue… What are we doing for dinner? I'm starving."

"Glad you asked." He made three clicks on the radio. "Relax on the couch and I'll pour you a glass of wine. Yes, from a bottle with a pretty label."

In minutes people appeared from the bath closet in the hall. Before Randy said a word, she could smell the hearty, greasy, meaty aroma.

"Charlie said your favorite was grilled steak, salad, and lime sorbet. He wanted you to meet the crew out here. Meet Lewis, Allen, and Simmons." They tried to maintain a straight face when they arrived dressed in black slacks, white shirts, and red bow ties. In their hands were trays of freshly grilled steak and the trimmings.

"Y'all are so thoughtful to welcome me. I could present a long speech discussing how thankful I am, but I'm starving. Let's eat!"

"Here are plates. Where are the steak knives?" asked Randy. She heard the click of opening knives. The room burst into laughter. "I'll cut a plate of trimmings for Baby Kittie." Instantly, Randy became Baby Kittie's best friend as she wrapped herself around his ankles.

*****

"Meowwtt. Meeooooow."

"What is it, Baby Kittie? Where's my watch? I was sure I set the alarm. Did you hide it? Is that a kitty smile? You are such a sassy kitty! Sleeping on our own furniture reminds me of home at the ranch. Did you choose the soft colors?" Baby Kitty rolled on the soft sheets, purred, and blinked her dark eyes.

She'd slept too long. Every bone, every muscle ached. She hoped there was coffee downstairs. After dinner she'd wilted. Checking kitchen inventory was the last thing on her mind. JoAnne left nightgowns and sexy underwear in her grandmother's dresser drawers lined with pink-scented tissue paper. Stacks of dark slacks with zipped pockets, no-iron shirts, and dark polo shirts were in neat rows on the closet shelves. Despite her lack of knowledge of a dress code, her choices were obvious. Besides, it might be too much to run downstairs to start coffee dressed in sheer lingerie, at least on her first morning. She brushed her teeth, shook her hair into something of a style, wiggled into one

44

of her boring black outfits, and headed downstairs. She opened the drapes and the wide glass doors to smell the breeze blowing through the grass in the cow pasture.

She snickered to find an electric coffeepot ready to go with a red arrow drawn on a yellow sticky note pointing to the start button. She immediately saw the envelope leaning against a shiny silver tray. She stared at the note and momentarily delayed opening the packet. She hoped it was from Charlie; she would be disappointed if it wasn't. She couldn't wait and impulsively tore off the flap and peeked inside. She read a "C" at the bottom of the note.

"Sweets, welcome. Be home soon. Love you, C."

She could smell Charlie's cologne. Oh, she missed him. The beep of the coffeepot brought her back from reminiscences of the dreamy week in Moscow touring the beautiful historic city. To be respectable she ate lunch in the hotel dining room after visiting with the ladies in the hotel's silver locker, and spent the rest of the day and evening in bed with Charlie.

She wondered who had selected the crystal-footed cake plate. It looked German with the etched flower design. Under the domed lid were fresh croissants, a wedge of brie cheese, and silver demitasse spoons to dip orange marmalade from a squatty wire-bound antique canning jar. She loved orange marmalade. On the gorgeous silver tray were European teacups, saucers, and stacked petite breakfast plates. She oooed when she saw the demure hand-painted orange blossoms on the plate's delicate rim. Her grandmother would tell her the linen napkins edged with hand-crocheted orange lace were too lovely to soil. She searched for a paper towel in the pantry. On the counter was an elegant silver bucket filled with ice. A French cow pitcher was filled with cream waiting on the refrigerator shelf. She was enjoying being a kept woman, at least for a few days. She grinned and suspected

45

Gustoff had sent the European china, but asking would break Frank's rules against acknowledging team members. There had to be glasses somewhere. She'd find them one day, but for the moment she grabbed a teacup to hold her iced coffee. She tore a croissant and filled the middle with a slice of brie and a smear of orange marmalade for a breakfast sandwich. She licked the marmalade from her fingers. It wasn't exactly a low-calorie selection, but she was starving.

She was still looking for a clock. Even the oven didn't have the time. "Baby Kittie, tomorrow we have to resume our morning jogging program, or we're going to be as rotund as the moo cow poking her head through the fence to nibble on the manicured grass in our yard!" Baby Kittie ran to investigate, scampering across the wide strip of yard separating the cows from the condos.

"Hey, Bonnie, you awake?" She recognized JoAnne's voice and could barely open the heavy carved wooden doors into the walled garden to welcome her.

"Come on in. Grab some coffee! I was in the garden designing the flowerbeds in my head," said Janice.

"You collected pictures of gardens in our housing design college courses. Hydrangeas were featured in all of your garden designs," JoAnne commented.

"Our thoughts are the same. Hydrangeas are my favorites. What if I mixed the traditional mop-head types with the lacey Asian hybrids?"

"Remember when we were the committee in charge of the annual spring cotillion? The sorority house wanted to wear dresses to harmonize with the landscaping and charming hydrangeas. What chemicals did you *liberate* from the chemistry lab to sprinkle on the plants to achieve such gorgeous pinks, purples, and pastel blues?"

"If I had *liberated* chemicals from the lab," — she winked — "I would've used Epsom salts for the blue color and lime for the pink, but unequivocally I have no memory of those events," she teased as she made theatrical efforts to point her chin into the air. "I remember spending the night repainting the porch banisters an antique cream because the shocking white trim conflicted with the dresses."

"Remember the paint spatters in your hair we concealed with sprigs of baby's breath?"

"And the afternoons sitting on the wide antebellum porch of the sorority house for the yearbook pictures," added Janice/Bonnie.

JoAnne knew they had to avoid the comfort of their years of personal histories. "The teacups are charming," she sighed.

"I agree!" JoAnne probably had also received packages of Gustoff's delicate European china cups and teapots. She knew she couldn't ask. "Thank you for the clothes."

"You're welcome," said JoAnne. "We enjoy having you in the neighborhood again. It's been a year or two since you worked in DC. You were one of my favorite guests for Miller's office functions."

"I was the ultimate DC fill-in at events for friends here. Your parties were such fun. And besides, I stayed at an adorable B&B down the street. You didn't have many options but to invite your former college roommate," Bonnie said and chuckled. "Where are the twins? You have to show me pictures."

"We made one set of pictures and put them in a safety deposit box. It's too risky to have pictures at home or in the office. Things are still unsettled at the agency. Frank sent weapons to hide in the house."

Bonnie started to giggle as JoAnne unloaded her purse placing a dozen Glocks on the kitchen counter. "Here's a box of loaded clips and extra ammo."

"I feel like a weird Easter bunny hiding the guns." Baby Kittie followed carefully inspecting each location.

"Remember, the weapons could save your life and others on the team," cautioned JoAnne. "Now to fun things. There's an interesting mall close by. We can grab a late lunch. I left you a handful of basic things, but if you have time for some shopping we'll buy a few dressy suits and evening wear for official functions at the State Department. I'm your personal shopper. Carrie prepared your uniforms."

"What's your sense of the house décor?" Bonnie asked.

"It's divine. The apartment has the spirit of you and Charlie: comfortable cosmopolitan. I'd forgotten you played the piano."

"Don't you adore my grandmother's baby grand? I was tickled to be the one who inherited it. I enjoy playing songs from classic musicals and fun camp songs. I haven't looked through the piano bench to discover if my folks sent a stack of my sheet music. After only seven years of lessons, I'm a solid beginner pianist."

"I don't remember you ever playing the piano at the sorority house."

"I played the player piano. Remember those WWII songs on the rollers? Some of my favorites were 'Don't Sit Under the Apple Tree' and 'Chattanooga Choo Choo'."

"Yeah, remember the Great Gatsby party we held and took turns working the piano peddles?" recalled JoAnne. "Get your shopping list. We have to get moving."

"I wasn't sure if there was coffee in the house, but looks as if the concierge coordinated everything. One thing to put on our shopping list is clocks. I can't imagine a house with microwave and ovens without clocks. What time is it anyway?"

"A few minutes before two. How soon will you be ready to go?"

"Let me grab my purse. Listen to me. Well, another item for my shopping list. My papers are in my slacks. I have cash."

"The field office gave me a set of credit cards for you, Captain Bonnie Watkins. We're going to have an enjoyable time shopping!" said JoAnne as she rubbed her hands together.

CHAPTER SIX

It was Tuesday, her day off from entertaining Mr. Tao's clients. Sue Li followed the same routine each week. First stop was an exclusive candy store in Alexandria. At the second stop, her driver dropped her and her bodyguard at the Freer Gallery, the entrance on Independence Street, to view the impressive Chinese porcelain collection. Sixty minutes later, he met them at the Jefferson Street door. The driver used to accompany her at the gallery, but after months of repeating the same routine every Tuesday, he stayed in the car, as Timmerman had predicted. The plot would work only if her uncle didn't replace her driver. During the summer she wore the same silk suit the color of pale blue hydrangeas and a white blouse with a soft fabric tie at the neck. She ensured her driver saw the two boxes of chocolate truffles in bright pink bags she smuggled into the museum in the same oversized leather satchel week after week. Today she nibbled on the decadent chocolates while enjoying the displays of Chinese exhibits. Eventually, the candy in the gaudy pink bags would be replaced with explosives—the key to her freedom.

Sue Li's spirits were lifted when they drove under the colorful Chinatown Gateway Arch, a gift to Washington, DC, from her home city of Beijing. But the arch covered the street near her uncle's Oriental restaurant, which signaled they would be arriving soon. The arch reminded her of home. She felt comfortable and homesick for her spectacular historic city when she heard endless chatter among the restaurant employees. She wondered if their petty arguments were staged for her uncle to resolve. Her uncle's Chinese delicacies were creatively displayed on Oriental platters on a central table, delivered via his personal jet hours before. She would skip the pickled eel today. He didn't seem to mind; he was deep in conversation with a towering American man in a dark suit seated at the table in the back of the dining room. The visitor's eyes looked at her as if she was the talented courtesan she was, but not the business professional she wanted to be. She'd met men like that before. A man in a dark jacket and sunglasses stood nearby.

After dinner her uncle would return to China having completed his business. She hoped his guest would leave before her uncle's departure. It would be problematic to deny his advances if her uncle had given permission. She'd worked to please a select clientele, to create the allusion of love and tenderness at a price. He seemed the type who would expect her to perform as if she was a girl in the porno movies her uncle produced in his slum brothels. She suspected it would be a *courtesy* visit as her uncle had instructed many times for his friends. She gave him a sweet smile anyway to please her uncle. She joined the other girls at the tables and retreated into their giggles of Chinese laughter. She was relieved when the two Americans left.

"Sue Li, please join me for tea before I leave," her uncle stated from across the room. The room was suddenly deadly quiet when he spoke. She scurried quickly to his table.

"Tell me progress on Janice Brown. Is she still friends with Charlie Smith?"

"She arrived in DC. We followed her. We had her home address in Florida from her passport when she came to China to investigate the fruit flies on the grapefruits. Her ranch in Illahaw has few roads in and out. We planned well and waited until movers arrived to transport her things to DC, to a condo in Virginia. Word went out to recruit a decorator with a short deadline at the same address. I made sure I was awarded the contract. Ron Jones from the Spa in Georgia and his interior design staff came to assist me on the project. I haven't seen her with Charlie Smith. We will kill her, my uncle. I promise."

"Good, my niece," he said as he slipped his hand under her skirt. "My visitor was interested in spending time with you, Sue Li."

"Yes, I saw him," she told her uncle, and offered a well-practiced warm smile knowing soon her uncle would be dead. Soon she and her bodyguard would be free to stay in the US with their lovers. She only had to wait until Timmerman arrived home.

CHAPTER SEVEN

Bonnie was supposed to report to her assignment at the VA outpatient diet clinic on Monday, but the building inspectors had yet to clear it for occupancy. Apparently, there was a long punch list of to-do items before the renovations of a tired strip mall would be finished. She didn't mind; she'd spent the morning organizing her files in her adjacent office. On Tuesday she wore a patriotic blue summer linen suit to visit the appropriate offices at the State Department to establish her identity and to learn how best to be helpful. It was Wednesday before she reported to work.

The outpatient diet office looked as if it has been there forever, even though today was the grand opening. Mid-century plastic chairs and ratty folding tables set the ambiance.

"Glad you could join us, Captain Watkins. Hope we didn't interrupt your tour of the State Department."

"Thank you, Sargent Major. Seems we're going to be busy today. Glad you are here to coordinate the details." The sargent major wanted to be somewhere else, anywhere else, she was sure. Being assigned to work the sign-in desk at the diet clinic was probably a less-than-desirable assignment. He was slender and balding on top with a deep tan. The starched creases in his uniform shirt and khaki trousers reflected in the toe of his polished lace-up boots. She quickly deduced working with Dobbs would require extra effort to retain him on her side. He wasn't pleased with a decision to put a hold on Carrie's transfer from Walter Reed, along with two dietitians assigned to assist with the outpatient clients, he told her. She suspected he felt he was stuck with her. He shoved a paper across the polished counter in her direction. "Here's the list of patients you are to counsel today."

She glanced around the former grocery store to find a location to hold a private conversation, but decided she'd have to whisper. "Sargent Major, is it okay if I talk to clients in the front corner of the room?"

"It's your show. Go ahead."

"Thank you." She was being overly cheerful working diligently to appear friendly. She retrieved the clipboard, walked toward the group of twenty or twenty-five patients, and called the first name from the sign-in sheet. He raised his hand and she approached him. "Hello, I'm Bonnie, the dietitian. What can I assist you with this morning?"

"It's my diabetes. Doc wanted me to come to the diet clinic."

"Certainly, a trusted strategy. My goal is to facilitate your efforts to plan strategies and examine options. I try to find the perfect solutions to comply with physician's suggestions, however, sometimes I don't provide the right advice at the first meeting, or I fail to ask the right questions to understand what's going on. Promise in advance you will allow me a second chance if the scheme needs adjusting. Managing diabetes is a process. It is a day by day effort. Don't expect optimal control in one day or one week. No one learns to be a sniper in one afternoon, do they? Do you care if other people who have questions concerning diabetes meet together? Would it be permissible to have them join us? What rank did you have when you were on active duty?"

"I was an E-5. I served in Vietnam."

Before he could answer her other question, she raised her voice but tried to pitch her tone low and robust. "Sargent Green is inviting anyone with diabetes to join our group."

While everyone was moving their chairs, she walked quickly to the sargent major's station. "Sir, do we have a coffeepot?"

"No. One was supposed to be here," he grumbled.

She grabbed her purse and walked hurriedly to a group of men gathered around the desk. "Can I ask a favor? Here's some cash. Go purchase us a coffeepot, coffee, cream, and sugar. Well, y'all have made coffee before. Purchase us doughnuts or cookies, breakfast sandwiches, bagels, whatever you can find for breakfast du jour. Today is the first day of the clinic. We have to celebrate, don't you think?"

They looked at her as if she was looney.

"Attention!" called the sargent major. He faced the American flag and flags for each of the services and began the Pledge of Allegiance. Once concluded he continued, "Welcome and good morning, men and ladies. Welcome to the outpatient diet clinic. First mission is to name our center. A crew is securing us a coffeepot. Captain Bonnie Watkins is our chief medical officer. Questions? Dismissed."

"Uh-rah!" rumbled through the room.

She returned to the diabetes group and asked the members to introduce themselves and provide a one-minute description of their military service. The group was mostly retirement-aged men, but there were a few younger and a small contingency of women in the room. By the time the introductions were completed, the refreshment crew had returned and started making coffee. They'd even found a bouquet of colorful balloons tied to a welcoming pot of white chrysanthemums with yellow centers. She quickly reviewed basic tips of the five strategies for diabetes control:

monitor, medication, diet, exercise, and food for sick days. Smells of coffee distracted the group. "I think the coffee is ready. Grab a cup and we'll have time to answer questions individually."

The morning went quickly. "Sargent Major, how do I obtain a copy of the sign-in sheet? Somehow the clinic needs to place notes in their medical files at Walter Reed. And what can we do to group individuals with similar diet problems? I was going to ask your opinion if we hold diabetes clinic in the morning and meet with everyone else after lunch. You're the one with those stripes on your sleeve, indicating you've commanded thousands of men, and I'm unsure of the chain-of-command, my first day and all. Can you please help me organize this?"

He nodded.

"Thank you for helping today. Things went pretty well. Things will be better tomorrow!" She tried to be enthusiastic, but suspected Sargent Major Dobbs would soon have other pressing assignments.

She couldn't believe Management, aka Charlie and Frank, would let her drive back and forth to the clinic. She enjoyed the freedom of driving her own vehicle again. With the people who seemed to hover around her, she rarely had time alone. She'd missed listening to tapes of her favorite Southern rock bands. She loved Charlie and guessed the constant crowd of his or Frank's associates was worth having him involved in her life. She started to add "again," but they'd dated only one summer and rendezvoused here and there when their travel locations overlapped.

She drove by a park a mile from the Veteran's Center. She recognized these military personnel already knew exercise. She was going to propose doing a lecture while the group walked to the park. Hopefully the blood sugar monitors she'd requested arrived with extra strips. They'd test blood sugars before the hike, complete the walk, and check blood sugars when they returned. Of course, Dobbs would have to agree, but she knew the clinic attendees would be surprised at the reduction in blood sugars with minimal exercise. "Oh, there's an office supply store." She stopped and purchased supplies for class. She wondered if a hundred pocket notebooks were enough. She'd ask Dobbs to put them on their office supply order. The class participants could maintain records of blood sugars and food intake to determine what foods elevated blood sugars, and which ones had minimal or no influence. There were general trends, but it varied tremendously from person to person.

Driving back to the condo, Bonnie was thinking of plunging into the cool waters of the pool. At the outpatient clinic, wide windows overlooked the parking lot, and as the day progressed, the low western sun filled the room with light but also unfortunately had a giant greenhouse effect. She worried if the patients were getting overheated as they sat attentively in the sauna classroom. By midafternoon the air-conditioning system made a loud groan and died. Someone stood, faced the air conditioner, and as he began singing "Taps," the rest of the room stood holding their ball caps against their chest. She sent the refreshment committee to buy metal tubs from the hardware store. Others volunteered to drive to the Class VI store to stock the tubs with ice, sodas, juice, and sports drinks. Somebody found a fan and pinned a handwritten sign on the receptionist desk with the words, "Health Spa," which didn't amuse Sargent Major Dobbs. She wanted to laugh, but could tell he needed her support. She suspected he also needed time to warm up to the idea of being in charge of an outpatient diet clinic. She suspected this assignment didn't have the interest nor the danger compared to his recent projects.

At home, Baby Kittie met her at the door and watched as

she tossed her low heels and wiggled out of the regulation Army uniform. Bonnie saw the ties to her bikini top disappear under the bed. "Baby Kittie!" There went her plans to swim in the lap pool. She wasn't the skinny-dipping type, especially in a pool at a carefully watched compound. After playing hide-and-seek with Baby Kittie, she grabbed the phone to call Randy.

"Randy, nothing urgent, but I have a request."

"Sure. Shoot! Wait, I'll be there in a few minutes."

"Okay. I'll mix a pitcher of sangria." But first she had to find her Levis with the cargo pockets and a T-shirt.

She was slicing oranges, limes, and lemons to toss into a pitcher of red wine with a six-ounce can of limeade concentrate. She was pouring the sangria into chilled wineglasses when Randy arrived.

"Randy, reporting as ordered, ma'am."

"Cute. Randy, cute. Be serious. The air-conditioning is out at the clinic. Have you seen those paper fans with the thin wood handle used on hot days in Southern churches?"

"Yeah! When I was a kid, I remember the fans at my grandmother's church."

"Could you possibly order a thousand fans as soon as possible?" she asked in a Southern whine. "And, if there's no delay for printing and the costs aren't too exorbitant, have them read, 'I'm a fan of the VA Diet Clinic.' Is it too corny?"

"No, you can pull it off. You have any other requests, Captain Bonnie Watkins?"

"Well, since you asked... Yes. I'm hankering for homemade peach ice cream churned in an old-fashioned hand-cranked ice cream maker. I can practically taste the luscious sweet custard with tart ripe peaches with a touch of salt from the salty brine in the wooden tub which usually leaked into the metal tub holding the custard mix. Carrie and I are going to the flea market this weekend. I'm hunting for a churn with a wooden bucket. I guess I could get an electric churn, but where's the fun in that? Oh, Baby Kittie is craving a tub of smoked mullet spread, if you travel to Cedar Key anytime soon."

"She does? I'll write a note. Big or a giant tub?"

Baby Kittie jumped on the counter with her reply, "Meeeowwwt!"

"Definitely a giant tub." They both laughed.

Randy wondered how she knew. This weekend he was traveling to Florida to meet with Frank and Roger at the strip club south of Gainesville, an hour's drive from Cedar Key.

*****

She'd hoped the second week at the clinic would be easier than the first. She arrived early, but the room was already full.

"Good morning, Sargent Major."

"Good morning, Captain."

She was shocked he responded. "Call me Bonnie."

"You can call me Dobbs."

She smiled. "Do I smell coffee?"

"Yes, ma'am. We started the coffee for you. The grocery store sent us yesterday's unsold doughnuts and pastries. I tasted one or two, and they appeared to be okay. They established a charge account for the clinic to secure morning pastries."

"How nice. Means I still have work to do on the teaching schedule. How's this for a topic? 'Trade Carbs for Doughnuts, Carb-Swapping 101'?"

"What?"

"Sorry. Y'all talk military slang, and I guess dietitians do as well. We call carbohydrates, carbs. I also use the term 'BS' for blood sugars, which I've heard has other meanings in some circles." She gave a sly smile. "Dobbs, you've gotten things well organized and created a comfortable place for everyone. I'm relieved we're running a people-centered clinic, and one with few regulations and boundaries. I'm rather new to the military so don't hesitate to tell me if I'm bending the rules too far."

"I've heard of your recent recruitment."

He confirmed what she had suspected. From a distance Charlie, Frank and Randy were smoothing rough edges for her.

"You're doing fine. You set the tone when you started the workshops by recognizing the men's service. Word of mouth has spread in support of the diabetes classes. When Frank pitched the idea, I honestly was prepared to accept the program would be short-lived. But, you've convinced me otherwise. I called Walter Reed and ordered the diabetes consults to be sent here. I also called the hospital commanding officer for a delivery date for the staff he promised," said Dobbs.

"What, and break up our fabulous friendship?"

"Captain, you and I both are aware we are top-heavy. At a moment's notice, we can be yanked out of here and sent to who knows where. We both want the program to continue after we're reassigned. You have an extra concern—you have to be mindful to leave a light footprint and to avoid a traceable record."

He knew her history. She guessed she looked confused. Frank had told her to talk to only Charlie and him and preclude discussions of her situation even with team members. She simply smiled.

"You and I are a lot alike," he continued. "We're starters. We take raw materials and create. The people who replace us will have an excellent pattern to refine and follow."

Bonnie nodded. "I totally agree. Yesterday, I noticed some of our crowd came early and stayed throughout the day; others dropped in for half a day, either in the morning or in the afternoon. What if we started the classes on the hour? I'll move through the lessons each day, but will start with a different lecture as the first morning topic and will repeat it as the last lecture of the day. This will allow people to stop by on the way to work or on the way home. By the end of the week, they will have heard five lessons. I'll post a weekly grid sheet at the desk. I'll do anything to create an atmosphere to make diet counseling as painless as possible. I hope to finish a form letter to give to employers and another for their physician to list patient's self-determined health goals."

"Would you consider offering a night class, and close at noon on Fridays?" asked Dobbs.

"You're proposing the change for *this* week?"

"Thursday night!"

She wished Randy was there to ask about plans for safely traveling back to the condo in the dark. "Hopefully I can find something to fill my time during a long weekend if we left at noon on Friday. But I work for you; the final decision is yours."

"You're damn right!" Dobb'\s chuckled.

*****

"Good night. Thanks for dropping me off." Her Thursday night ride waited while she unlocked the heavy carved doors to enter the enclosed courtyard. She waved as the car slowly drove away. The evening was warm. She looked forward to cooler weather. Fall was still weeks away. "Baby Kittie? What are you doing on the porch?"

"Meow." The tortoiseshell calico happily returned to her perch on the glass top wrought-iron table, chasing moths circling the soft patio lighting along the edges of the flower beds. She could have sworn she left her kitty upstairs watching the cardinals play in the magnolia tree by her bedroom window. She needed to talk with Randy to at least consider having the shuttle driver accompany her into the house before they left. Baby Kittie scooted under her feet as she opened the door to the kitchen hall.

Bonnie headed to the refrigerator for a glass of wine. She

61

and JoAnne toured the Class VI store on their last shopping trip. She didn't have a clue how to select wines. It didn't matter if the vino was white, red, blush, aged, oaky, or buttery; she simply made her selections by the labels. Flowers were her first choice followed by birds and animals, but there weren't many labels featuring animals. Choosing the bourbon was uncomplicated — she bought Wild Turkey. She opened a can of cat food and added a handful of cat nibbles to Baby Kittie's bowl. Usually when she rattled the box of nibbles, Baby Kittie was at her feet. "Where are you, you little rascal? Baby Kittie?"

"Geeerrooowlll, Geeerrooowlll!

"Baby Kittie? Where are you?" She felt a chill. She grabbed her Glock from the kitchen drawer, one of many delivered by JoAnne at Charlie's insistence. She checked the magazine and pushed it snugly into the handle. She pulled the slide toward her to load a bullet into the chamber making it ready to fire.

Baby Kittie continued to howl. She heard frantic banging. Something shattered as it landed on the floor with a thump. Pounding footsteps rushed across the floor upstairs in the bedroom. She held her gun tighter. She kept her back against the railings to steady her aim as she moved one foot at a time quietly ascending the dark stairs.

Something furry brushed her leg. She wanted to scream but it would convey her position. Baby Kittie continued to growl. She pushed against the wall on the platform at the top of the stairs between the bedroom suites. She patted the wall with her left hand. "Where are those light switches?" She clung tightly to the Glock in her right hand. She quickly snapped the lights and waited.

Baby Kittie rushed to her side, faced the door, and made an angry hiss, then darted back into the dark room. Sounds of scurrying and screeching followed. "It has to be another cat!" She took a deep breath and moved slowly around the corner through the door opening. Gray fur disappeared under the eyelet bed ruffle. Suddenly, she saw the long skinless tail. It was a possum! She chuckled and quietly closed the door trapping the possum in her room.

She moved the picture to retrieve the emergency phone hid in a wall opening between the rooms at the top of the stairs. "Baby Kittie, time to call in reinforcements."

"Ma'am, are you okay?"

"I have possums upstairs in the bedroom. Bring traps."

Within minutes, people were arriving through the tunnel entrance in the downstairs hall closet and the upstairs closet connected to the office on the first floor via a circular staircase. Their guns were drawn. "Bonnie?"

"In the bedroom!"

"We must have had static on the connection. Who did you trap?"

"Baby Kittie has them cornered, but at least one ran down the stairs. Do we have any have animal traps?"

"You're kidding, aren't you? How in the h-heck did they get in here?"

"My thoughts exactly." She put her hand on her hip. "I wanted y'all here with me, in case I'm wrong and the possum is a diversion." She opened the door and there perched on the toilet was a mama possum with five or six babies hanging on her long gray fur. "Somebody grab a bowl to offer her water. We have to prevent those little ones from losing their grip and drowning."

"We could rescue them."

"Have you seen those fifty-two teeth? I count seven sets of eyes. Possums can birth as many as fifteen babies. Check under and around everything upstairs. There's bound to be a few siblings. And check downstairs. I swear something furry ran past me when I was on the stairs. The drapes are wiggling. Did anyone check behind the drapes?"

"No, we're still searching the other rooms."

"Found two in the guest bedroom."

"I found one under the dresser," added one of the crew.

"Find me a dustpan and a broom, or a pancake turner," she hollered. "The littles ones are two or three inches long. We may be able to move them in a dustpan."

"Baby Kittie is howling in the kitchen in front of the cabinet by the sink"

"Look inside for the kitty nibble. She probably wants you to retrieve food for the mama possum. Bowls are on the shelves above the dishwasher." Bonnie's tone suddenly turned harsh and demanding, "Guys, get up here now!"

"Did you find another one?" one of the team joked.

"Everyone to the bedroom! Immediately! That's an order," Bonnie hollered.

"We'd never contemplated we'd hear that from you, Bonnie." One punched the other with his elbow as they moved toward the second floor.

"We have a problem. The window is broken and there's a bloody print on the wall by the window." She pulled back the drapery panel. "Here's how the possums entered the apartment, but those aren't possum prints!"

She heard one of the crew on the phone reporting back to "Mom."

"Mom, rowdy neighbors came over while we were at the movies and left dirty handprints on your white sofa. Okay, we'll talk when you return home."

She wondered why anyone would break into her apartment.

In minutes a dark van pulled into her driveway and was ushered into the enclosed garage. Bonnie's Jeep was kept in the garage belonging to the adjoining office apartment. An attractive young lady bounded the steps carrying a tackle box under each arm to the second floor. She was dressed in khaki slacks and a navy polo shirt. Her ball cap read in bold yellow letters, "FBI."

"Bonnie, meet Special Agent Gilman Summers. We call her Gil. She worked with us before she transferred to a high-profile job with the FBI. She lives in the building by the gate."

"Pleased to meet you. We found a bloody handprint on the wall by the window, along with a family of possums."

"Can't help you with the possums but let me look at the prints."

The room was quiet while they watched her slip her hands in blue gloves and place yellow evidence markers around the room. She efficiently took pictures of the glass on the floor, the window, the drapes, and the handprint. "Find me a ladder, Randy. I'm going to carry the drapes back to the lab. Cross your fingers we'll recover epithelial cells or a strand of hair. While she retrieved a paper evidence bag, a ladder appeared. "Anyone have forensic training to lend a hand and bag this glass? Lots of curved edges. I suspect the glass was cut. Randy, send a crew outside to secure the area under this window. Get a bucket truck pronto to examine the tree without destroying possible physical evidence. And people," she added, "don't touch anything. Stay across the room by the door. The scene is extremely organized. I suspect this was a professional break-in. I smell the scent of explosives probably used to break the bulletproof glass in the picture window when cutting failed. Creative design, by the way, Randy."

"Randy, what are we going to do with the possums?" questioned Bonnie.

"Oh, forgot to tell you. Friends from the US Forest Service are on the way to relocate the happy family."

"I'll keep the mama and her brood in the bath," she

65

volunteered. "Can someone bring me a chair?" Once seated, Baby Kittie jumped onto her lap to supervise.

"The mama possum seems perfectly content with her brood resting on the bathroom rug. Thank you, Baby Kittie, for sharing your nibbles." She reached down to scratch her ears. "Ten babies on my count. What was the critter that ran down the stairs?"

"A squirrel. Baby Kittie cornered it in the kitchen. We opened the patio door off the kitchen hall and he or she gladly retreated. But on the subject of retreating, we have to move you for a few days until we repair the window."

"I'm going to cut hunks of the drywall and carpet to conduct the analyses. Sorry, Bonnie."

"I'll talk with the building manager to organize the repairs." She looked at Randy and raised her eyebrows. "Baby Kittie and I have a bug-out bag in the Jeep. Okay if we retrieve the uniforms?"

"Maybe tomorrow since the closet door is open."

"You're right." She gasped. "The doors were closed when I left this morning. Randy, what are the options for my wardrobe tomorrow?"

"I'll call Dobbs. I hear the Forest Service crew downstairs. I'll be right back."

In minutes, the men dressed in khakis and green polo shirts efficiently corralled the possums using dark plastic panels, into an animal carrier.

"Bye-bye, Mama Possum, right, Baby Kittie? Thanks, guys, for helping a damsel in distress."

"We were glad to. Tiny possums can die of hypothermia if we don't move them to our heated environment at the recovery center. We lose a lot of them at this age when there are too many and Mama loses count, or too big to sleep in Mama's pouch and are left in the cold. She's a noble mama to have saved ten. Virginia possums are the only native marsupial in the North American continent."

"Can I ask you a question? Do possums climb trees?"

"Yes, I've seen them in apple trees to pick fruit, but at this time of the year with babies in tow I doubt she would risk climbing a magnolia tree. Despite the drawings in children's books, they don't hang upside by their tail. Why do you ask?"

"Oh, simple curiosity. Do you have volunteers at the rescue center?"

"As a matter of fact, we are desperate for volunteers. Lots of babies this time of the year following spring romances." They snickered.

"Do you have a business card? I'll check my schedule." She immediately remembered the veterans staying at the strip mall and wondered if they would consider volunteering for a pet-sitting project. She needed to talk to Dobbs.

"*Management* has invited you to stay at an exclusive hotel tonight. Dobbs issued a uniform policy for Fridays as casual Fridays. You and Baby Kitty ready to go? Got your gun?" asked Randy. "Here are binoculars and ammo for your bug-out bag."

"Thanks." A Glock was tucked safely into her backpack, Charlie's orders. She had to refrain from a giggle and smiled thinking of the casual Friday dress code. Only she and Sgt. Dobbs wore uniforms.

Chapter Eight

Few cars were on the road driving into DC when they'd left the condos. It was close to midnight by the time they'd organized teams to investigate the break-in. She was in awe seeing the national monuments bathed in evening lights in the distance. The lights twinkled on the Potomac River. "Look at the powerful buffalos guarding the bridge into Georgetown, Baby Kittie!" She was trying to sound as if a burglary at her apartment was a day-to-day occurrence. She tried to divert her concerns toward enjoying the stunning DC landscape.

"The bridge was built in 1883 to provide access to the business district along the Potomac River," added Randy, her driver for the evening.

"With streets of romantic historic townhouses in Georgetown, I forget this area was a major shipping center to and from international ports."

"These cobblestone streets don't forget and are too bumpy."

Rarely did Randy sound apprehensive. She figured the recent events with safety implications had his attention. She ignored his negative vibes.

"Why did you ask if possums could climb trees?" he asked

her.

"The assumption was the possums climbed through the broken window from the magnolia tree. I can possibly theorize the squirrel jumped from the tree to the window, but I propose someone broke into the apartment through the window and went downstairs to retrieve Mama possum and her brood in a waiting cage."

Randy grabbed his radio. "Mom, I didn't have time to clean downstairs at the guest cottage. Can you call the cleaning lady? Love you, Mom!" He returned the radio to the console. "I hadn't considered there may be evidence in the rest of the house after we found the bloody handprints upstairs. Frank will send a second team."

She didn't make further comments on something she'd discovered Randy had overlooked. "I've admired the artist's portrayal of a peaceful spirit in the *Nuns of the Battlefield* sculpture to honor the hundreds of nuns who worked in field hospitals during the Civil War for both sides. It's unfortunate that it was 1924 before their loving service was properly recognized. Sixty years later, I bet few of the heroic women were living to have enjoyed such an honor."

"Yeah, what a missed opportunity."

"It's been a while since I've been on the Georgetown side of DC," chatted Bonnie. "There's DuPont Circle and the gorgeous three-tiered fountain in the middle of the roundabout. The view of bygone architecture framed by aging oaks could have been one hundred years ago. Randy, you're a builder. I'm confused with the layers of building styles in Georgetown. Are the red-brick-trimmed buildings with contrasting black wrought-iron late Victorian? Or maybe Romanesque Revival or Classical Revival? Can't you envision ladies in long dresses sitting at their desks in the bay windows and curved alcoves maintaining their correspondence with a feathered quill pen? When I was working a contract in DC, I remember somewhere in the area was a farmer's market. They had the most flavorful homemade cheeses and local honeys. In the fall they gave shoppers a basket to fill with apples. Who knew apples had so many shapes, sizes and colors? One weekend I even attended a watercolor painting course held on the sidewalk at the market. I painted apples. The pictures are at the ranch somewhere. The number of apple varieties was captivating. I guess I shouldn't have been surprised. With oranges there are early and late varieties, each with their individual tastes and qualities. Only local stores can carry the interesting rare varieties, right off the tree. I remember helping my dad test our oranges for sugar levels to schedule picking the fruit and selling them to the processing plant. Apples must be the same. You would've loved the hot cider made from fresh-squeezed juice served with fried apple doughnuts rolled in cinnamon and sugar. Oh," she moaned, "they were practically orgasmic!"

"What?"

She knew his mind was somewhere else or he would have bantered with a snappy reply.

"Here's where you're staying. We enter through a private entrance two streets away. There's a rumor the FBI designed thirty-two secret doors and rambling passageways through the hotel rooms. I hope Baby Kittie doesn't get lost."

"Meow!"

As she read the name on the hotel marque, "The Mansion on O Street," she wondered if this was where Randy had been inspired to build tunnels in the condo complex. They pulled into an ordinary-looking garage at a two-story brick Colonial. After going through a maze of security checkpoints with keys and keypads, they parked in an underground parking lot. Randy unlocked a door to one of several elevators along one wall. When the elevator opened, a man in a tuxedo welcomed them and handed Randy a room key. Baby Kittie leaned across Bonnie's arm carefully observing. The concierge smiled briefly, extended a white-gloved hand, and suggested a path to the room.

Randy opened the utilitarian-looking metal door into a commercial-looking hall, and once past the metal door Bonnie was immediately impressed. But she knew she had to wait until the door was closed. Baby Kittie jumped down and ran around the room. "Randy, this resembles my living room at the Ranch at Bay Branch!"

"You're kidding, aren't you?"

"No, I'm serious. The whitewashed shiplap on the walls and the handcrafted pie safe of mismatched boards is the same design as the one my grandfather built for my grandmother's birthday right after they finished the house in Illahaw. Even the huge brick fireplace is the identical design! The brick has the same look as the bricks at my grandmother's house. She told me the bricks came from a house built in the late 1800s by a British family, the Addisons. The English country house was hit by lightning near the same time as the outbreak of WWI when my grandfather and his brother were drafted and sent to France. Their house was a mile from the Ranch at Bay Branch, depending on how many wildflowers I picked. My grandfather and great-uncle visited the Addison family in England and sent my grandmother a letter for her to send money to purchase the neighbor's former English estate. Grandmother sold the sheep, the calves, and most of the cows to have enough cash to complete the deal. The family attorney send the money and waited. She said she neither had the cows nor the cash, which is the standard in cattle sales, even today. Ships bringing supplies and mail to England were being torpedoed. It was months before she knew the purchase was confirmed, and with no knowledge if my grandfather was coming home after the war."

Randy seemed to be in another world.

"Guess what my grandmother said was the first thing she did when the attorneys confirmed the purchase of the English land? She salvaged the brick from the English house to build a real fireplace. She and my grandfather had crafted a sticks-and-clay fireplace themselves, which generally was very efficient, but they had to maintain a careful watch because stick-and-clay fireplaces had a tendency to catch fire and frequently leaked during rainstorms where the fireplace joined the house."

"How long has your family been in Florida?"

"Depending on which genealogy chart you examine, somewhere between 120-150 years. We have relatives from Ireland, Scotland, and England. With aunts, sisters, and cousins who have dark hair and sultry eyes, Grandmother suspected some of our relatives may have also come from Spain in the late 1500s and settled at St. Augustine, but it's probably fun gossip rather than fact. Some of the family arrived at Ellis Island in New York, but most came to Savannah in the 1820s and started drifting south. Members of the family came from Scotland to escape the potato famine in the 1840s. My great-great grandmother purchased the land at Bay Branch in the 1850s a few years after Florida became a state in 1845."

"I had no idea Florida had such diverse populations."

"Florida had been an historic international destination well before the theme parks arrived searching for the elusive Fountain of Youth, but mainly searching for land and treasure. At one time or another Florida lands had been controlled by Spain, France, Great Britain, and of course, the United States." She was still touring the transformed maintenance office. "Randy, look at these polished oiled floors. Reflecting on my grandparents work to salvage the English house, I wonder if the English sideboards and the Hepplewhite chairs in grandmother's house came from the old house. Her chairs weren't covered in leather but the rustic table could be the twin to grandmother's table at my farmhouse. I wonder what was done in the bedrooms."

"My responsibility was to purchase the list of furnishings. Another crew did the decorating."

"Randy! Look at this white-on-white muslin quilt with its gorgeous off-white embroidery. Where did you find a king-sized canopy bed? How creative using strips of muslin to create a loose canopy tied at the corners leaving the frame exposed." She'd admired the prints of Washington's Mount Vernon on the Potomac River hung above the bedside tables. She was twirling around the room mesmerized by furnishings she'd previously viewed from behind a rope on a tour of historic homes during a college field trip, and tours of DC with Charlie.

"Are you staying here tonight? There's another bedroom," Bonnie asked.

"No, I have another assignment, but someone will be at the door at 0700, oh yeah, seven o'clock in the morning to deliver you to the outpatient diet clinic. I'm told you have a fully stocked kitchen. But back to your question, I'm to stay until someone relieves me to introduce you to your security detail. The password for you is Montana. Ask for the password. That's our protocol. Any questions?" He glanced at his watch. "While we wait, let's raid the kitchen. Did you have a chance to eat before we left?"

"No, I'm starving, since you mentioned it." She couldn't wait to explore the kitchen. "In the refrigerator there's a plate of sliced meats and cheeses, sourdough and rye bread, and a basket filled with jars of gourmet mustards. There're pint jars of chilled corn relish and maybe potato salad. Both have today's date on the label, could be the made date, or expiration date, but it smells okay. Found cream cheese, Brie cheese, and hot pepper jelly, a couple of yogurts, and a whole shelf of soda and juice. The stems on the grapes look fresh. Here's a dazzling cut-crystal bowl of apricots, pears, and apples. In the cabinet there's a shelf of crackers and chips. What can I fix for you?"

"Did you find the grits?"

"I wonder if twenty-five pounds of grits will be enough. You bought white, yellow, instant, flavored, and stoneground grits. Obviously y'all were expecting me to stay here for a while."

"If need be, we're prepared. But back to dinner, I'll assemble a sandwich and grab some chips, but I can do it."

"Oh, Randy, look at the bottles of wine with labels and drawings of Monticello, Jefferson's home. Y'all are going to spoil me. I can't carry the treasures with me, but this cute tea towel has a printed copy of Abraham Lincoln's favorite molasses pecan pie recipe. It sounds delicious. You can't go wrong with molasses and pecans. Here's a basket of DC tasty extravagances: gourmet blended teas from Mount Vernon, a pack of Pez dispensers featuring the faces of famous presidents, Virginia pecan pralines, and gourmet chocolates in hot pink boxes. Are you sure I can't bring one or two things with me?"

Randy gave her a nasty scowl.

"Baby Kitty found nibbles on the bottom shelf, cat litter, and a litter pan. I'm gonna pour me a glass of wine from the bottle with the garden on the label. Can I pour you one?"

"What are you eating?"

"It's probably murder for my waistline, but Baby Kittie and I are hungry for salty taco chips, cream cheese, and spicy corn relish. Maybe we'll research how it compares to cream cheese with pepper jelly on crackers. But look at these elegant porcelain plates with a green border and the bread and butter plates with the botanical scenes. The price labels are still on the back. Honestly, I had anticipated paper plates with plastic silverware."

"I have a confession. With the plan you'd be joining us in DC, Management assigned a crew to outfit this apartment. The security was the best here. I'd met you for maybe thirty minutes in Daytona when we took Charlie to the clinic, and in Russia at the chateau, but there were a lot of things happening. Roger knew you the best. His crew sent photos of your house at the Ranch at Bay Branch. JoAnne mentioned we should look at Mount Vernon and Monticello for ideas. The ladies in the gift shops looked at the pictures of our great-aunt's farmhouse and suggested the dishes, and also gave us the addresses of antique stores for the other pieces. We told them your health was failing and you were moving to DC into my dad's converted garage, slash guest house. We practiced our story. Pretty creative, huh?"

"I'm flattered at the efforts to welcome me into the group. You could have dumped me in a fleabag hotel. Even here you could've chosen early prison décor. This suite is extravagant. I noticed there are no windows behind the drapes, simply black-painted window frames. Incredibly clever."

"At least you won't have trouble with broken windows or invading possums!" He chuckled, and glanced at his watch again. "The location is close to Embassy Row. It's almost impossible to get a reservation. This room was used for storage, but met our needs. At the entrance we added the rough concrete wall and left the stained concrete floors. The construction crews wore construction clothes when they came and went. We wanted the hall view of the room to retain the look of a maintenance area, in case someone walked by as the door opened. Hiding in plain sight can be challenging."

"Yes, I can imagine." She remembered the elaborate efforts it took to disappear in an airport during the flights from Moscow. "How's the sandwich?"

"Acceptable, but the sandwich would be extraordinary with

a couple of wedges of a garlic pickle to eat with the pastrami."

"I'll speak with Management."

"My replacement is behind schedule. We're so deep in the building structure none of our usual electronics work. We had to go old-school and install a landline. I'm going to call in. The phone's in the third drawer of the china cabinet in the kitchen. Same system as the condo: remove the receiver and you're connected. "Hey, Mom. Can't find the mangy dog. Yeah, I'm still looking."

Bonnie could sense Randy was rattled. He usually responded in a neutral way, similar to Frank and Charlie. She wondered if there was an escape route. Surely, they wouldn't have only one entrance in and out. "How did you discover I liked jigsaw puzzles?"

"Pictures of the farmhouse showed a bookcase filled with puzzles. We didn't have time to install a TV and entertainment center."

"Where did you buy these marvelous rugs?" She was trying to kill time and avoid asking the obvious questions. Randy's conversation was disengaged.

"At the same antique store where we bought the leather-covered chairs. The rugs had been used in a steakhouse as wall art. We felt the rugs with subtle greens and grays in geometric patterns blended with the framed watercolors of the Mount Vernon landscapes. You'd be proud we passed on the antler lamps and moose head."

"I would have loved those!" She sighed. "Y'all apparently didn't visit my folk's house across the pasture. Dad and my brother have a collection of antlers with high Boone and Crocket scores. But the sophisticated country manor furnishings appear in harmony with the multinational flavor of Georgetown. I'm amazed the decorating mission was accomplished on such short notice. The apartment reminds me of home. This will be comfortable. Randy, it's getting late. Would you mind if I grabbed a shower and went to bed? Wake me when your replacement arrives."

"Yeah. I'd be glad to."

"Baby Kittie loves playing with puzzle pieces. She'll like the puzzle of Smithsonian Castle on the Mall. But beware Baby Kittie picks pieces by color and will push the ones in the same hue off the table and onto the floor. She also hides pieces. Check under the furniture if pieces go MIA."

"It's you and me, Baby Kitty. Bonnie, I'm raiding the liquor cabinet," Randy said as he grabbed the feline and headed to the kitchen.

"Where did you hide the Wild Turkey? Randy, you're holding out on me!" she bantered.

"I'll have one waiting when you finish your shower."

In her bug-out backpack were two outfits identical to the ones she'd had on: dark polo shirts and dark cargo slacks with zippered pockets below her knee to hold her official papers. She brazenly considered wearing a top in dark purple or burgundy, but would save the wardrobe experimentation until there were calmer events around her. She wasn't in a hurry to shower, but had exhausted her list of mindless conversation despite the high grades she'd received in table chatter at her Mississippi alma mater years ago. After the craziness of the last few weeks, she'd enjoy sitting on a Southern veranda filling the afternoon with lighthearted tête-à-tête. She carelessly tossed her head to dry her hair. "Okay, Randy, where's the bourbon you promised?" she chattered as she walked into the living room.

"Sure, Sweets. I have one waiting for you!"

There stood Charlie. His smile was inviting, his six foot frame, sexy. His Levis and DC T-shirt did nothing to hide his muscles. Why couldn't they simply tell her Charlie was in town? "You're Randy's replacement? Are you sure you can handle this assignment? I've been known to be difficult," she teased. She couldn't wait to kiss him and enjoy his arms around her. The week they spent in Moscow seemed eons ago. Oh, she was hopelessly in love and drank the bourbon in one long gulp. She pulled him closer and curled her leg around his. He held her tight, but his kiss was warm and soft. They kissed across the room, down the hall, and into the bedroom. Discarded clothes followed their path. She took a deep breath, a breath which tingled her toes, then willingly surrendered to his body.

"Morning, Sweets! I made you some coffee," he said as he placed a glass of iced coffee on the bedside table. The chauffer will be here around 0700."

"Have you been awake long?"

"Yeah, jet lag, I guess."

"You should have wakened me? I love morning sex with you. It's magical. Or we could have simply shared a cup of coffee. I sure missed you. Are you going to join me in the shower?"

"Oh, I wish, but I have meetings this morning. Can I get a kiss before I leave?" She propped on her elbow and wrapped the sheet around her naked body to cover her breasts. She was eager to please.

"I'll deliver dinner tonight. I hear you and Sargent Dobbs close shop at noon on Fridays. Can't wait to hear of your work at the outpatient clinic. If you need anything, talk to Randy or Dobbs."

"They can't give me your dreamy kisses!" she whimpered. "I revel in the memory of your passionate kiss the entire day. When you retire, I hope there are many sunrises in our future to share morning kisses. Are we staying here tonight?"

"Check with Randy for an update." He was startled, her

comments unnerving. She was talking of their retirement. Had someone leaked information of his future plans? Did she know?

"I didn't find a washer/dryer unless you propose to be naked the entire weekend while I wash the clothes in the sink?" she teased.

"You're making me blush, but the image had crossed my mind. Gotta run, Sweets. Love you."

*****

Bonnie's driver arrived at her door precisely as scheduled and with the correct password. She and Baby Kittie sat quietly during the drive to prevent distracting their driver as she maneuvered through the crazy DC morning traffic.

"Baby Kittie, you're pawing at your neck, did you get a tick from the possum? Let me look at you." Baby Kittie crawled onto her lap. Bonnie tenderly separated the hair and saw a small cut on the back of her neck. It couldn't be a scratch. If it was a tick bite, those were usually a round irritated area, but this injury was a straight line.

"Thank you, Sargent. It was a delightful ride this morning. I appreciate you driving by Lady Bird Johnson Park to view the colorful summer planting along Memorial Parkway. I have a passion for wildflowers. The double loop at the Iwo Jima roundabout has inspired my day."

"You're welcome, ma'am. We've heard you have magnificent wildflower gardens in Florida. I figured the flowers in the Lady Bird gardens may brighten your day!"

"They were exquisite," she sighed. "I appreciate everyone trying to welcome me into the community. Thank you for driving me to work today. Are you spending the day at the clinic?"

"No, I report to Walter Reed. I work in Carrie's office."

"Tell her hello for me." Ordinarily she would have been flattered by the personal attention but after the break-in, she was perhaps being overly cautious. She walked into the outpatient clinic as if nothing was wrong, and slid her backpack under the reception desk. "Baby Kittie, meet Sargent Dobbs. He's in charge, so be polite."

"Meowww."

"I was warned to give your cat top security."

"Dobbs, I have problem," she whispered with a smile as if they were discussing the day's schedule. "Look at the cut on Baby Kittie's neck between her shoulders. What if the blood found in the condo was from a kitty attack on whoever did this to her? I found the injury during the drive this morning. I figured it was best to look routine. Besides, where else was I to go for a morning iced coffee with cream?"

"Hey, Bonnie brought her cat," echoed through the room, and the tortoiseshell calico jumped to the floor and joined the class."

"You look…"

"Be careful, you may reveal top secret information," she said beaming a brazen smile. "Anything happening?" she asked as a group entered the conference room.

Dobbs continued his conversation to be heard across the hall. "The stroll to the park has become a morning run. You ordered team flags, as well as T-shirts and running shorts. And you demanded they had to be here today. You had some nasty words which I took the liberty of repeating indicating you didn't care what it cost! The supplies should be here this afternoon."

"My thoughts exactly, I'm sure!" She giggled. "Dobbs, Management will never let us work together again."

Once the area around the desk was clear, Dobbs whispered, "I'll call a vet to examine the cat. I was asked to tell you Randy will be back in a few days. And I wondered if you would consider accompanying the ladies in our entourage to lunch and a shopping trip this afternoon. Did I tell you about the international hotel working with us? Their corporate recruiter will be in town the first of the week and have invited several of the crew to interview. The ladies told me they need business attire."

"Gotcha. How thoughtful to invite me," she said and winked. "As a matter of fact, I do have some shopping to do." Under her smile she added, "If I've been targeted again, are my fellow shoppers prepared for a security response? Also, when you talk to Management, can you find out if there are any limits on my credit cards? And will my driver be briefed on protocols to deliver me somewhere after the shopping trip?"

"Plans are to return here. By lunch, details will be in place for the shopping trip and where you're sleeping. What are the topics for today?"

"Find out if the interviews include a meal. I can introduce a topic for Monday on eating with the boss. Tips such as avoiding soup and spaghetti which undoubtedly spatters on your clothes, but I'll cogitate on a catchy title by Monday. For today, do these topics sound Friday-ish? Foot Care, Friendly Fats, Fudging, and Friday Feedback. I'm hoping the group will tell me how to structure the classes to meet their schedules. I'm working on a notebook of lecture outlines. Optimistically, our pattern could be shared with future outpatient diet clinics. Dobbs, I've been looking through the physician referrals and it seems we're focusing solely on diabetes."

"Right. Carrie and her team are handling the other diets at Walter Reed and Bethesda. The highest number of physician referrals were for diabetes and were also the classes with the poorest attendance, fewest follow-ups, and the worst outcomes. But we've beat those statistics. I've even had to 'borrow' additional chairs."

"Were chairs one of my demanding requests?"

Dobbs smiled but refused to answer.

"There's one last thing you must tell me! When will I be given a T-shirt?" She lightheartedly pounded her fist on Dobb's desk.

Dobbs looked at his watch. "Attention!" called the sargent major. He faced the American flag and flags for each of the services and began the Pledge of Allegiance. Afterward he made his announcements, "Welcome and good morning, men and ladies. The Friday clinic will be closing at noon. Questions? Dismissed."

"Uh-rah!" responded the group.

As the morning continued, Bonnie saw a uniformed veterinarian appear at Dobb's desk. "Okay, who's hiding the cat?" announced Dobbs. "The vet is here to check she doesn't have fur balls." A group promenaded to the reception area with Baby Kittie in tow. Bonnie gave Dobbs a thumb's up.

At the lunch break, people drifted toward the parking lot since on Fridays the clinic officially was on hiatus for the weekend, although in reality, people came and went twenty-four/seven. She checked in with the vet. "How's she doing?"

"Removed a tracking device. Dobbs is taking it to our IT people, in a metal box of course."

"Thanks for making a mall-call."

"Glad to. Helped myself to the lunch buffet; busy afternoon. Call us anytime."

She sauntered across the room to talk with Dobb. "Any word on my lodging? Can I go back to the condo since the tracking device has been removed?"

"We found tracking devices slipped into the hems of your uniforms, thus, returning to the condo is a no-go, and the renovations aren't completed. We're bringing in the electronic crew to check your condo and the other condos in your building and throughout the complex."

"Oh, I hadn't even considered the other renters. I can't go back to the hotel since Baby Kittie had the tracking device when we were there last night. Whoever is following us could have identified the location and may watch the entrances. They might have also connected me with the operation at the Red, White, and Blue Veteran's Center. Well, this is above my pay grade," she said and sighed.

Sargent Dobbs took a deep breath gathering his thoughts.

Before he could respond, she rallied, "This is my cue to head to the mall for lunch and shopping with the crew. Do we have reservations?"

"Yes, taken care of. Kittie is staying here with me and her adoring fans, and there's no limit on your credit cards, Captain Bonnie Watson. Enjoy!"

Lunch in Old Town Alexandria was a pleasant diversion. Reservations were at a private upscale restaurant, an exclusive place where there were no prices on the menu, the waiter placed the napkin in your lap, and finger bowls were brought before dessert. "I'm going to order one of everything on the menu to taste something novel! Order anything. Sargent Major Dobbs is paying the tab."

They giggled. The young women shared stories of working on foreign assignments. They talked of exotic flavors they'd sampled and others they adamantly avoided. She could certainly agree with their opinion of durian, a tropical fruit with the taste of pineapple but the aroma of dirty socks. Everyone agreed the fruit was definitely an acquired taste. Bonnie admired their independence, often the only woman in their unit or one of a small team. She wondered if they succeeded because of some innate trait or characteristic; maybe from genetic material coming from hearty stock, as her dad, a rancher, would say. Or was it the service training they received? A wave of insecurity momentarily overcame her. She was well accomplished in her field of nutrition, PhD and all, but was a novice in the world of the women who sat with her at the round table. But now she was in their world; in Charlie's world. Charlie told her she'd learn and she'd become proficient at the skills she needed. The frustration was how to prepare for a life of the unexpected.

The mall would have been a brisk walk, but instead they drove the van and parked near the center of the complex in the parking garage. A business wardrobe was different than living out of a duffel bag, and moving from one assignment to another. "I'll share my mom's guidance on business attire and don't smirk," shared Bonnie. "'Never wear clothes that touch your skin.' The ladies on the news channels and TV soaps seemed to have ignored her advice. I can hear snickers," she teased.

"Hey, Bonnie!" She recognized JoAnne's voice. She was relieved to have backup to answer questions of fashion selection.

"Ladies, meet Cindy. She's worked in lots of government offices in DC and can answer your shopping questions. Medical people aren't known for their stylish business attire. We wear scrubs or hide quirky wardrobe choices under lab coats."

"How are things going?" Cindy whispered under her smile.

"Simply splendid. Thanks for asking. Hope you don't mind I gave you an alias. I'm in hot water again and wanted to provide you some distance."

"Probably best. Pay attention when the group leaves on the elevator. You're to go with me when the group starts home. Buy some sunbonnets." JoAnne left telling the group in a loud commanding voice, "I have other shopping to complete, but best of luck on the interviews and work on your tans during the weekend at the beach retreat!"

"The beach!" They were overjoyed.

"A surprise from Dobbs and the Veteran's Center," boasted

Bonnie. "Oh, buy a sexy sun hat and a summer sweater to wear on cool evening walks on the beach." Bonnie sashayed to the accessory counter and decided on a melon-colored hat with a wide floppy brim and stripped ribbons cascading off the back of the hat. A lime-green sweater with three-quarter length sleeves caught her eye. "Don't forget bathing suits! They're past the makeup counter."

"Makeup counter? Do we have time for a makeover?"

"Yes, of course! Y'all are going to be dangerous!" announced Bonnie.

"We hope so!"

"Don't forget a non-military purse to carry a folder for copies of your resume. Consider purchasing an overnight bag. In some circles those snappy OD green backpacks are the latest fashion, but..."

JoAnne reappeared and helped with the rest of the shopping. Bonnie tried to stay focused on the excitement of the ladies and their shopping spree. But at the same time, she wondered if the lady she swapped clothes with at the highway rest stop was going to be the contact in the elevator. When she saw her, they both smiled. The elevator maneuvers were flawless. She stepped into the elevator, swapped hats and sweaters, and JoAnne and Bonnie exited two floors before the shoppers. Once in the faded sedan, she and JoAnne broke into hysterical laughter. "JoAnne, I recognize this is serious stuff, but you have to concede it is fun, until I stop and wonder why someone is tracking me."

"Right. While I was helping with the shopping, I quietly told the ladies of your escape strategy. Your double has the beach reservations." JoAnne ignored her companion's comments. She'd seen it before with people learning field operations. She had to admit her former college roommate was doing far better than anyone had expected.

"I wish I knew if this had anything to do with my involvement with Charlie, or if this predicament is my doing. I can't understand why. My consulting contracts have gone well. None of my hospital sites have failed their inspections. My consulting rates are high but cheaper than having to hire a full-time company employee with benefits. My folks aren't involved in a land deal or negotiations to sell the orange crop. It's a bit early in the year to sell this year's calves, although Dad will be sorting the calves soon. If anything, they would be trying to buy my brother's influence. You've heard the Southern adage, 'Daughters marry; sons manage the farm'."

"Right," mechanically responded JoAnne. But Bonnie was correct in her assessment of the seriousness of the situation, especially since no one had a clue as to why she was being targeted. Her involvement with Charlie made the situation complex. His world could have nothing to do with the attacks on Janice, the woman in Charlie's life. She wasn't sure Bonnie fully understood the depths of Charlie's dedication to her. She hated to admit it, but his love for her made him vulnerable.

"Where are we going, JoAnne?"

"We're heading to Fort Eustis, near Williamsburg. Dobbs has friends there to support the story. Temporarily, you are going to be Mrs. Dobbs. She's traveling in California staying off-base with her sister, making your cover story difficult to verify. We made ID cards to present when you enter the base. Baby Kittie is the guest at the bunkhouse at the Veteran's Center and seems *purr*-fectly satisfied with the excessive attention."

"She is an entertainer, isn't she? Let's grab a couple of sandwiches, salads, maybe a few yogurts, and a romance novel to retreat in my room this weekend off the radar. I also need gloves and socks. I couldn't exactly buy them at the mall with the conversation we were having about heading to the beach. Has

Charlie been updated?"

"He's out of the country, I think."

Bonnie wondered if JoAnne knew Charlie had spent the last evening in her bed. She didn't contradict JoAnne's report, but it sounded as if tonight she would be sleeping alone again, and without Baby Kittie.

Chapter Nine

JoAnne orchestrated having one of the wives drive her to the Veteran's Center on her way to work in DC. When Bonnie returned on Monday morning, she hoped casual Friday attire was still in force, but Sargent Dobbs was in a crisp, sharply pressed regulation uniform when she arrived. She wanted to cringe.

He immediately noticed. "Oh, I'm glad you're in casual attire. It helps maintain a lower profile. We're working on installing some type of image-diffusing film on the windows and brought in a rolling blackboard. You'd be easy pickings for a sniper. When you lead class discussions, try to vary your position. Sit in the crowd, move around, and place the blackboard between you and the window, if you can."

She was relieved her limited wardrobe wasn't going to be an issue, but was apprehensive at the news of being declared a sniper target. She put on her Southern smile, what else could she do? "Dobbs, the sign above the entrance is magnificent. Did you suggest the name, the Red, White & Blue Veteran's Center?"

"We had a contest last week. It was the winning entry with over a hundred entries. The winners were awarded a steak dinner we grilled in the parking lot. The painted signs at the curb with the directions for parking give the building an air of legitimacy, don't you agree?"

"I adore the food posters."

"Carrie found them when they were cleaning the dietary storage area in the basement at Walter Reed preparing for the move. The guys made frames from found lumber."

"They certainly brighten the room. We actually resemble an official diet clinic. All we need is a basket of plastic food!"

"What?"

"Insider dietitian joke, Dobbs, my apologies. When did you find time to paint our meeting room?" The dreary beige walls had been painted a crisp white with wide playful waving horizontal stripes of red and blue which extended across the back wall. She was already thinking of locating twinkling snowflakes for the holidays. "I was beginning to be fond of warehouse drab," she teased.

Dobbs chose to ignore most of her critique of the decorating. "You'd appreciate the grocery store at the other end of the strip mall is sending trays of pastries and yogurt, but also trays of cut vegetable with a choice between cottage cheese dip or a hummus dip. They also thought we would enjoy a cut fruit salad and a basket of whole fruit."

"It's liberating to have choices. Food habits are enormously individualized. It must be troublesome to transition from food choices determined by the mess hall to a world of 'my' choices. Following a special diet is complex. What worked when they were twenty may be different at retirement age. Dobb's, I am still amazed the Veteran's Center came together almost overnight."

Baby Kittie glanced her way and preferred to stay with the class members. Bonnie suspected her kitty had mentally put her in time-out for abandoning her the entire weekend. She was seeing the same faces she saw day after day in the classes last week. They came early and stayed late.

"Our first group of volunteers arrived. Will thirty minutes be enough time to present an orientation?"

Bonnie surveyed the assembly of volunteers. The group had a lot of gray with the average age of post-retirement. "Thirty minutes should cover everything. I'll train the first group and let them train the new group while one of us observes the training. Would you let them choose a spokesman? Or should we draw a name out of the hat?"

Dobbs hesitated but nodded at the second option. The hat option won.

"Let me ask you something in case the volunteers ask. How many of our crowd would you estimate are homeless?"

"More than there should be."

"I wondered where they sleep."

"Bonnie," he whispered. "Frank and I are friends, which you probably figured out by now. One of our companies won this strip mall in a poker game. Once the diet office was proposed, the storefronts in between the hardware store and the diet clinic were converted to a series of community bunkhouses for our veterans. We finished the work during the weekend. We left the storefronts, installed bathrooms, and connected the barracks rooms with a hall at the back of the building. Finding you employment legitimized a proposal we'd been working on for some time."

"How do we prepare meals?"

"The food service departments from the area bases send surplus. The military creates the menus and signs production contracts to supply food years in advance. In a time of crisis it's an efficient system, but day to day, units may have modest flexibility on the number of meals they produce, often resulting in extra. If inspectors are there, the food goes into the garbage, but most days they send us what's safe. The medical shuttle also covertly transports food packed in chilled boxes marked 'Confidential US Military Medical Files.' We had them constructed with waterproof washable linings. Other foods are also sent by a local hotel. Initially they hired some of our people to wait tables for a banquet. When they heard of our program, they'd been donating unserved banquet dinners, but of greater value, they've been hiring our veterans for positions at their DC hotel and other hotels within their franchise. I thought I'd tell you in the event you observe anything in violation of health standards, you wouldn't hesitate to immediately implement corrective actions. For attending the diet classes, we award cash cards which allow folks to buy lunch and a few personal items while on base for medical appointments."

"I wondered why we've had a packed house. I suspected it wasn't my eloquent lectures on carbohydrates," she teased. "Where's our kitchen?"

"Staff from Fort Lee's culinary academy has dropped by to give us a little advice. Some of our veterans graduated from there. One of the stores in the strip mall was a restaurant, and when the mall closed they left the industrial kitchen equipment. In one weekend we cleaned, scrubbed, moved a couple of walls, and installed walk-in coolers and freezers. If you have a minute, would you inspect the kitchen facilities? Eventually, the health inspectors are bound to show up. Hate to be dinged for something obvious."

"I'll call Carrie to send over a set of standardized inspection forms. We'll look very squared away and organized when the inspectors ask for our records. Thank you for the peanut butter and jelly station to make my favorite sandwich."

"We noticed and even made sure there's orange marmalade especially for you." He chuckled. "Grab a cup of coffee. We've added an ice machine, a cooler to store cream for your coffee, and soft-serve ice cream machines for Baby Kittie."

"Thank you. I won't ask how you knew iced coffee was my favorite. Baby Kittie has wrapped the crew around her paws. By chance, did a special delivery package arrive?"

"Oh, sorry. The boxes were delivered on Saturday."

"Did you peek inside?"

"Yes, I thought we'd wait for you to unveil them. But I took the liberty of sending several boxes to Carrie and her staff at Walter Reed and Bethesda. They were a tremendous hit!"

"Glad you suggested it," she teased. "I hope the air-conditioning will be fixed today. Hint, hint!"

Dobbs nodded his head. "Question: The military spouse's organization have asked to borrow our space on Tuesday nights for scrapbooking. Any conflicts?"

"There is plenty of space and oodles of room for parking. Maybe the wives will even arrive a bit early to hear the featured afternoon topic. I vote yes, but you're in charge."

"Damn right! Can you be here tomorrow night? I'll introduce you to your evening security detail before I leave. They can escort you home, which I hear is a different address. I have a command conference tomorrow."

"No secrets in this unit, huh? Well, I have another favor?"

"Another one? Your favor quota is only three per week," he said in a mischievous tone.

"Can you arrange for a medical tech stationed here? I'm sure the physicians have medically cleared our enrollees," she said as she raised her eyebrows. "But in case some of our crew are aggressively experimenting with beginning steps to manage their diabetes, or are working on the detective skills to learn personal blood sugar patterns, we may have some individuals with unsafe blood sugars."

"Like what?"

"Blood sugar which may be too high or too low. Worst case, they may require medical assistance. Can you ask Carrie to send us a copy of the hospital protocols on blood sugars, specifically what blood sugar numbers mandate a trip to sick call? We have to avoid a real emergency at the clinic and avoid any reason to close us down. Frank told me to stay off the radar. We have to ensure that this project is a success."

"Agreed! When you have a minute, ask me which one of the national veteran's groups have offered to sponsor a potluck on Friday night for our people."

"Well, ask me to tell you of the opportunity for volunteers at the Forest Service's wild animal rescue shelter," she said in a coy tone.

Dobbs looked at his watch. The hands on the dial indicated it was eight o'clock. "Attention!" called the sergeant major. He faced the American flag and flags for each of the services and began the Pledge of Allegiance. After the pledge, Dobbs' comments began, "Welcome and good morning, men and ladies. This is a monumental day. We have survived the opening of the Red, White and Blue Veteran's Center." A roar of applause yells and uh-rah's filled the room. "Questions? Dismissed."

"Dobbs, it is a pleasure working with you, if I forget to tell you," Bonnie said as she raised her glass of iced coffee in a salutatorian salute.

"Thanks. What are the topics for this marvelous Monday morning?"

She read the topics of the flyer she'd created during the long weekend. "Move them Blood Sugars, Make Mine a Muffin, Medication Monopoly (How to avoid *Do not pass go* and *Go directly to the hospital*), Mutts and Meows: Pet Therapy, and the last topic, Meeting Menus for Job Interviews, as I promised. The iced coffee is delightful, by the way. With the popularity of the morning jogging program, it would be prudent to review safety protocols on how to avoid low blood sugar during exercise. And remember, Mondays through Thursdays we're going to stagger the lectures during the first-time slot and the last one in the afternoon to accommodate our commuters.

"Tic. Toc." He pointed to his watch. "We'll talk at lunch," he said and laughed. "Get out of here, Captain."

*****

The next morning, the Red, White and Blue Veteran's Center appeared as if it had been in the community for years despite drying paint on the walls. Volunteers suggested their uniforms to be dark blue short jackets and vests which Sargent Major Dobbs immediately procured. Many came dressed in red and white to highlight the new décor. A medic was assigned and established a table behind a folding screen. Thus far the only ones needing medical advice had been the retired volunteers. A set of balance scales appeared along with a chart of weight loss by teams with names of fruits, and another chart of blood sugars by teams with names of vegetables. She wasn't sure what the hash marks represented, but based on the numbers, Team Kumquats were ahead on weight loss and Team Eggplant winning the blood sugar challenge. A bookshelf assembled from found lumber and discarded red bricks displayed nutrition brochures.

"Good morning, Captain. I didn't realize you were here," greeted Dobbs.

"My ride had an appointment in town, and she dropped me off early. I wanted to look at the nutrition brochures to hone the talking points for classes today to be consistent with the other military diet clinics. I was thinking of doing an extended lecture at the grocery store in a few weeks. Who would I ask?"

"I can organize those details for you," answered Dobbs.

"The scrapbook workshop is tonight. Did the extra tables arrive? What time should I expect them?"

"The tables should arrive before noon. I was told the scrapbookers will be arriving at 1800, but I received heads-up notifying the coordinator could have been a drill sergeant in another life. Look for them early. I'll have someone save you a sandwich."

"Is Baby Kittie behaving?"

"Are you kidding? I found a volunteer sheet for cat sitters filled for a month."

"Dobbs, have you seen anything on the experimental program using companion pets to support military personnel adjusting to life back home? After seeing how everyone loves Baby Kittie, I was…"

"Oh, no! Don't even ask. There's no such thing as one pet."

"Certainly, Dobbs. I totally agree. But I was thinking of something different." She quickly recovered. He'd read her well, actually, it was exactly the questions she was going to ask. "How many volunteered to assist at the wildlife rehab center?"

"I'll check. I'll include it in the morning announcements. Come on, it's time for reveille."

"What's with the bugles?

"We were given a whole box of bugles and other instruments. Do you play a musical instrument? We'll talk about the bugle project later," he groaned.

She hoped he would choose someone else to organize the bugle project. Surely one of the volunteers would be musically talented. Her family asserted she played the piano as if she had two hammers in her hands. She grumbled of course, but unfortunately, as much as she enjoyed playing, they're critique was too close to the truth.

CHAPTER TEN

It was Tuesday. Sue Li was looking forward to visiting with the other girls at lunch as she and her bodyguard ran the routine visit to the candy store and the Chinese collection at the Freer Gallery. She'd lived with her uncle before there were memories of her birth family. For a brief moment she imagined a loving family eating on the luxurious Chinese plates in a modest home of Chinese design. She took a deep breath. She wore her pale blue silk suit; it made her feel sophisticated. She was surprised when she arrived at the restaurant to find her uncle in the corner booth. The table lamp had been turned off. He motioned for her to join him.

"Sue Li, my niece," the uncle greeted her warmly, but she recognized the snarl of his smile when he talked to her.

"My niece, I told you, Brian Timmerman too arrogant!" he ranted. "Many miscalculations." She wondered what Timmerman had done. She didn't dare ask. She could feel his anger as he spoke. She was still waiting for Timmerman to call. If the plot carefully crafted by her, Timmerman, and Ron was successful, they would rid him from their lives forever. She had to maintain her composure for only one hour; just one hour. Eventually she'd be free. She was young when she was sent to live with her uncle. All the women who worked for him, he referred to as his niece or nieces. The women in his brothels raised her, as they did many female children of his relatives and employees. The uncle controlled her life — he and his bodyguards.

Her uncle was talking in mixed Chinese and English detailing her list of failures. She maintained eye contact on his face, on his moving lips, but her thoughts focused on her love of Timmerman and their future plans to be married. Soon, they would be together. Things had been arranged with one of her guards. The guard easily fell in love with Brian's selection of an attractive American woman, which would guarantee him American citizenship. In saving him from the harsh factory life in China, she was saving herself.

"You miss your Mr. Brian Timmerman, my dear. You be with him soon. This our contribution to make China great. We do what is required to control world's produce market. It China's destiny. Ancient Chinese warriors say, if you control food, you control the people. This my part," said Mr. Tao in a proud, boastful manner.

She nodded politely. She's heard his speech many times before on his visits.

"I have special project for you in San Francisco, my niece. I promised your family you soon deliver a boy baby to carry on family name. Brother sent to Army and not returned. My doctors will fix. We apart too much lately. You very skilled. I miss our together." Under the tablecloth, he slid his hand along her thigh, his cold fingers slipping under the edge of her silk panties. She closed her eyes and focused on keeping her body relaxed. "Thank you, Uncle," she whispered.

She had terrifying memories of many visits to *his* doctors before and after each visit with her uncle after her eighteenth birthday. He said it was to make her beautiful. She was kept isolated from the older working girls until he found another birthday girl to train. In California, Timmerman took her to an American doctor, a real doctor. In one of the surgeries to "make her beautiful," she had been "biologically sterilized," she was told. She was unsure of the medical words, only she wouldn't be able to have children.

Her uncle didn't mention Timmerman and Ron in the plans to move to San Francisco. She, Timmerman, and Ron had been together for ten years, since college in California.

"Uncle, you not worry. This time my plan will bring you success and bring you pride." She bowed and took several steps back before turning away. She smiled a happy smile. Soon, Timmerman's plot would kill her uncle and she'd retire. She wanted to buy a house in Chevy Chase with flower boxes and white shutters to cover the windows.

CHAPTER ELEVEN

The day went quickly. Bonnie glanced toward the door and saw a blustery, lofty lady rolling a huge suitcase behind her; it had to be Mrs. Nelson. "Mrs. Nelson? Can we help you?" Bonnie looked around with one of her stern schoolteacher expressions, and half the room were on their feet to assist their guest.

"Are you in charge?"

"No, our NCO-IC is Sargent Major Dobbs. I teach the diet classes."

"Okay. I guess you'll do."

Thankfully, Dobbs had preemptively warned her and the group to be on their best behavior at the morning assembly. Out of the corner of her eye she caught Baby Kitty being whisked away to a cloistered location.

"The Fort Belvoir scrapbooking team will be arriving shortly," rapidly fired Mrs. Nelson. "I understand Sargent Dobbs has given permission for the Walter Reed team to meet here on Wednesdays, Fort McNair on Thursdays, and the Pentagon group on Mondays. The Pentagon has all services, but I've been the regional DC scrapbooking coach for four years, and therefore I'm including them as one of the Army teams. The Army competition

SASSY SUE ABBOTT

is in two weeks. The winning Army team will compete against the Navy, and Air Force teams in the greater DC area competition held the first week in August. My ladies will require coffee and snacks. Questions?"

"No, ma'am."

"We'll get along fine. What's your name?

"Watkins, Bonnie Watkins."

"Don't recognize the name. Do you have anyone in the military?"

"No, ma'am."

"Too bad."

Bonnie saw the activity behind Mrs. Nelson, and the eyes looking her way giving her a nod. When she raised her eyebrows they quickly returned to clearing the tables. Oh, wait till I talk to Dobbs. When did he volunteer the room for the scrapbooking workshops on Monday, Tuesday, Wednesday, and Thursday night?

"While we have a room full of volunteers, where should we place the tables and chairs?"

"Near the coffeepot. It gives the ladies valuable minutes to work on their project. And where are the restrooms?"

At precisely 5:45, eighteen ladies appeared. They stood in a row and drew numbers from a coffee cup corresponding to numbers drawn on yellow folded cardboard tents evenly spaced on the tables. Exactly at 6:00 p.m., Mrs. Nelson drew a piece of paper from another coffee cup. "The two projects for tonight are: 'Way Out' and 'Once Upon a Time.'" She removed the stopwatch from her blazer pocket. As the countdown was shouted—three, two, one—the ladies rushed to the assigned tables.

Bonnie and the rest of the room were mesmerized at the precision of the organization. Several clinic members sat with Bonnie ready to respond to orders Mrs. Nelson may dictate. At

100

fifty-five minutes, Mrs. Nelson announced, "Five minutes." Once the five minutes passed, she announced, "Mandatory ten-minute rest break." Bonnie and her crew rushed to the refreshment table as if they were a pit crew at the Daytona 500. "Two-minute warning," her voice rang throughout the room. At the one-minute warning the ladies stood by their tables. The countdown sounded again. At three, two, one, the ladies joined in and began their projects as everyone shouted, "Begin!" On the half hour Mrs. Nelson announced, "Thirty-minute warning," and signaled ten-minute time intervals. Exactly at eight o'clock, she gave the order, "Stop. Tools down." The room cheered, including Bonnie and her veteran's entourage who were totally consumed by the activities.

"Ms. Williams, could we impose upon you and members of your team to be judges for tonight on the appropriateness of their page to the two themes? Please rank each project from one to ten. I'll be the judge of the skills used. Write your evaluation on these scorecards. Questions?" But before they could take a breath, Mrs. Nelson responded, "You have fifteen minutes."

Bonnie and her team looked at each other, frantically grabbed pencils and scorecards, and rushed around the table. Bonnie felt obliged to offer encouraging comments at each exhibit. "What adorable kids. You went to Yellowstone! How colorful."

Mrs. Nelson quickly reprimanded, "Judges will please refrain from making comments until the scoring is completed." Bonnie grimaced to the giggles of the scrapbookers and the rest of the observers who had filled the room. "Pencils down," was shouted.

Mrs. Nelson walked quickly to gather the scorecards and laid them out on the table. "The top scoring based on artistic scores was Mary Chandler," she announced and handed her a coffee cup featuring the Washington Monument. "The judge's pick for appropriateness of the theme was Carolyn Brown." She was awarded the coffee cup featuring the Jefferson Memorial. "Congratulations to everyone. You are super creative. Finish the pages you've started and we'll select the top ten of the four themes to submit for the competition at next week's combined workshop. We're down to the final days before the competition. Usually, the winning teams receive an expense-paid trip to Camp Dodge, Iowa, but due to a sudden housing shortage, arrangements are being made for the winning team and their families to travel to Patrick Air Force Base in Florida, near the beach and other attractions. There's a rumor the Air Force teams are boasting they will be the winners. I don't have to remind anyone our reputation is at stake."

A light rain covered the tree-lined streets and the parking lot. The ladies quickly gathered their supplies. Volunteers held umbrellas while the scrapbookers scattered to their cars and disappeared. "Thank you, Ms. Wallis, for allowing us to meet at the Veteran's Center. The VFW meeting hall had a kitchen fire. The fire marshal closed the building for three weeks before renovations can be started. The ladies' dedication to the competition has been commendable." Bonnie admired the passion in her voice. "Someone told my husband of Dobbs' project and the enormous conference room available after hours. Men, thanks for the coffee."

"Ma'am, we can move your supplies to your car."

"Thank you, Ms. Waters. I'll be back tomorrow at the same time."

"See you tomorrow. Be careful driving home," politely responded Bonnie. Once Mrs. Nelson was outside the building Bonnie asked, "Who can obtain intel on Mrs. Nelson before she comes back tomorrow? She seems awfully familiar with the specifics of our outpatient diet clinic."

"Except your name is Captain Bonnie Watkins."

"Probably best. If she thinks I'm a civilian, I can't be held too accountable," she smiled. "At least the scrapbook ladies will be here for only two weeks. Cancel the dancing girls, guys."

"Meowwtt," echoed Baby Kittie.

Chapter Twelve

Sue Li's much anticipated Tuesday excursion turned sour when the phone call came. Her uncle sent word he was joining her for lunch. She showered, carefully shaved her body, and wore the expensive perfume her uncle liked, in case his visit extended beyond lunch and she was to entertain him or his guests.

Driving to the restaurant she and her bodyguard followed the same routine, but lingered a few minutes longer in the museum knowing her driver would be angry. She was hoping his verbal abuse would overflow into the Chinese restaurant; anything to gain sympathy from her uncle.

Once she gave her uncle the pink boxes of handmade candies, she skipped the pleasantries and went straight to reporting on her assignment. "Uncle, Ron confirmed Janice Brown was a student of the scientist from Florida who discovered our lab in Mexico. He had a fishing accident near the plant and was buried in the mud. Your important friend in the White House arranged for her to visit the ship to look at the fruit flies. We planned to kill her in China in case her professor had sent a message about the chemical lab in Mexico, but she left too soon. Ron lured her to the spa, but the scheme became complicated when she brought Charlie Smith who needed surgery. There were too many other people to kill both Smith and Brown. Timmerman was sure he killed Charlie Smith in Mexico after he inquired of the whereabouts of blonde woman, the CIA agent who also found our lab."

"I patient man, Sue Li…"

"Uncle, everyone trying to kill Ms. Brown. We tried following her when she left the spa in Georgia, but she disappeared. Tracking the transmitter on Smith, my Brian Timmerman arranged to kill them in Colorado, but the pilots didn't finish the attack once the helicopter exploded. Even your brother in Moscow tried to poison her at the hotel in Petropavlovsk, but he failed. She was with Charlie Smith, but different rooms. I haven't heard from Brian, Uncle, have you? Maybe he has details concerning Charlie Smith?"

Her uncle poured tea into blue and white Pinming cups. His eyes remained focused on the teapot.

Sue Li spoke wanting to avoid his criticisms, "Uncle, with Ms. Brown dead, your honor will be restored. I saw her on the flight from Anchorage to Seattle. I have plan. She will pay."

His tone changed. "Your plans have failed, Sue Li," he said in an icy character.

She abruptly stood, wanting to leave. Disappointing him had not been pleasant in the past. As she was leaving, Mr. Tao clinched his fist and pounded the table.

CHAPTER THIRTEEN

"Good morning, everyone. I smell coffee." Bonnie chirped as she walked through the Veteran's Center.

"Good morning, Bonnie," was their reply in unison as if they were in third grade. "We have apricot coffee cake with an almond topping. Carb count is twenty-seven grams for a two-inch square."

"I'm impressed." She could play along. "How many grams of carbs are in one serving of a carbohydrate? And how many carbohydrates is generally an appropriate goal per day?"

"Fifteen grams of carbohydrates per serving," came from the back of the room.

"Daily carb goal depends upon body weight and activity levels. My notebook calculations estimate between 200 to 225 grams of carbs per day, unless I exercise, and then I'll eat one or two extra servings of carbs based on duration of exercise plus a factor for cold or extra hot weather. I'm still working on verifying those calculations."

"Based on *my* weight, 150 to 175 grams of carbs per day is my goal. Since I was fitted for my prosthesis, my activity level is increasing by the day. I'm keeping records of decreasing blood sugar when I exercise. Have to plan for a snack to avoid low blood sugar."

"Wow! And how would you recognize when to increase carbohydrates for exercise duration and changes in temperature as you've correctly learned?" she quizzed.

"By keeping a log of blood sugar before and after physical activity cross-referenced with the carb intake and weather."

"By Jove, you've it!" she exclaimed in a British accent flavored with a Southern twist.

"What?"

She realized the crowd was unfamiliar with the script of *My Fair Lady* when Eliza Doolittle was learning the finer arts of a European society. "Super job! Y'all are fantastic diabetes detectives," she rephrased. "What topics should we include today?"

"We have several first-timers."

"Welcome," she said addressing the group while making a demure bow. "I'm going to let you 'old-timers' undertake teaching responsibilities today. I'm behind posting progress reports in your medical files. Someone may notice I'm having too much fun. Do we have a copy machine somewhere?"

"Yes, ma'am!"

"Is the 'yes, ma'am' y'all will teach Diabetes 101, or 'yes' we have a copy machine?"

"Both! Newbies, report to the southwest side of the building," was shouted across the room. "The copy machine is in the kitchen by the phone."

She started looking through the stack of counseling referrals, reading each patient's file one by one. She hadn't had time to develop a generalized progress report and was trying to gather her thoughts to standardize a checklist of completed topics and skills. From the stack of crumpled yellow paper in the wastebasket, her thoughts were far from organized. She considered the project as a work in progress.

"Ma'am, I brought you an iced coffee. If you have a minute, I have a problem. I didn't intend to interrupt."

"You're our medic, aren't you? The first time we met, you were in scrubs with long hair and a three-inch beard. Thanks for the coffee. Please forgive me. I didn't recognize you right off. Glad you could join our group. I'm Janice Brown."

"No problem. I'm Dan Rudolph O'Connel, Devil Doc to most around here.

"Have a seat! What's going on?"

"I would've discussed this with Sargent Major Dobbs," he started slowly.

"Oh, of course."

"I compile an inventory of medical supplies when I leave at 1600. When I report the next morning at 0730, I've find things are missing. If residents need anything, they write it down on the supply adjustment sheet stored in the top drawer."

"What kinds of things are disappearing?" she whispered. Her first thought were the problem medications such as pain pills, narcotics, or hypodermic needles.

"First, I panicked hoping it wasn't any of the controlled medications locked in the med cabinet, but it's insignificant things: bottles of aspirin, tongue depressors, and the experimental bandages treated with antibiotics. I don't care if they appropriate aspirin or the tongue depressors but the experimental bandages are essential to a research project conducted by one of the docs at Walter Reed. I'm supposed to chart changes and duration of the wounds using the specially treated dressings."

"Anything else missing?"

"Office supplies: pencils, sticky notes, and surgical scissors. I'll be in a retirement home before the system replaces the scissors!"

"Can I assist with the official report?" She held her breath. *Please say no*, she hoped. She'd have to find the specially numbered form. The Army had forms for everything. She couldn't ask Dobbs until he returned from the conference.

"No, not yet. I was hoping you would watch for anything suspicious."

"I'd be glad to. How are the blood sugars doing?"

"Our crew is doing fine. The classes appear unusually casual, and I wasn't sure they'd be successful. I've been watching your technique. You let the client tell you how they're going to try to improve their blood sugars. Rarely do you stand and lecture, you move around, talk in small groups. It looks kinda willy-nilly, but it seems to work."

"You probably studied patient education methods in your medic's training. The approach is consistent with the adult learning theory. I ask the group what they want to learn. Our crowd has strong survivor instincts and is successful on many levels. The theory plays upon those traits and when planning the lessons, I present the information the group has determined is the most important as they perceive it. Other essential information is stuffed in here and there to accomplish their self-determined goals. I try to encourage a patient to verbalize what they are trying to accomplish—it increases the probability of success. I'm glad it's working. You are usually busy; how do you find time to assess the class progress?"

"I look at the log sheets on my breaks. I was an accountant before I was drafted. The Army didn't need accountants, but needed field medics. I served in Vietnam and Europe before transferring to DC for additional medical training. In college between accounting classes we would compete on how quickly we could tabulate columns of numbers in the phone book. I can scan blood sugar reports quickly."

"I bet you can spot trends in an individual record in a minute!"

"I've been having coffee with the endocrinologists at Walter Reed to discuss our patient's medical histories. They appreciate your notes indicating patient's personal goals. I'm gaining experience checking vital signs for the older volunteers and their friends who tag along. I don't mind; they're former military or wives of former military. The VA hospitals are overwhelmed with treating battle injuries which leaves minimal time to provide routine wellness monitoring. I'm glad I can support the volunteers here at the Veteran's Center, and glad they can be members of our group. They create a touch of home. We appreciate the little things they do. They listen to our war stories or give advice on how to talk to family or girlfriends. But it works both ways. I saw one of our vets grab two cups of coffee and carry it to one of our volunteers who was sitting at the front windows staring into space. Some of our people are talking of forming a construction team for minor household repairs for the volunteers. Understand, it's only a rumor. One of our volunteers needs safety bars in the bathroom and another needs a ramp to walk into and leave the house after hip surgery. We admire the volunteers' continued contributions to the military community, even with their medical problems."

"I agree. Regarding the missing medical supplies, I'll watch people in your area when you're at the hospital. I'll let the construction team approach Sargent Major Dobbs when they're ready to initiate the household repair project. They may want to consider estimating a budget, making a list of supplies and needed skill training to prepare for the meeting with Frank. Dan, where did you serve?"

"I did three tours in the desert after a stint or two in Vietnam and Europe. I'm training in emergency medicine at Walter

Reed and will be transferring out in nine months. One of the docs suggested I volunteer here at the Veteran's Center for the community experience."

"Thanks for your service both in the military and here at the Veteran's Center."

"I'll let you return to your charts. But before I go, what's the story with the box of bugles and brass instruments?"

"Talk to Dobbs, but it's my understanding the instruments were donated. Do you play?"

"I try. Who knows, we could start a band. Thanks for the information."

The stack of completed patient folders was slowly increasing. She was being mindful to leave a light footprint in the records and signed the charts with two sets of squiggles along with the official dietetic credentials. She felt proud of the progress until she looked at the clock. In horror she screamed, "It's five o'clock. This room must be squared away in fifteen minutes. General Scrapbooker will be here any minute!"

Mad pandemonium erupted. Baby Kittie screeched out of the room spinning her paws on the polished floor. Brooms appeared. Cloths were wiping down the plastic chairs. Tables and chairs were moved near the coffee station.

"Wash the coffeepot!" someone hollered.

"Where's the ground coffee?"

"I'll run to the store for coffee creamer."

"Don't forget treats! Grab three or four boxes of something from the bakery — anything! We'll eat the leftovers later," she responded. "And buy us a package of pretty flowered paper napkins and a potted plant."

"Five thirty. We're on countdown," was shouted across the room.

"Target at twelve o'clock. Places everyone."

111

"Smile," whispered Bonnie as the door opened. She ignored the quiet background chant, "three, two, one!"

"Good evening, Mrs. Nelson. Let me assist with staging the supplies. We have everything organized for the Walter Reed group."

"Is Sargent Major Dobbs here tonight?"

"No, ma'am. Our ranking officer is…"

"Sargent Phillips, US Marine Corp, reporting, ma'am. He stepped forward asserting his position. He was dressed in civilian clothes.

"We have many international members and must have tight security tonight, and again for Monday when the Pentagon group is here."

"Yes, ma'am." The room behind him remained silent knowing many in the group had been specifically selected to provide security for Captain Bonnie Watkins and her cat, but hadn't met the man who just took charge. They'd check with Dobbs when he returned before calling Frank. They apparently had accomplished their goal to provide security without being visible. It would have been easier to be obvious. "Troops, I need a dozen volunteers to provide security for tonight's meeting," he stated as if he was organizing a neighborhood watch or a major military engagement.

Mrs. Nelson looked pleased. Bonnie handed her a box of sharpened pencils to assist her with the judging cards. "Can I pour you a cup of coffee? The bakery is sending several boxes of nibbles. They should be here momentarily."

"No coffee, but thank you for the hospitality! I was worried this wasn't going to work and the unfamiliar venue would put the teams at a disadvantage for the regional competition. The DC region has won top prizes for the last three years! The work produced yesterday was winning quality. Can you and some of the group be the judges for tonight?"

"Oh, we would be glad to," replied Bonnie in an overly soft Southern tone. "Once the crew saw the refreshment table, interest in volunteering suddenly increased."

Mrs. Nelson ignored her comments. "It's five minutes before six o'clock. Nice to talk with you, Brenda."

She chuckled when even Mrs. Nelson was having problems remembering her name.

The evening followed the same routine as the night before. The security people made overt overtones as they patrolled the room and the parking lot in front of the windows. They would periodically meet and talked quietly using hand gestures pointing to various buildings or toward other stores in the strip mall. Their theatrics looked impressive, but Bonnie knew there were other layers of security beyond those readily visible.

At the break, Bonnie was standing tall at the refreshment table to serve coffee. Luscious trays sent by the bakery held slices of lemon pound cake, chocolate layer cake with chocolate icing, and another tray of sliced vanilla layer cake stuffed with fluffy coconut frosting. Several catering trays were filled with cookies stacked on paper doilies. She chuckled at the treats to feed an entire battalion.

"Tools down!" announced Mrs. Nelson. The judging followed. "The themes for tonight were 'Thru the Years' and 'All for One.' I'll judge the entries for the level of skills and technique. The guest judges will evaluate the appropriateness to the theme. Judges will refrain from commenting on the entries. You have fifteen minutes."

Bonnie chuckled when Mrs. Nelson included corrections for her indiscretion in the instructions to the judges, but worked to maintain a straight face. Quickly Bonnie's team made their decisions, recorded them on the scorecard, and returned the cards to Mrs. Nelson. Bonnie wrote on her scorecard, *Are Carolyn Brown from last night and Candice Brown tonight married to the same man?* She hoped Mrs. Nelson would read her note. She didn't dare say anything in public.

"The winner of the best technique and skill is Candice Brown, and the judge's choice for theme is Lucinda Rodriquez," announced Mrs. Nelson. Each lady was awarded a coffee cup featuring one of the Washington monuments consistent with the previous night. Bonnie noted the featured DC monuments were the Lincoln Memorial and the White House.

Phillips, the self-appointed leader of the security detail, spoke as the ladies gathered their supplies to move to their cars. "We will be honored to escort the ladies home or to the security office of their post or bases. Or ladies from our contingency could drive you home and our chase vehicle can retrieve our drivers. Just give us a few minutes to organize."

"No. Thank you, Sargent. We always drive together in a caravan. We'll ensure everyone gets home safely, but before I go, I wanted to talk to Belinda."

"Yes, ma'am. She seems to have disappeared for a moment. Have a good evening, ma'am."

Mrs. Nelson felt as if she had been told nicely to leave by Barbara's security people. He didn't ask to help, or take a message. How odd. She would have her husband talk to Sargent Major Dobbs in the morning. As quickly as the ladies had ascended on the meeting room, they were gone.

"Whew! All clear?" questioned Bonnie as she appeared from the kitchen to an empty room. She was gone for only a few minutes. "I was hoping to speak to Mrs. Nelson. I guess I missed her. Phillips, thank you again for stepping up. Mrs. Nelson obviously needed to be assured someone was in charge besides me. We have one remaining workshop this week, and four next week. Don't forget the veteran's community potluck is on Friday night."

"Ma'am. I'm your driver tonight."

"Thank you. You must have the information as to where I'm staying."

He smiled. "Come on. Grab your gear and I'll grab the cat!"

"Greroowwwlll."

"Baby Kittie, where is your happy meow? Maybe she wants to stay here. It's okay with me, if Management doesn't mind."

They walked out of the Veteran's Center and climbed into a four-wheel drive truck and headed west, away from the busy highways, away from DC. She saw Pennsylvania State road signs. She guessed she wasn't going south to Fort Eustis.

"Phillips, how did you get matched with this crew?"

"Joined right out of college."

He was being vague, but knew other team members rarely gave her details of their lives. She hadn't met many of the men and women who worked with Frank and Charlie. Somehow tonight was different. Usually someone she'd met introduced her to the incoming team. No one was there to introduce her. Frank may consider she was being overly paranoid. But regardless, she placed both hands beside her legs and carefully lifted each finger and gently rolled the finger on the front of the vinyl seat. She did the same on and under the armrest and on the visor when she commented on how bright the stars were without the clutter of the lights from metropolitan areas. He simply drove and didn't say a word. If she was wrong, Frank could send the vehicle to the car wash.

The clock on the truck's dashboard showed they'd driven for two hours. Her mind was thinking of the scrapbook pages she'd examined. Pictures of one family last night looked practically identical to pictures she viewed earlier in the evening. Both had pictures of the family at kindergarten graduations, at barbeques, and watching a parade dressed in red, white, and blue. How odd the ladies had the same last name—Brown—the same as her family name, which had caught her eye. But, there are lots of Browns in the phone book.

She couldn't swear the appearances of the husbands were identical, but their builds looked very, very similar. She couldn't compare their eyes. One man wore sunglasses, the other didn't. Each family had two kids, an older boy who looked eight or ten years of age, and a younger daughter with blonde hair. Both wives had long dark hair and appeared generally to be the same size. Surely, a man in the military wouldn't have two families; she guessed it was possible. She hoped Mrs. Nelson saw her note.

"Here's the safe house for tonight. I'll go in and retrieve the key."

While he was gone, she quickly spit on a tissue and stuffed it into the web frame under her seat. She was probably being silly. She was already dreading the early alarm to return to the Veteran's Center to attend morning reveille at eight o'clock. The routine was different from other times she'd been moved. She looked around the gravel parking lot, two cars with tags from Maryland and the other Virginia. She made a mental note of the tag numbers on the three vehicles and Phillip's red truck from the registration papers in the glove compartment. The motel sign was gone, the frame remained. She didn't recognize other landmarks.

"Here's your key. I'll be back in the morning at 0600. We'll stop at a drive-thru for breakfast. Put the chair against the door and close the drapes. Sorry the cable is out, but we bought you a DVR player. Do you need anything else?"

"Nope. I put a sandwich and a Coke in my backpack during the scrapbook workshop. See you in the morning."

After leaving her room, he ducked into the room of the other guests.

"Does she suspect anything?"

"No. I drove around for two hours past Pennsylvania road signs as we'd planned before circling back to Front Royal. She's been moved from safe house to safe house so she didn't question. Slip a note under her door indicating plans have changed before you leave: 'Security problems at the clinic. Shelter in place.' Sign it 'Dobbs.' Crazy Mrs. Nelson gave us a convenient cover when she wanted increased security at the meeting tonight. I have to return to DC before curfew. When they discover she's gone, I can't be missing and have events inadvertently link me with her disappearance and draw the focus of an investigation. No one saw us leave. No one followed us, we avoided toll roads. Thanks for taking the barriers down. Can you put them back when I leave? "

"Well done."

"Things ready for tomorrow?"

"The demolition team set the dynamite. I'll place the detonators and timers in the morning on the way out. Chemicals are staged for a meth lab. Should provide lots of excitement and confusion."

"Should destroy evidence, as well. What time do the contractors arrive?"

"They should be here around 0700."

"I'll set the timers for 0530."

"What happened to the guards?"

"Their bodies are in the room with the meth lab chemicals. I positioned them in chairs before rigor set in. They'll look as if they made a mistake in processing the meth and died in the explosion. We'll wear their construction hats if we have to be outside to confuse the time line if anyone should drive by."

"Did you catch Charlie Smith?"

"No joy, missed him. He appeared at the hotel in Georgetown but left before we could organize a tail."

"At least we can kill Janice Brown or Bonnie Watkins, whoever the hell she is."

"Timmerman would do the same for us."

"Still wonder why she killed him."

"We have orders. I don't want to know. Don't care."

*****

Bonnie straightened the window coverings as a ruse to confirm her mental notes and quickly wrote down the license tag numbers. She returned the hand-sized notebook to one of the zippered pockets in her slacks. She looked around her lodging and realized she shouldn't have teased they'd dump her in a fleabag hotel. This room would definitely qualify. The room had the look of roadside motels built in the sixties: a concrete shell with a noisy air-conditioning unit mounted in the wall above the bathroom sink. How convenient. She could brush her teeth and dry her hair at the same time. The room was nothing fancy — two double beds and a round table in the corner by the windows along with two rusty folding chairs. She used the clothespin she carried in her bag to close the used-to-be-fashionable yellow and orange flower-power drapes. The multicolored brown and yellow shag carpet felt sticky when she walked across the room. The word sleazy came to mind. "Just wait till I talk to Frank. I'm demanding a different travel agent!" She giggled.

She retrieved her Glock and thigh holster from the concealed compartment in the bottom of her backpack. Frank's team had the bag designed to look as if it was an everyday backpack. It took a minute to organize the web belt and the Velcro strips to wrap around her right thigh. Fighting with an octopus would have been easier. She swore to practice the gear-up routine to compete with Charlie and his crew. She'd heard their snickers. They could don thigh holsters with the same ease she kept her shoulder bag in place. She checked the security of her papers and cash in her zippered cargo slacks pockets. She found the Russian and German bills she'd forgotten to return to Randy from her trip from Moscow. Now, her major decision was which movie to watch.

In the paper grocery bag along with the DVDs was a set of bedsheets still in their plastic wrapper, towels with the tags remaining, several bottles of water, a bag of chips, and a receipt for $62.78. It was obvious these guys weren't trained by Frank or Gustoff to carelessly leave a traceable credit card receipt. *Shoddy technique*, she pondered.

The dusty bedspread in a geometric mauve and green was outdated, worthy of a museum, she mused. She unfolded the sheet to cover the spread, trying to avoid touching anything. She stuck the wrappers, price tags, and receipts in her backpack. She grabbed her gloves to avoid leaving fingerprints, mindful of Frank and Gustoff's training. Maybe she was overreacting.

She wished Baby Kittie was there to sit and watch the videos. The tortoiseshell calico liked to watch DVDs and lick the salt off the chips. The movie, *101 Dalmatians*, was her kitty's absolute favorite. Bonnie was convinced it was because Sargent Tibbs, a scrappy Tabby cat, saves the kidnapped puppies.

Thank goodness she'd found a travel alarm clock on the shopping trip with JoAnne. She set the alarm for 0500, plenty of time to shower and be ready to leave by 0600. Reveille at the clinic was at eight o'clock. She'd be back in time for the opening exercises as if it was simply another day. At least she didn't have to organize a nutrition class on Thursday night with the scrapbook ladies using the conference space. She was looking forward to leaving early on Friday. "Oh, no," she reminded herself out loud. "I completely forgot to order patriotic tablecloths and centerpieces for the veteran's potluck on Friday night!"

Chapter Fourteen

The Congressional after-hours cocktail conclaves were heading home. A light mist covered streetlights creating soft glows on deserted streets and quiet alleys in the heart of the nation's capital.

Three men in business suits arrived in a line of black sedans and were rushed through a side door into a private dining room to join Mr. Tao in one of Washington, DC's most prestigious hotels. Two men dressed in gray slacks, bulky blue blazers, and dark glasses remained in the hall by the door, and two others stood on the sidewalk outside the window of the dining room.

"Do you enjoy my modern hotel?" asked Mr. Tao. "Business make much money, bought ten US hotels this year. Profitable for my girls and Chinese companies. We learn much. Thank you for advice on how to put hotels in seashells."

"You mean, shell companies?"

Mr. Tao looked confused and whispered something to the other Chinese men seated at the table. They snapped their fingers, and plates of Caesars salad and prime rib with roasted potatoes appeared, carried by staff in tailored tuxedos. For dessert freshly sliced sugared strawberries were served on a rich shortbread cookie and topped with tart *crème fraiche* in elegant Oriental dishes. Waiters efficiently passed American coffee and Chinese tea, cleared the dishes, and withdrew through the door to the staging kitchen. Quietly, the door closed with a click.

The men in expensive suits had met with Mr. Tao and his entourage on many previous occasions and knew the protocol was consistent—first they ate, after which they discussed business.

Mr. Tao held his cup of tea. "Ms. Brown cost me three million yen when she uncovered Sun'Luk's grapefruit repacking plant in the Philippines last fall. Shoppers not know regular grapefruit from organic. Damn fruit flies she found in my boat in China. We kill her professor when he found lab in Mexico. Many years for Sun'Luk to recover. I patient man. I reflect Sun Tzu, 'Turn misfortune to advantage.' Damn Brown, she give copies of report to someone," said Mr. Tao, his voice fading as if his focus changed.

His guest made a mental note to have his people check what exposure Brown had uncovered.

"I am old. I not need this distraction. First, military found repacking plant in Philippines. Mexican government close bacteria lab. Sun'Luk was in position to supply Europe and the US with organic vegetables when the planned Staphylococcus aureus outbreak be blamed on greedy farmers in Mexico, California, Florida, and South America."

"Mr. Tao. We are working on a solution even today. Miss Brown has many ties with people who can do you and me much harm. We have to look at future opportunities, you will agree. We now are aware of her friendship with Smith, and he has been in DC for a long time. Mr. Tao, we have to accomplish our project and leave with clean hands. We both learned of Smith's friends in the Russian government, information which could be extremely helpful in the future. The information will allow us to build a better trap, wouldn't you agree, Mr. Tao?"

"Yes, as Sun Tzu has directed, 'Turn misfortune to advantage'."

"Exactly! Thank you, Mr. Tao, for the recordings of the Congressional Intelligence Committee planning session last week held here in your hotel. Damn politics. The information you gave us on their strategy for the upcoming election has been beneficial. The experimental software being designed by your computer people will be helpful for both the US and Chinese government. I look forward to seeing the beta version."

Mr. Tao smiled and slowly bowed his head.

"Mr. Tao, I apologize I must leave to attend a late-night meeting at the White House. I do enjoy your company. It is a pleasure to meet with you and your associates. We will meet again soon."

There was a series of subtle bowing before the men in expensive suits left for their meeting at 1600 Pennsylvania Avenue.

Chapter Fifteen

"You called on the secure line. What's up? What do you mean she's gone?" demanded Frank.

"I arrived at 2000," reported Dobbs. "The cat was howling and was running toward me. I figured the cat lost track of Montana. I felt she was probably visiting the ladies' quarters. I looked but didn't find her. Her bug-out backpack was gone. Mrs. Champion, who was going to drive her back to Fort Eustis, arrived minutes after I arrived. Montana didn't go with her. I told her our security needs changed and apologized for the confusion."

"Anyone else missing?"

"After General Scrapbooker left, the entire building rushed to a neighborhood beer hall. Curfew is at 2300. I'll call if anyone else is missing."

"Have you looked at the surveillance tapes?"

"The machine had been disabled. Sitting on the shelf, it looked fine, but inside the recorder a magnet had been placed against the tape which erased the images as they were recorded. This was professional sabotage."

"Damn! Has anyone realized she's missing?"

"The cat has howled from the moment I returned, but other

than the cat, I've kept her disappearance low-key. In the morning there are bound to be questions."

"Thanks, Dobbs. I'll be in touch."

Frank dialed Charlie's satellite phone. "Hey, bad news." He knew Charlie; they'd worked together since they both attended officer candidate school right out of college and served together through Vietnam. They had remained close. Knowing Charlie, it was best to lead with the worst information. "Montana is AWOL. The surveillance machine has been disabled. Appears she left around 2000 before Dobbs returned, but I haven't confirmed the time line. Most of the crew is out on a beer call."

"It's unusual for her to go off on her own, especially after Russia and the break-in at the condo. Get us access to satellite footage! Whoever organized this extraction will have avoided tolls and intestate with traffic cameras. She's been gone for less than an hour. She's pretty savvy beneath her Southern charms. My bet is on her, and heaven help whoever has temporarily relocated her. Push forward with whatever resources are required. Get us some air power. Call Dobbs to get a list of vehicles in our lot. Maybe friends can provide a satellite shot from last night. Put some birds in the air to track vehicles. Start at the beer hall near the Veteran's Center."

"Already working on it."

"Frank, you cautioned we were moving too quickly. You were right. We didn't have time to do sufficient background checks on the residents. Some we knew, others were friends of friends, which were probably okay. It must be one of the walk-ins. Patch me in when you find her."

"Will do."

Charlie wanted to drop everything and rush back to DC to rescue her, kiss her forever, hold her, and spend another long night in bed with her. But he had an assignment to complete.

When he saw her in Georgetown, she'd promised to catch him up on the romance he'd missed for the last ten years. Instead of cashing in her promise, he'd held her while she slept. Satisfying his personal desires to be with her, he'd put her in the middle of another tornado, and at this moment he was half a world away and couldn't do a damn thing to comfort her. He'd kept her at a distance since Key West. He had no other choice if he was to protect her.

Over the years, he'd come to reconcile that having her in his life would remain only a dream. When he woke briefly after the surgery, there she was. He relished in her whispers in his ear and the softness of her touch. At first, while on the pain medicine, he wondered if she was merely an illusion, a pleasing hallucination he had retreated into before. It was days before he'd actually realized she was truly there. But he loved her and after a long ten years she was back in his life. Reuniting with her wasn't the romantic wooing he had longed for, hell, he was in and out of consciousness after he was shot. But he knew she had saved him.

Maybe one day he could explain and apologize. He'd tried when they were in Moscow. He hoped eventually she would understand and forgive him. He should have stayed away when he realized she was at Mansion on O Street. They'd used the Georgetown hotel many times during the years, along with other government agencies and contractors. Few knew of the suite designed for her. It was risky to have been in the same city, and to spend the night with her. He wondered if someone had followed him and tracked her to the Veteran's Center.

Frank and Dobbs were perfectly capable to handle this and anything else, as they would for any member of their teams. Maybe he'd soon have another chance to share romantic moments with her; he hoped he would have a lifetime as they restarted their relationship. She was the one he wanted to spend the rest of his life with. He hoped she would stay. Whoever was behind these efforts to harm her was pushing the schedule.

He exhaled.

His exit strategy was already in play. They only needed more time.

CHAPTER SIXTEEN

"Phillips!" Dobbs met him at the door at the Veteran's Center. "Thanks for jumping in to aid Mrs. Nelson. We're doing a roll call tonight. Did you by chance see our dietitian, Bonnie Watkins, after the scrapbook workshop ended?"

"She was here when I left."

"I haven't had a chance to visit with you. How are things going?" asked Dobbs. "Are you still working at the construction company?"

"Yeah. Squared away, guys. We're doing a project in Pennsylvania. I appreciate I can stay here to save money. I have a girlfriend back home. We're saving for a down payment on a house."

"Sounds like things are going well. If we can assist in any way, holler. We're still figuring out what resources would be useful to our service personnel as they transition home."

"Can I throw a suggestion into the hat? Could you arrange for a speaker on home mortgages?"

"Fantastic idea! I'll pass along the suggestion to the veteran's group. They're going to be here for a potluck on Friday night."

"Thanks, Dobbs." *Tell people what they want to hear,* reflected

Phillips. If the explosion goes as planned, he knew at least five people who wouldn't be at the potluck.

Chapter Seventeen

Beep, beep, beep. Her eyes flashed open. She woke abruptly to the sound of industrial trucks backing into the gravel parking lot. It was 0400 a.m. Sometime during the movies she'd drifted into sleep. The bedside lamp wouldn't turn on, and the light switch with the pull-chain located above the sink didn't respond. The air conditioner was quiet. She wondered if the noisy air conditioner was running if she would have even heard the trucks.

She looked through the drapes and was shocked. Outside, across the windows, were boards and strips of plywood. They weren't there when she arrived the night before. The parking lot lights were out. The two cars were gone. Through the thin slats covering the windows she could view men in Levis and black T-shirts reading "Demolition Crew" in glowing white letters across their shoulders. DO NOT ENTER signs placed across the parking lot reflected in the backup lights of the truck. The workmen wore the same yellow security hard hats like the one Phillips had on the back seat of his truck. Workers were shouting orders above the truck noises.

"Where's the security crew we left last night?"

"Probably drunk somewhere."

"They were supposed to remove the doors. What were they thinking to cover them? Grab some screwdrivers and remove these doors. Where's the supervisor, Phillips? This will delay our schedule for hours. Glad we arrived early. Take the battery powered saws to disassemble the plywood strips. Break the windows to minimize flying projectiles when we set the charges on the explosives."

"Set the charges? Explosives?" She had to escape! She grabbed her backpack, ran to the door, and turned the knob. It wouldn't budge. She desperately banged on the door, but no one turned their head toward the noise. Her foot slipped on a handwritten note. "Hah! Security problem?" She stuffed the note into her pocket.

Through the minute cracks between the boards she watched dump trucks and backhoes assembling on the narrow country road at the edge of the parking lot. She hoped someone would hear her cries despite the noisy throaty diesel engines. It was barely light outside.

"Boss Man! Get the hell in here! Man, we have a problem. Got three dead bodies: Manchester, Ames, and Britton. Weren't they the vets we hired as day labor? Where's Phillips?"

"Hey, these chemicals weren't here last night. Look at these Bunsen burners and ceramic bowls. How's your chemistry? A skull and crossbones means they're deadly. What's this red label with a fire and the yellow triangle with the fireworks?"

"*Damn*! They mean grab those bodies and *get the hell out of here*!" he yelled.

In minutes blue and red lights were parked on the road, blocking the entrance of the parking lot. Chattering could be heard from the radios. The outside noise increased matched by the confusion she observed through the slits between the timbers. Suddenly her earlier distaste of even thinking of crawling on the sleazy carpeted floor wasn't a concern. Her hand searched the narrow dark space under the bed. Her fingers found a metal coat hanger. Several swipes of her knife produced strips of the bedsheet. She quickly wrote HELP ROOM 112 with lipstick and globbed lipstick on her lips to put a wet kiss on the message flag. She wrapped her gloved hand in a towel and broke the glass with the butt of her knife. She dragged a chair to the window and banged her feet against the boards, but the timbers wouldn't budge. She used the blade to hack a larger opening between the planks. The fabric strip was tied to the thin wire. The signal flag was pushed and working the wire through the narrow gap between the boards covering the door and windows. It had to work.

She was trapped. She had to catch the attention of someone, anyone, to free her from the motel room. She was determined to break the focus of the crews responding to the bodies at the other end of a long motel complex. At last, the flag cleared the boards and immediately dropped to the sidewalk. Her heart sank.

Uniformed officers were quickly unrolling yellow crime scene tape around the area blocking access from the road. With Pollyanna optimism she knew anyone who walked by her room would surely notice the crumpled cloth lying on the sidewalk, her desperate cry for help. People previously tearing down the timbers covering the window were ordered to leave by police officers. She snapped back into reality with determined zeal. Finding the bodies had bought her some time. She cut another strip and added the same information. She mentally dared this flag to jump from the wire. She whittled a larger space between the slats. The second attempt to squirm the signal flag through the wood slats was faster and successful. She wiggled the wire waving the flag back and forth. It was bound to snare someone's eye. She heard her alarm clock sound. It was five o'clock. The

132

approaching sunrise increased the odds someone would discover her signal. She kept waving her SOS banner.

Teeny streams of light peeked through the wooden seams. Hammering and cussing by the workmen blocked other sounds. Suddenly, people were yelling, *"Bomb! Get out. Bomb, run! Clear the area!"* People rushed toward the road.

Bomb? She was locked in. Her flag had been fruitless. She looked around her prison and was aggravated when she suddenly saw daylight streaming around the edges of the air conditioner box where it met the wall. She had focused solely on activities toward the parking lot and hadn't even considered what was behind the building. Why hadn't she considered escaping through the air conditioner opening? If she hadn't noticed it, maybe her captors hadn't as well. She could escape and hopefully go unnoticed.

She ripped the plug from the wall, grabbed her backpack, and carefully braced her feet on the green linoleum counter under the air conditioner. The counter was slippery. Standing on top of the sink, she hoped the thin metal legs of the counter wouldn't buckle. She cushioned her shoulder with the backpack as she pounded her body against the air conditioner's plastic frame. In the first attempt her foot slipped. She rebalanced. She shoved for the second time and the air conditioner tumbled to the ground below. She was amazed how easily she moved the rectangular machine. She was proud of her success until she looked through the gaping opening. The drop was further than she'd anticipated.

She jumped down and stripped the sheets from the bed and pushed them and the tacky spreads through the eighteen-by-twelve-inch opening. She tossed her backpack to the ground. Headfirst she squirmed through the tight opening being careful to avoid accidentally shooting her foot with the gun strapped to her thigh. She was planning a summersault landing, although she hadn't done those since her bout of gymnastic lessons at 4-H camp. The building rapidly began to shake. Events unfurled in seemingly slow motion. Walls were crumbling and beginning to disappear around her. The force of the explosion catapulted her away from the collapsing structure. Her landing was brutal, but a gully filled with leaves softened the fall. She was momentarily stunned, but took a deep breath, no pain, thank goodness.

Flames jumped through the walls, as if waving good-bye through her escape hatch. The heated dusty air made her cough. Clumps of the concrete, timbers, and sparks landed in the dry leaves around her. She had to move. She scrambled to her feet. Found her backpack. The light from the fire behind her guided her retreat deep into the shaded forest.

CHAPTER EIGHTEEN

"Morning, Frank," stated Dobbs. "Wanted to touch base before our people began to scatter. Wish I had favorable news, but I don't."

"She didn't call! Damn. I've barely met her, but I have the feeling she'd check in, if she could," Frank added. "You would have called if you'd heard from her. I'd hoped we could have turned things around. Glad we're not betting men, Dobbs."

"Don't forget that's how we won the strip mall, remember?" Frank's laugh was hearty.

"I scheduled Dan, our medic, to do a lecture on diabetes medications to minimize concern for her disappearance. The troops are eating breakfast. We'll have reveille at 0800. Classes start after another hour following coffee. The cat attacked Phillips when he returned last night. The kitty usually likes everyone."

"Was he late?" asked Frank.

"No, but he helped the scrapbook ladies load their supplies. I asked if he saw Montana leave, but he said he didn't."

"You said the cat growled at Phillips? Where are we on the background check on him? Where did he serve?"

"I had the same idea and went through the personnel records

135

last night. The background checks have been completed on everyone else. Most are from units we've worked with, but his paperwork hasn't come back. Our people said they can't verify any of the information he gave on the application, which is irregular," Dobbs explained.

"Is he still in the building? I'm going with the cat. Detain him. Oh, and also secure his vehicle. What does he drive, anyway?"

"A red Dodge pickup; NY License 5555-121."

"I'll pass it along to the crew who are looking at the satellite feed. I'm sending you a forensics team to search his vehicle. Have them dust for prints, swab everything, tear it down to the frame. Montana has a quirky style, but smart. Tell the team to look for something out of the ordinary. Who knows, we may get lucky."

Dobbs returned the receiver to the cradle. As if a magician had waved a wand, Baby Kittie appeared from out of nowhere, landed on the counter, and rubbed his elbow. "You were right, kitty. We're going to detain Phillips!"

The feline jumped to the floor and ran ahead of him briefly entering the rooms as they moved down the hall. He knew the kitty had found her prey when he heard the growls.

CHAPTER NINETEEN

A sharp pain shot through her knee with each step. *Pick up your foot, pick up your foot, dragging your foot will leave a trail*, she ordered herself. She had to keep moving.

The landscape behind the motel sloped into a wide crevasse. It was less painful walking downhill. She leaned against a craggy oak trunk to rest. With an aching knee, she knew she didn't dare sit. *Move, Bonnie. Move*, she reminded herself. She found the dark knit hat kept in the outside pocket of her backpack and stuck her hair inside. She dug her fingers into the soil beneath the leaves and smudged the dark rich dirt on her face. Sleeping in her black long-sleeved polo shirt and black cargo pants did have benefits when she needed to leave quickly. The gloves had protected her hands during the explosion and the landing. She wondered if she should've made a point to leave fingerprints. In a fire she doubted the fingerprints would have survived.

Embers from the fire lit the sky as if they were tiny stars. The sparks ignited spontaneous fireworks in the dry leaves on the hill around her. The crisp underbrush could quickly become an inferno. But where to go? Warm air rises and could pull the wind upward to the top of the hill. The draft may pull the fire around her, over her head, over her body. She struggled through branches toward her left, toward the road half a mile away.

She'd put her trust into the hands of Phillips. He told her he was her escort, and she believed him. *What a mistake*, she scolded herself. Strangely, now it seemed comical. She'd giggled when Frank's crew told her to ask for a password. It reminded her of the crazy TV spy show, *Get Smart*. But she should have asked for the password. The mistake could have been fatal.

She checked her weapon. The parts seemed fine, but she was far from a gun expert. She tested the magazine holding the bullets. It seemed to be snugly inserted into the handle of her Glock. She'd had a few lessons from her dad's friends at the hunting camp on how to shoot a gun and from Charlie when they were in the WWII tunnels in Unalaska/Dutch Harbor. She felt her thigh to reassure the spare magazine remained in her zippered pocket, although her thigh was tender; probably meant another nasty bruise. The sun was rising, but was low on the horizon enabling the hills to provide dark shadows to shield her from eyes of the workmen and firefighters assembling along the road. In a distance, the activities of firemen in yellow slickers resembled a hive of bees. Their focus was the fire. Waves of explosions were pushing the work crews further and further to the far side of the road away from the building.

She wondered what had happened to Phillips or his associates. Had they blended into the crowd? He wouldn't be working alone. She'd assumed people at the Veteran's Center were friendly, but now wondered if foes had infiltrated the crowd. She understood Frank's stern advice to talk to only him of her situation to protect the team. Her foot slipped and she tumbled over a log. In the shadows she hadn't seen an undersized pond, but flat on the ground her perspective changed. Maybe it wasn't a pond, merely a large puddle, but it was wet.

She remembered her dad telling her if she was lost in the pinewood at the ranch to quit moving and simply stop. Stay where the rescuers calculate you may be. She'd sit by the pond and blend in with the dim shapes in the shaded ravine and wait. If fire approached, she'd duck into the pond. As the day progressed, she'd move slowly along the ground to stay in the shadows. Surely, someone at the Veteran's Center would notice she was gone. Maybe someone would find her signal flag, but after the explosion and fire, her hopes waned.

Flames marched through the building on the hill above her. It would be hours before a forensics team would be allowed anywhere near the building to start their examination of the three dead men found in Room 134. On the evening TV news, following an explosion, muscular men in dark glasses and ATF jackets took command of the scene to investigate the bombing. No ATF or crime scene investigation vehicles had arrived. Frank and Charlie seemed to have a way around organizational turf wars, but did they even know she was there?

Somehow fate had saved her from being another body in a sleazy hotel room. Was Phillips in another room, dead? Or had he organized the operation? She wished she knew. She wished she knew why she had been held captive. She sighed and wished she'd put another sandwich in her bag. She usually carried peanut butter and orange marmalade sandwiches in her pockets.

CHAPTER TWENTY

"Where's the coffee?" growled the investigative team members as they slowly gathered into the Frank's field office at the junkyard.

Frank poured himself a cup. He'd read their expressions and knew their answers before he asked. "Give me the bad news."

"No joy. We wish we had good news for you, Boss." His crew avoided using identifiable names, even if the names changed frequently. "We're hunting a needle in a haystack. We've spent the night at National Security Agency (NSA) going through satellite pictures. We made the assumption she was taken by a car or truck. We eliminated abduction by plane or helicopter since they would have had to file a flight plan, especially near the heart of the government. Federal Aviation Authority (FAA) reported no unscheduled flights or last-minute requests for takeoffs last night. Friends at local law agencies have been getting people out of bed to gather video recordings from banks, drugstores, liquor stores, and anywhere else with surveillance cameras along roads leaving the Veteran's Center across four states. We're in the process of cross-referencing the films."

"I called base security to check if the scrapbook ladies arrived home safely and to ask if they saw anything unusual," responded Frank. "I even talked to Mrs. Nelson, aka General Scrapbooker. She said she wanted to talk to our hostess, but Phillips was there and seemed to rush her out of the building. I cannot underscore the importance of finding our lost dietitian," emphasized Frank.

"We understand, Boss. We are not going to consider the alternative."

"Dobbs called with a possible lead," offered Frank. "Start at the Veteran's Center and track a red truck belonging to a guy named Ross Phillips. Maybe it can narrow the search, or could simply be another rabbit to run. The background check has given us a big fat zero on him. According to Dobbs, the cat tried to attack Phillips. He's been working for a construction company. Track where he went last night. Once he is eliminated, we'll start looking at other vehicles leaving the parking lot at the time when the scrapbook ladies left and Montana disappeared."

The communication's operator hollered across the room. "Boss, Alcohol, Tobacco, and Firearms (ATF) is rolling an investigation team to an explosion at a construction site near Front Royal, Virginia. Where's our red truck guy?"

"Dobbs and the cat are detaining him. Do we have any physical evidence to put him at the construction site?" asked Frank.

"He works construction somewhere. We're tracking down the details! The video tech guys are backtracking vehicles from the construction site. I'll cross-reference with vets employed at the location."

"Send a search team and cadaver dogs to the locale of the explosion. I doubt they will turn down the manpower. Go in uniform to investigate. Tell them we had people working there. Wait, Montana wore dark tops and black cargo slacks. Have some of your crew dressed in black. She's scrappy. If anyone could survive; it would be her. I'll call Dobbs and Charlie."

A hand shoved a report in front of his face. "We have four men assigned as day labor to the location of the 911 call reporting the explosion. We're verifying names."

"Quick response. Tic-Toc. Call when you have details." Frank punched in a long series of numbers. Before he could say a word, Charlie asked, "What's the news on Montana?"

"Nothing yet, but I'm sending a crew to a suspicious fire at a construction site that hired some of our people. It's a long shot. Once on the scene, our people can provide a firsthand report. We have a crew at NSA looking at surveillance film. The cat is blaming Phillips."

"I appreciate the call. I have an uneasy feeling this is related somehow with Timmerman. He's dead, but the whole situation continues to nag me for some reason. We're still examining the extent of his network. Call Miller and JoAnne. Whoever is after Montana may have seen the ladies together. We must have missed something. Find her, Frank!" The line went dead.

He agreed. What were they missing? Right now, his sole focus was finding Montana. He'd figure out the motive later. He followed up with Dobbs. "Handcuff and gag the suspect. Cover his head. Deliver him to the field office."

"I have a room of volunteers ready to assist," quickly responded Dobbs.

"We have to be reasonably friendly. Tell your people to be careful with what they say," stated Frank. "He's probably CIA. You're aware of the problems we have over there."

Dobbs gave a nod, and across the room the self-selected security committee jumped into action. He heard Baby Kittie's growls coming from the hall as they were moving their guest. "Done, Boss."

"How's the cat holding out?" asked Frank. I heard she's

been howling since Montana disappeared after the scrapbook workshop. Strange. When Montana was traveling the cat was a perfect lady."

"On your toes, men, or the cat will replace us," joked Dobbs. "Gotcha."

"Not kidding." Dobbs laughed. "I'll tell Baby Kittie you'll check in with news or progress."

"You're aware the feline will do anything for drive-thru soft-serve ice cream. I'll have someone deliver her a cup."

"Thanks, Frank. Carrie clued us in on the calico's fondness for frozen custard. The soft-serve ice cream machines arrived over the weekend. I'll call with any updates. Out."

Frank chuckled and shook his head. He called Miller, then JoAnne.

The phone at the Veteran's Center was busy. Dobbs saw another line flashing.

"How was the command conference, Dobbs?"

"Good morning, General Nelson. Superb as always, sir. I arrived home last night."

"Mrs. Nelson said you'd called to ensure everyone arrived home safely. Thank you for providing extra security for the group. She shared that Sargent Phillips was somewhat rude as she left last night. She wanted to speak to the young lady who was acting as the hostess. I reassured her Phillips was unaware she was my wife. Even if she wasn't, poor customer service, Sargent Major."

"Yes, sir. Our clinical officer...hostess...is MIA. I'm directing the investigation. We are still trying to determine the time line. It is unknown if she disappeared before Mrs. Nelson left with her group, or after. There may have been events in play which distracted Sargent Phillips. Please convey to Mrs. Nelson my greatest apologies. We are delighted the scrapbook workshops can utilize our space after hours."

"I'll pass along the information, but speaking of the scrapbooking workshops, last night, Mrs. Nelson received a note from the hostess, Bethany, if I remember. She asked if Mrs. Nelson noticed two of the attendees had similar pictures of the same man. She wondered if anyone had overheard comments from the two ladies. One Mrs. Brown was on Tuesday night, and the other Mrs. Brown on Wednesday. I ran the identities quietly by our personnel director. One Benjamin Brown is a Lt. Colonel in the US Navy, the other man, Major Bradley Brown, is US Army. On paper, both reported they were graduates of the US Service Academies. Pictures from the two personnel files look identical. Dobbs, you have available personnel resources. At the best, we have a man with two wives. Worst case is our security systems have failed to identify a man with two identities. Both men have high level appointments with access to some of the nation's most closely guarded secrets. Dobbs, your people can work off the grid, work off the radar, and can look in areas my people can't touch. Call me to assist with any resources required."

"Will do, General."

Dobbs glanced at his watch, 0750. Reveille and morning announcements were scheduled in a few minutes, enough time to update Frank. Who would have projected benign scrapbook workshops would trigger an investigation into the security of military personnel assigned to the nation's capital?

"Frank, Phillips is coming your way. General Nelson called. He has a project for us. He wants us to investigate two men featured in pictures Montana saw at the scrapbook workshop. It appears either we have a husband with two families, or possibly a man with two identities. He said both had last names of Brown. I don't have a good feeling about this."

"You said Brown?"

"Brown! It could be a coincidence. But I doubt it. Any other

144

time, I'd put the project on the back burner, but it may be related to Phillips and the disappearance of our hostess. If Phillips isn't who he says he is, the Browns may not be either. The general said one is a Navy officer, the other Army, both reportedly graduated from the service academies."

"Dobbs don't misunderstand my suggestion, but send some of our ladies to look at their backgrounds under the guise of a secret award to be presented by General Nelson. They look less threatening. Send along somebody nerdy with a camera around their neck to photograph any files that may be helpful. Aren't the hotel interviews today? When are they scheduled?"

"This afternoon."

"Maintain the schedule, Dobbs. After the interviews we'll fly the teams to West Point and Annapolis to check the men's applications and academic records. I'll secure clearance to have someone meet them who can access their personnel files and background reports. I'll send a limo to drive them to the hotel and later to deliver them to the downtown helo pad. Before they leave the Veteran's Center, brief them on the importance of this assignment. The research trip is on a need-to-know basis. You're familiar with the protocols. Tell them to limit discussions of this or any other projects they've worked on. If the interviewer asks, tell them to inform the employer, 'Sir, I am not at liberty to discuss my past assignments, as I would not discuss my assignments with your company.' We should avoid any comments causing a future employer to question their priorities. Coordinate with any necessary resources. Where are we on locating Montana?"

"Frank, the general reported Phillips was rude to Mrs. Nelson last night. Phillips told her Montana left after the workshop ended. Phillips told me she was at the Veteran's Center when he left. Either way, he left near the same time as Montana. He's on a list of veterans working for a construction company. It's a long shot. If he transported Montana, she may be at the construction site. The cat is convinced he's responsible. Once you've eliminated him as a suspect, we can move the investigation in other directions. A crew is en route to an explosion at a construction site. It's our best lead at the minute."

"Thanks, Dobbs. Your people sent word they'll tour the area for a couple of hours. I'll notify you when Phillip arrives. We've gonna let him sit a while in our concrete guest suite."

CHAPTER TWENTY-ONE

The crew from the motel assignment returned to DC to debrief. They met their handler in a dirty basement in a wood-framed house on a remote Virginia farm.

"How did things go last night?" asked the coordinator of the extraction team.

A tall stately man sat at the end of the table listening. He avoided these meetings when Timmerman was in charge. It kept his hands clean. The Embassy in Moscow sent the report of Timmerman's death through official channels which circulated through his office, including the identification of Janice Brown as the shooter. Mr. Tao had introduced him to Timmerman. Timmerman dated his daughter here and there when they were both in college in Long Beach and had even escorted her to official functions over the years. It proved to be the perfect cover scenario for the last ten years to keep Tao informed, and to give Timmerman a safety net occasionally. He like being part of the game, but from a distance.

"Our part went well. Brown is locked in a hotel room. She didn't suspect a thing. She's there to stay. We set the timers for 0530. We should hear something any minute. Our next mission is the elimination of Smith."

"What about Miller?"

"His wife works for the new CIA section chief during the transition, which complicates things. We care for our own. We can kill them later. The deaths should look totally unrelated. It's been only few weeks since the loss of Timmerman.

"Hey, the explosion just hit the emergency channels."

"Pretty darn clever putting our people in local permitting departments to provide direct information of construction and demolition projects. The arrangements may have many future benefits. Will Phillips be okay?"

"Ross left in plenty of time to return to the Veteran's Center for bed check last night. If he hadn't returned it would've attracted attention. With the explosion today, the construction company will be shutting down until the investigations are complete, and will officially lay everyone off. When the call comes, he'll tell the Veteran's Center he's heading home to Oklahoma and disappear. He'll contact us once he leaves and resurfaces.

"Gentlemen. Thanks for the update and the hard work," said the stately observer. "Hate we had to sacrifice three men to get Brown. Have to return to the Hill. There's a close vote in the Senate in a few hours. I may need to break a tie."

"Thank you for your oversight during the transition after Timmerman was killed, sir."

He nodded his head; didn't look back. His bodyguard who had stood in the shadows followed him from the room.

CHAPTER TWENTY-TWO

"Who's in charge, sir?" Frank's team leader asked the sheriff's deputy blockading the road. He'd been on their side of bombing investigations many times and knew the assignment never came at a convenient time, and never when you were rested or organized. After an event it took a few hours to even begin the inquiries. He doubted there would be a second round of explosions to injure emergency crews once they arrived on site. The area was isolated without news coverage.

"Talk to the men in the mobile command unit by the barriers."

He knocked on the metal door. Somebody responded, "Enter."

"Sir, I'm from the Washington, DC Military Command," said the team leader using the rehearsed lines Frank had provided. "We had a team of veterans working at this construction site who failed to report in last night. Can we be of assistance?" He handed the man wearing an ATF jacket, a business card. If called, the number would be answered at Frank's field office.

"What command?" asked the representative from the Office from the Alcohol, Tobacco and Firearms.

"Sir, if we are in the way, we'll head back to the office."

149

"It's too early to look for bodies.

"It's worth checking if we can locate and save the injured if they were thrown from the building."

"Go ahead. We have ambulances on the way."

"Thank you, sir." Frank's team leader walked out of the trailer, looked toward the van and nodded his head. He walked to the three bodies spread out in the parking lot, lifted the tarps covering their faces, and took discrete pictures with a handheld mini-camera. There were no burns on the bodies or clothing. He concluded they had been killed before the fire. Dried blood patterns seemed to suggest three bullets in the center chest. He couldn't detect gunpowder stippling with the dark crusty blood-soaked clothing. Skin on their lips, faces, and arms were gray with patterns of dark splotching. Someone had thankfully closed their eyes. He estimated they'd been dead for at least twelve hours. They were killed before Bonnie disappeared at the conclusion of the scrapbooking workshop. He breathed a sigh of sadness for the men who had survived hostile battlefields only to be killed trying to earn an honest wage. Thankfully, Montana wasn't under the tarp in the parking lot. A scrap of white cloth blowing across the parking lot caught his eye. It was burned, half of it remained. He carefully retrieved it, the half he held in his hand read, "Help — Roo" with a glob of red. He meticulously folded and placed it in a paper evidence bag. No one seemed to notice. Frank's team leader hoped it wasn't blood.

The dog-handlers walked down the road to survey the perimeter before moving to the area behind the building. They avoided firemen from local fire agencies battling active fires in the woods. On the way to the site, they'd collected clothes from her condo and shared them with the search dogs. The military dogs worked quickly and quietly, unlike deer-hunting dogs who would yelp when they caught a scent. The teams started in the area nearest to what they estimated to be the site of the largest explosion and expanded the boundaries. The dogs' acute canine noses busily searched under leaves, in gullies, and around stacks of rocks as they raced to the top of the hill and back to the trainer looking for injured or human remains. The routine was repeated many times. After several hours they shrugged their shoulders toward the team leader. He was standing at the road overlooking the valley behind the building.

Bonnie saw the dog teams when they arrived and watched apprehensively as they explored the area. She'd put her trust into the hands of another individual, and wasn't going to repeat the error. She knew if she moved she'd be spotted immediately. The silhouette of the man on the hill seemed to be in charge. He had a gun strapped to his thigh and was holding a long slender gun across his chest. She watched him closely. Was he one of Phillips' group? Hiding under the oak limbs stretched out on moist ground, she hoped to be unnoticed. If they saw her, she was an easy target. The dogs were coming this way. She tried to slow her breathing. In the movies water confused search dogs; she hoped they would simply lope past her.

The team leader motioned for the teams to work the area closer toward the road. One of the dogs stopped and pointed. They'd found her.

"Bonnie?"

"What's the password?" She sat defiantly. The dogs were rubbing against her.

The team leader called on the radio. "She wants us to give her the password. Call Frank and ask him. He didn't assign us a password."

"Let me talk to Frank," she snarled. They handed her the phone. He was on the line.

"You okay, kid?"

"Yeah! Y'all have to hire a different travel agent. The dog-welcoming committee was a lovely touch, but Baby Kittie is going to be truly jealous."

"The guys have a jacket for you. It reads 'DC Military Command.' Put it on. Go with them. They work for me. We'll talk in the van."

"You okay to travel?" asked one of the team.

"No problem," she said in a reassuring tone. Damn right, she'd walk out on her own, even if her knee was throbbing! She loaded into the van with the other dog handlers. "Where am I?"

"Point Royal, Virginia. Did you plan to stop and purchase a postcard?" they teased.

"No, he drove me past Pennsylvania road signs before coming here. I was going to put this place on my list of hot spots on where to stay near DC." The crew snickered. They had fresh memories of solemn retrievals of lost comrades. She shook off the wet kiss as one of the dogs licked her face. One of the team handed her a disposable wet towel to remove the mud and the kisses.

The team leader had the driver stop the van in front of the ATF trailer but past the wide windows. He headed inside. She slumped down into the seat. The ATF agents didn't even glance toward him. "We're heading back to DC. No joy. The site's too hot for the dogs. Holler if you want us to come back. We'll try again."

Down the road, they handed her a Gatorade, a peanut butter and marmalade sandwich, and a radio.

"Kid, how in the hell did you get in the middle of this?" asked Frank.

"I didn't ask for the password." She could hear the passengers chuckling in the van.

"Have you ever done any genealogy work?"

152

"Really? You're asking a Southern female if she's familiar with genealogy?" She laughed.

Before she could formulate a snappy reply, he responded. "The team will drop you off at the airport. Your tickets and luggage are at the Delta counter. Baby Kittie said she'd stay with us. One question before I let you go: who transported you to the motel?"

"Phillips. He said he was my escort. I have the receipts from the linens they purchased and a handwritten note someone slipped under my door. Maybe you can secure fingerprints. Oh, I tried to touch everything in his truck. I recorded tag numbers for the two cars in the parking lot when we arrived. I'll leave those with the team. Don't forget the veteran's potluck scheduled for Friday night. I was supposed to purchase patriotic tablecloths and centerpieces today. Can you cover for me? And thanks for finding me."

"Mrs. Nelson wanted to talk with you regarding two ladies who had pictures of the same man in their scrapbook entries at the workshop," said Frank.

"I saw those pictures when I judged the scrapbook pages. I wrote her a note on the judge's scorecard. I was disappointed I missed her," Bonnie said.

"That's why you're traveling and the rest of us are staying home."

Her curiosity was piqued, but knew she could ask later. She was sure there'd be background data in the packet at the airport.

"Kid, don't forget to leave your weapon with the crew. Out!"

He punched in the number of Charlie's satellite phone. "Retrieved Montana. Putting her on a plane to London. She'll be wheels up in two hours."

The van stopped at the outside curbside check-in for Delta Airlines at Dulles Airport. A metallic sign on the door of the van read, "Mountain-Climbing Tours." It must have been added at the bathroom stop; it wasn't there when she loaded into the van. They handed her a ball cap and a backpack with the same logo. "It will explain your camper attire."

"Gotcha. Thanks, guys." She tried to turn her head to avoid the Slurpee licks from the German shepherds, but they slobbered her anyway. "And puppies," she said. She squinted her eyes and grinned.

Once in the terminal she found the ladies room, changed her clothes, and wiped the rest of the mud and dog kisses off her face as best as she could. She packaged her current outfit from her camping escapade in a pre-addressed shipping box found in the backpack. On the way to the international security station she casually dumped the parcel addressed to Frank's mailbox in Ochopee, Florida, in the blue post office bin.

She had the same seat as her inbound flight from Alaska, the first row by the window, seated by the same man in hunting attire. "Ma'am."

"How's the fishing?"

"Fine, just fine," he said as he smiled.

As soon as they were airborne, Bonnie propped her head against the shaded window and was out. Five or six hours later she woke when her seatmate's elbow nudged her shoulder. "You missed dinner. You ought to eat something, or at least drink some fluids. Frank's orders!"

"Okay," she wearily responded. "I'll ring the flight attendant to bring me a Coke and something salty," she said and yawned. "What time do we arrive?"

"Around three o'clock a.m. You'll have to navigate Customs on your own. Carrie will meet you in the lobby to ride with you to the hotel."

"You have three hours to catch some sleep. I'll wake you in

time to brush the leaves out of your hair."

"Thanks. You don't appreciate my back-to-nature look?" she mumbled and was asleep. It seemed as if she barely closed her eyes when she felt the nudge indicating she had fifteen or twenty minutes before the plane began final approach. Consistent with the previous flight, her seatmate used the same routine to facilitating her being the first passenger off the plane by struggling with his luggage from the overhead bins blocking the exit. She walked past the drug-sniffing dogs. They had friendly eyes. She wanted to hug them but they wore yellow vests with "Don't Pet" written in several languages. She walked passed baggage claim and headed to the exit. There were no glitches at Immigration and Customs using her Bonnie Watkins passport.

As planned, there stood Carrie holding a handmade cardboard sign reading, "Dr. J. Brown." She was somewhat shocked when Frank allowed use of her given name, Janice Brown. To protect the team, he usually insisted she be called by her alias. "Dr. Brown, Dr. Brown," Carrie said, waving. "Glad we could locate you at the mountain-climbing class. Everyone is pleased you were available to present Dr. Reynolds' paper at the International Food Engineering meeting later today."

Dr. Reynolds was one of her favorite professors at her Mississippi alum. Later in graduate school she was assigned to be her major professor to coordinate her studies. Colleges required courses in many areas related to food which is the heart of health and nutrition. The diverse curriculum prepared dietitians for the many hats they would wear during their careers. There was something in play; she had no idea what, which seemed to be the normal routine when working with Frank and Charlie. "What time is the presentation?"

"At ten o'clock. You can read her notes in the cab. Let's find breakfast."

"And some strong coffee," urged Janice.

Once in the cab, Carrie remarked, "Attractive wardrobe." She snickered. "The technical conferences in England are a little more formal and a bit stodgy."

"What? Adding a pair of pearls to my coordinated black-on-black cargo pants set I'm sure will gain the approval of the fashion police. Where can I purchase an outfit at this hour?"

Carrie smiled. "I went shopping yesterday afternoon when I was told you were on the way. We have appointments at the beauty shop in the hotel at seven. The first customers are scheduled at six. There is a high demand to beautify travelers before catching morning flights."

"Do we have slides and handouts?"

"Yes, and yes. Dr. Reynolds said to tell you hello. She received a sudden consulting opportunity she couldn't pass up."

"Oh, how interesting." They both smiled, avoiding laughing, knowing Management probably made the convenient arrangements. "After lunch do I have time for a nap?" asked Janice.

"Well, no. Your folks are in London."

"What?" she whispered. She wondered if it was safe to talk in the cab. Were her folks in danger? But it seemed lately everything she did put someone in danger.

"Here's our hotel," Carrie announced.

At the reservation desk she was prepared to present her Janice Brown identification and passport. Her Bonnie Watkins credentials used on the Delta flight from DC were securely zipped in her pockets. During the walk to the room, Carrie continued to brief her on the activities planned. "Between your folks being here and the meeting, we had to go with Brown. Some of the professors from Mississippi may remember when you were a student there. We were afraid we would alarm your folks if we

156

used your cover identity. Your folks have been in France for a week tracing where your dad's father and uncle fought during WWI and visiting cemeteries."

"Dad said he's always wanted to travel to France. This is the tenth anniversary of my grandfather's death. He served at Verdun. His brother was listed as missing in action and years later his body was found buried in a collapsed tunnel. I bet they are searching cemeteries for his uncle's headstone. I wonder if Dad is going to visit the Addisons who were our neighbors at the Ranch at Bay Branch until a few years before the WWI. They live somewhere in England in a community named Featherlawn. It's been a long time; I may have the wrong hamlet. Ask my dad."

"Plans were to meet your folks this afternoon for tea, but the DC team indicated you needed to rest. You sent your folks a telegram and left tickets for a double-decker bus tour of London. We hired a tour guide who is a specialist in genealogy, and you can tell them you arranged to complete their excursion of England. We're going to Featherlawn tomorrow. You recall the two families named Brown you pegged at the scrapbook workshop? You apparently uncovered a possible high-level security problem."

"I hadn't even considered a security risk. I was concerned about the potential heartbreak of two delightful families captured in the photographs," Janice explained.

"The DC office is trying to confirm there are actually two men; both have been on foreign assignments with lots of travel. The men look identical, and both apparently have high-level security positions in DC. We are frantically exploring their backgrounds. Investigative teams were at the service academies yesterday and another team in New York. It appears the Grandmother of one or both men was from the same community your neighbors were from, Featherlawn, England. She married a man named Brown based on the court records in New York."

"This is an unbelievable coincidence. Why in the world did the bride travel to New York?"

"Frank is hoping you can put the pieces together, between the start of a successful outpatient diet clinic in a converted strip mall, and your recent mountain-climbing expedition, of course," Carrie teased.

"And he wants the information as soon as possible, I presume."

"Exactly!"

"By the way, what's the title of the presentation today? I ought to start morphing into my college professor persona," Janice asked.

"Here's the folder. Frank told me to feed and hydrate you. Management does have their style, don't they? Here. Drink a bottle of water. We have to hurry and shower or we'll miss breakfast and our appointments at the beauty salon. Oh, I'm also going to tell Frank in addition to the beautician visit, you also demanded we book a spa and massage this afternoon because of your sore muscles. I made us an appointment for three o'clock before our dinner reservations at eight."

"Thanks, Carrie. You've been talking to Dobbs. I seem to be developing into an extremely demanding person lately. I'm glad you're here. Thanks for coordinating the details."

"Okay, okay. Shower or we're gonna be late. And to be honest, your hair looks a mess!"

"Can I demand breakfast be delivered to the beauty shop? Are you staying here?"

"Yummy idea on the breakfast," said Carrie. "I'll call room service. I'm down the hall. I'll be back in thirty minutes."

CHAPTER TWENTY-THREE

The hot water was heavenly, or maybe it was the scented lavender soap. Carrie was right, her muscles were sore when she stopped to contemplate. Her knee ached and she had bruises here and there, but basically, she told herself, she was fine. Jumping out of buildings was certainly a skill she didn't learn in the gymnastic classes at 4-H camp. She was tired and was getting giddy. Oh, how she craved a glass of bourbon on ice and a long nap, but reluctantly searched for the coffeepot and pushed the start button.

She heard a knock, checked the peep. It was Carrie. "You're a savvy shopper. The dress is definitely European and is the latest trend in the fashion magazines I glanced through at the airport. The navy-blue wrap dress with the belt pulled tight reminds me of a trench coat."

"You have the petite waist to pull off the look," said Carrie.

"The oversized collar trimmed in snowy white piping is beautiful. The pearl necklace is elegant."

"Didn't you demand pearls? I called the concierge and he asked the lobby boutique to loan us a string of smoky pearls. They are beautiful, aren't they?"

159

"Yes, I love them. The sexy shoes go well with this sexy dress. There's enough fabric in the skirt I could hide a full arsenal strapped to my thigh. I hope you aren't expecting to dye my hair hot pink at the beauty salon! And Carrie, you can't tell my mother of the stockings and lingerie."

"They call those 'small' over here."

"Well, I can certainly see why!" She was holding the tiniest pair of panties she'd ever seen. She wished she could show off her sexy outfit for Charlie. She'd twirl and he'd unwrap the dress in an instant and there'd she'd stand in hot pink lace panties and matching camisole, a hot pink lace garter belt and a push-up bra. She liked when Charlie liked her lingerie, but she could never resist his kisses at sunrise.

"I hope you don't mind I ordered enough breakfast for the three other ladies with appointments in the beauty salon, which overlapped with ours."

"Me? Any reason for a party is my motto even at six o'clock in the morning. Come on! Can't miss the breakfast goodies. I'm hungry."

"Good Morning, I'm Cressida," said the hostess greeting them with fluted glasses of champagne. "By special request we're serving an exploration of British morning cuisine. The full English breakfast features a proper fry-up with streaky bacon, pale banger sausages, and savory slices of black pudding served with grilled heirloom country-grown tomato halves. Also, being served is a clay casserole of baked beans to eat with fried bread."

"Umm, this is exquisite. Tell me the recipe for black pudding? It's delicious. It looks similar to aged pepperoni sausage, but with a slightly different texture," said Janice.

"I'm glad you enjoy the pudding. Traditionally it is a sausage made with animal blood, fat, oatmeal, onions, and spices. But this is a hotel vegetarian specialty made with black beans, squid ink, fresh herbs, and chopped wild mushrooms. Isn't it mouthwatering? It's a favorite with the younger guests."

The fry bread was different from fry bread sold at Native Indian festivals in South Florida. British fried bread resembled sliced whole wheat bread browned on both sides in a buttered fry pan. The crisp buttery bread was absolutely delectable smeared with baked beans and topped with bitter orange marmalade. It was certainly an unusual combination, but it was yummy. Orange marmalade was her favorite, even the British bitter types. Growing up she loved her grandmother's sweet orange marmalade, especially when she was older and was invited to pick the fruit from special orange trees her grandmother had grown from seeds. For many cooking activities she was allowed to stand in a chair, but when making marmalade Grandmother's rule was her head had to reach the line Grandmother had drawn on the doorframe. It seemed years before she gained the height to stir the pot of hot bubbling liquid at 220 degrees. Growing to another line she could assist Grandmother in pouring the treasured hot fruit mixture into jars. *Paddington Bear* was probably one of her favorite childhood books simply because he also loved marmalade sandwiches. Fatigue was letting her mind wander. She took a long sip of her coffee.

"For the 'hen egg' dish as a component of any proper British breakfast, our chef has carefully stacked scrambled eggs as the bottom layer. In the middle is sautéed eggplant seasoned with rosemary and the layers are topped with boned, smoked herring filets." As she served the hen egg dish, the hostess deftly lifted the individual metal rings revealing the succulent tiers. "On the side the chef is serving a wedge of pan-grilled bubbles and squeak. If I may translate for those unfamiliar with our cuisine, bubbles and squeak is an English delicacy of seasoned mashed potatoes mixed with julienned strips of steamed cabbage."

Janice announced in a playful tone, "I'm trying some of everything, strictly as a matter of research."

"Champagne, anyone?" asked the charming hostess. She spooned delectable samples using silver utensils onto delicate English bone china plates from the rolling buffet cart as the beautician washed and curled their hair. Once she and the ladies had their mouths full of delicious treats, the hostess continued, "The English breakfast is a meal which can be eaten at any time during the day. To complete the repast, Builder's Tea is often served. It's an intense tea brewed from a tea bag in a mug unlike a proper tea steeped in a heated teapot," she stressed. She mandated the tea was best served with milk and several teaspoons of sugar. They agreed. "Since you must have a busy day, I added tarts of lemon curd garnished with candied violets for 'Elevenses,' a light snack of a meal to eat at eleven o'clock in case lunch is delayed.

"We'd applaud, but our nails are wet! Thank you, Miss Cressida."

"Would we be imposing if we inquired the origin of your delightful name?"

"Lots of people ask. My mum studied Shakespeare's plays at the university. I was named after her favorite heroine from the play, *Troilus and Cressida*. She said the play was written in 1602."

"What a fascinating family history."

"Shakespeare wrote romantic stories. *Troilus and Cressida* fell in love, but tragically the romance was not meant to be. Shakespeare apparently wrote several versions and other writers have adapted his original story. In one, Cressida is smitten with a military man. He leaves on assignment and while he's away, her heart wanders toward someone else. In another rendering, after spending the night together, Troilus is heartbroken when Cressida is taken from him in a prisoner exchange during the Trojan War. Mum said the early productions were pure porn with love scenes acted on stage!"

Everyone giggled but Carrie politely changed the subject. Janice was grateful. With the circumstances in her current life she desired to avoid thoughts on failed romances. "Janice, I made us reservations with the makeup artist while our nails dry. Cosmetics in London is more...more...how do I say this...well, it's *more*."

Janice understood when the artist applied red lipstick, not a hint of rose, but day glow red, red, red lipstick. "I resemble one of those voluptuous models on the cover of a romance mystery!" She and Carrie giggled.

"Come on. Hurry, the meeting starts in an hour. Did you have a chance to read the presentation?"

"Barely, "she whispered. "The topic Dr. Reynolds was presenting isn't overly exciting. I'm hoping no one will deduce if the lackluster lecture is my performance or the subject matter."

"What is the topic?"

"The effects of polymer linings on the development of Mallard browning reactions in canned fruit juices."

"Oh, yeah, I understand. But as gorgeous as you look, I doubt anyone will even care. I hope you don't mind, but I included lunch for your folks on the city tour. You should have a couple of hours this afternoon for a nap."

"Mind? You deserve a raise!"

*****

Janice and Carrie met the Browns in the lobby in time for their dinner reservations. "EJ, it's lovely to see you," greeted her mom. She was bubbling with highlights of their travels. "Imagine the only way we get to visit is to meet in London. It sounds cosmopolitan, doesn't it? We went on a sightseeing trip of London on the famed red double-decker buses and lost track of time. We barely arrived at the hotel in time to dress for dinner.

London is such a regal city. We left you a thank you note at the desk for the tickets. Did you get it? Your invitation was such a surprise when we received your telegram in France complete with reservations to this elegant hotel and tickets to the tour and lunch today."

"When the last-minute request came to present Dr. Reynolds' paper at a conference in London, I jumped at the chance! I called the ranch and the crew said y'all had taken off for Europe. I couldn't resist inviting you to stop in London on the way home. With the meeting this morning, the concierge suggested the tour arrangements."

"I remember Dr. Reynolds," said her dad. "She came to the ranch on one of her trips to work in the research lab at the USDA Citrus Processing Center near us. Wasn't she friends with your professor who disappeared in Mexico on a fishing trip?"

Sadly, she remembered her professor's body had been found near the bio lab in Mexico buried in the mud where they were manufacturing a resistant form of Staphylococcus aureus. She'd wondered if he had been killed for uncovering the devious plot by Chinese produce importers to introduce the prolific bacteria to crash American and Mexican agricultural markets. She had shared with Charlie and Frank her theory that if the North American produce markets were poisoned, it could result in Chinese domination of the world's fresh fruit and vegetable supplies. Apparently, the plot was masterminded by Timmerman, unless he was acting on orders of someone else. Thankfully, Frank said the Timmerman intrigue had ended.

"Reynolds was working on color stabilization of orange juice at the time, wasn't she?"

"Dad, she was greatly appreciative of the fresh-squeezed orange juice you prepared for her initial chemical analysis of the juice components for the preliminary pilot study. She received the grant, and I presented her data at the conference this morning."

"It was my pleasure. It reminded me of being in the food production lab at the University of Florida. You look tired, EJ, but your mother is pleased you've invited us to join you. Your mother would be ecstatic if you visited the ranch a little more often. Your nutrition consulting business keeps you too busy."

"I miss you, too, Dad." She wanted to diffuse his focus. "I can't wait to hear details of the tour of the WWI battlefields. Did you photograph La Havre and Verdun where Grandfather was stationed? Oh, I'm sorry. I was so excited to see you both I completely forgot to introduce Carrie. You remember Carrie, she's my office assistant while she's in graduate school."

"Yes, she's been at the ranch a couple of times. Recently, we've seen her more than you, EJ. Carrie, you're always welcome. How is the degree coming along?" asked Mrs. Brown.

"Oh. It's a challenge to complete the course work. When Janice invited me to come to the meeting, I couldn't turn down the opportunity to travel to London. I figured I could study on the plane as well as I could at the library," she said as a typical graduate student. In reality, she was a straight A student.

"We decided to blow the budget and both came to the meeting. Come on, Dad." EJ grabbed her dad's arm. "I hear the restaurant makes a mouthwatering grilled steak."

"Thank goodness!" whispered her dad. "You mom has developed an addiction for French sauces and microscopic portions. In France you can eat pasta at three meals a day. What is it with those doll-sized cups of coffee? I had to order at least three or four to get a decent dose of caffeine! And let me say I was under-impressed with the famous kidney pie. How did you recognize I was dying for a steak?"

EJ restrained her giggles. Her dad was her dad. She grabbed his arm and the crowd headed to the dining room. Her mom ordered the roasted monkfish, Carrie ordered the rack of lamb. She and her dad ordered the steak. "I'm certain the steak won't be as scrumptious as the ones you sizzle on the grill at the ranch, but I'm starving!"

"EJ, your telegram hinted you wanted to visit the Addison family. We're inviting ourselves to go with you," strongly stated her mom.

"Remember when I used to ride my horse to the Addison's house to ramble through the ruins. I'd hoped one day I'd meet the family who built the magnificent house."

"You were such a tomboy and haven't changed. I see you have a few new bruises."

She ignored her mother's assessment. "I used to imagine I was a princess in an English castle. Of course, the remaining structure of my pretend castle was a few bricks clinging to the building's foundation. I'd carry a quilt and ate my peanut butter and orange marmalade sandwich under a tree which had grown inside of what I imagined to be an enclosed courtyard."

"Rumor had it those bricks were transported from England," contributed her dad. "Clipper ships sailed to Fort Myers where the bricks were loaded into shallow paddleboat barges and traveled through the Caloosahatchee River to Lake Okeechobee. When the water was high, the barges left Lake Okeechobee moved north through the Kissimmee River to Fort Bassinger. My grandfather said everyone with oxen and a wagon was hired to deliver the brick to the site of the house located on a sandy bluff above Mossy Creek which joined the Kissimmee River.

"The view was beautiful from there," added EJ. "The creek was shaded by graceful cypress trees and wandering limbs of live oaks that reached into the water. I would lie in the sun on the wide branches and watch the clouds."

"My father said he enjoyed seeing the Addison family when

he visited while stationed in England during WWI," reminisced Mr. Brown. "He and his brother hadn't seen them since they were young kids. The Addison's house was struck by lightning in 1910. Despite the heavy downpour during the night, by morning the house had burned to the ground. The family never returned."

"When my dad and uncle were in England they requested weekend passes to stay with the Addisons," added John. "My dad received his military assignment first and left for Verdon. His brother waited for his station. When the war ended, he tried to locate his brother, but with no success. He returned home and crossed the treacherous North Atlantic in November of 1818. He said he was sick for the ten-day journey and slept in the lifeboats in the cool air. The family tried contacting the Addison family hoping they'd heard from his brother Anderson, but no one replied."

"Dad, do you remember how many kids were in the Addison family? Did Grandpa ever mention if the children were boys or girls?"

"No, I don't remember him ever saying."

"I found a genealogy guide who specializes in locating families in England from the war-torn years. He wanted background on family details. There are a lot of Addisons, apparently. I couldn't remember the community they lived in?"

"Wasn't it Featherlawn?" chirped her mom. "Y'all must be tired. We are." Her mom squeezed her dad's hand. "What time should we meet you for breakfast? You're coming with us, aren't you, Carrie?"

"I'd hoped you'd ask. I'd love to go if there is room."

Eva Belle was the ultimate Southern lady, observed Carrie. Janice resembled her mother in many ways: petite with a soft voice, both women often underestimated. Janice and her mother had dark hair and warm, calm dark eyes. On one of her visits to the Ranch at Bay Branch she'd watched Mrs. Brown walk through the cow pens with a twig in her hand and even the meanest-looking steers gave her a clear path.

"What if we meet for breakfast at seven thirty?"

"Right-oo. I'll tell our guide to meet us at nine."

*****

Janice and Carrie stopped at her room after dinner. "I didn't realize your folks called you EJ?"

"When I went to college in Mississippi, my folks suggested I pledge a sorority. You probably overheard they wanted their daughter to be a Southern lady. Dr. Hess, who was Dean of Women, believed using initials wasn't *cultured*. She would say the word with a fake French accent if you were in her office, which I seemed to be on a regular basis. She talked endlessly of the importance of being cultured." They both snickered. "She insisted I go by my birth name which is Elsa Janine Brown, after both of my grandmothers. Don't get me wrong, I loved my grandmothers, but as a young child not understanding family politics, I wanted to be called Janice. My dad proposed the initials EJ as a family compromise. Dr. Hess wouldn't have initials, but was satisfied with Janice. Dad has the same initials as mine, EJ Brown, for Edward John Brown."

"No wonder you are able to switch from one name to another with such finesse. You've been using multiple identities for years."

"Well, whoever the hell I am right now is exhausted. The fatigue is catching up with me. I feel drunk and none of us had anything to drink with dinner."

"Did you just tell me to go to my room?" Carrie laughed. "I'll drop by in the morning and we can go downstairs together."

"Thanks, Carrie."

Back in her room Carrie reported in to Frank. "Kept to today's schedule. She made a convincing performance at the meeting. She's talented at meet-and-greets and even remembered the names of the professors from her Mississippi College. Her folks arrived and we're going to Featherlawn in the morning. She's dog-tired, but a real trooper."

"Have you coordinated the security?"

"Yes, sir. Our people filled the rooms in our hall. Military police have the rooms near the elevator and stairwells. Called in some of our retired military to fill the beauty shop this morning. I wanted to have a secured audience in case things were said, but Montana was solid. I've staged appropriate tourist groups at possible stops on our trip tomorrow. We'll have various advance and chase vehicles along the way. The driver is one of the crew. Your contact from the US Embassy is impressive. He secured an armored van complete with concealed weapons."

"Tell me again what time you are meeting in the morning."

"Breakfast at 0730 and van leaves at 0900."

"I'll alert the air base to have a plane standing by. Thanks, Carrie. Out."

*****

The knock at the door startled her. Janice looked out the peep expecting Carrie.

"Get in here! You are the last one I anticipated meeting in London. What are you doing here? Oh, I said that wrong. I just didn't expect you to be here. This is a wonderful surprise."

"I heard you were out of Wild Turkey and ice." Charlie flashed the bottle toward her.

"I can find two glasses."

"Your nightgown is driving me crazy, silky beige with spaghetti straps. Take it off, take it off," he said grinning. "Sorry I had to leave you in DC. But I hear you've been practicing mountain-climbing since I left. Should I consider the Alps for our

169

holiday trip?"

She smiled and gave him a coy grin.

"Sweets, are you alright? I was so worried and so proud. You jumped twenty feet from a second-story window."

She threw her hands on her hips. "For your information, it was an opening in the wall for a noisy air conditioner which I had to kick out. Luckily it wasn't a fancy well-constructed motel. My landing wasn't as embarrassing as falling off a horse in front of Dad's ranch hands. The real risk wasn't the fall, it was I had to touch the creepy crud on the grungy hotel bed linens I pushed through the window to soften my fall. I'm glad you're here. I've missed you." She leaned in for a kiss pressing her body to his. Her emotions expectantly overwhelmed her. A tear ran down her cheek.

"You're crying. Oh, I'm sorry, Sweets. I didn't intend to upset you. Honestly, I was impressed as hell you escaped from a building minutes before it exploded."

"I'm fine, Charlie." She sniffled as she sipped her bourbon.

"Yes, you are. You're exhausted. I'm glad you love me. The last couple of weeks have been brutal and you've put in some long days. I wish I could've sent you to the romantic bed-and-breakfast near Key West."

"Planning to dump me again?" She pouted with a proper amount of indignation. "I'm waiting until you can go with me and I dare anyone to send a helicopter, float plane, or even a carrier pigeon with a message for you!"

"Something tells me you still haven't forgiven me for abandoning you in Key West."

"Well, maybe with a few luscious kisses..."

"Thanks for helping us with this security investigation. Tracking down the connection of the two men named Brown is crucial. It is essential we discover if the two men are a major security risk. Your family history is the ideal cover to enable you to ask the right questions without ruining the men's careers, plus you have an inquisitive nature."

"Are you telling me I'm nosy," she said with a pretend sulk.

"Who knows, you may even be related! Solving the Brown mystery isn't why I'm here. The plans gelled quickly. The guys who abducted you probably assumed you died in the fire. We felt it best to maintain the illusion until we complete our investigation. The timing of this trip was advantageous."

"Any idea of who they were? Somehow, I knew things weren't right. I tried to leave as many clues as I could."

"Thank you for those. It gave us the evidence to start our own investigation. ATF takes forever to distribute their report. We can't wait. When it looked as if you were traveling to London, I made arrangements to intercept your trip to spend a few hours with you. I love you. I don't mean to sound sentimental, but you've made my life complete. Have you heard the song, 'Addicted to Love'? It's corny, but you are so important to me."

She moved to procure another long juicy kiss. "I'm glad you could join me. I've spent more time with you in the last few weeks than during the past ten years. I'm hoping this trend continues."

She was already dreading when he left. She knew he couldn't stay long. "Isn't this a marvelous suite? The neutral color scheme reminds me of other hotels we've stayed in," she teased and raised her eyebrows. "No pretty pots of lilies, though. The night view across the river is romantic with a wee bit of fog, as they say in London. Look at the House of Parliament on the Thames bathed in lights. I can't believe I am here with you. I can't wait to show you the gigantic soaking tub." She pulled the drapes closed.

"Of course, we select hotels for you based on the size of the tub."

"Didn't Frank protest? This is a really, really expensive

hotel."

"Not a peep. I told him you had given me a specific list of demands. Besides, it's only fair with those nasty bruises you've acquired on our behalf. Does makeup come in aerosol cans?"

"Cruel, Charlie. I may soak in the tub all by myself!" she teased.

The rain forest shower gently sprinkled their naked bodies as they soaked in the bottom of the tub. Charlie massaged her body with warm rose-scented oil and turned on the jets. Water rushed in and mounds of bubbles covered them to their chins. "I have to admit the hot water feels absolutely fantastic!"

"My soap bubble castle is taller than yours," he teased.

"No fair. Mother Nature gave you an unfair advantage!" she bantered.

"Sweets, sit right here." His hand reached for the controls. "Sip on your bourbon, close your eyes, and focus on the jets as they massage your feet."

"Oooo, my muscles are turning to jelly."

"Do these ease the soreness on your back?"

"Yumm. I could stay here the entire night, if I wasn't afraid of drowning."

"Do you enjoy these jets?"

"Ohhh. Quick. Oh, kiss me. Kiss me. Kiss me! Oh, Charlie," she closed her eyes and cooed.

Her urgent commands were interrupted by Charlie's embrace. She wrapped her arms around his neck and curled her legs around his waist as he lifted her from the tub. She tingled as Charlie's hands roamed her body, as he kissed her lips, her face, and nibbled her ears and neck. The room seemed in slow motion as they moved to the bed and made love under the soft sheets.

"I wish this night could go on forever, but I'm to meet the genealogy tour at seven-thirty. What time are you leaving?"

"Gosh, I love you! How did I get so lucky? Set the alarm for five."

"Four-thirty?"

CHAPTER TWENTY-FOUR

They had blindfolded Phillips when they detained him at the Red, White and Blue Veteran's Center before he had time to leave. They drove for hours. He had no idea where he was. At one point they stopped; voices changed and someone jabbed a hypodermic needle in his thigh. The reception in the basement of the Frank's office was less than cordial. The room was damp and cold. He had no sense of time with the drugs they'd given him. His mouth was dry. He suspected he'd been out for six or eight hours.

The crew had considerable discussion of how to deal with the man who had kidnapped Bonnie. Some options were appropriate, Frank told them, but a bit extreme. They had fallen in love with her as a teammate. She had fought for them and had earned membership on their teams. His crew wanted to torture and kill Phillips. Most of the men had been Navy Seals or Army Special Forces. They were still working on transitioning their skills, when dealing with obstacles, into civilian career opportunities. Today, he was glad they were available.

Frank was grateful Bonnie had survived without broken bones or nasty injuries needing stitches. With the time difference, he put Carrie on speakerphone on a secure line before she and Janice met the Browns for breakfast. "Hey, we have Phillips in custody. How's Montana doing this morning?" He hoped with their medical training the reports from Carrie and Janice would diffuse the growing hostile forces within the room.

"Tired and terrific." You should have seen her at the meetings yesterday in a sexy navy dress and red stiletto heels. She had a few bruises, but between the dress and makeup they were well hidden. In those nerdy Army-issue reading glasses, she had the attention of the entire seminar. She refused to let me have her hair dyed bright purple." She could hear the laughter through the receiver.

As he'd anticipated, Carrie's comments were positive and reassuring.

"Anything on the evidence you can share?"

"Montana, you left excellent evidence to start the investigation. I'll let the research teams update you on the forensics findings," offered Frank.

She tried to identify the voices as the team presented their reports. "First, Phillips' fingerprints didn't match the ones on the store receipt and note, but from the time stamp, we tracked the purchases to the store location. The store's video camera indicated Phillips accompanied the man who bought the supplies. The assumption is the unknown man on the video was Phillips' co-conspirator.

"Second, the store gave us the information on the credit card used. A team is following the lead." Frank suspected the lead would go nowhere, but at least it gave the team something to do. Information on the card may reveal something in itself. A name on the card wasn't identified in the search through the investigational computerized felon's database, but many agencies and states were still in the process of submitting prints.

"Third, facial recognition is slow. The computerized system is still in the baby steps phase and the store videos are of pretty poor quality. We may send the tapes to NASA in Florida. They have the best technology for film-enhancing these days. They developed computer programs to improve transmissions from the Hubble telescope.

"Fourth, the flag you made contained sufficient evidence for the lab crew to identify the explosives used, which enabled us to track where the explosives were made, purchased, and by whom. The lip print gave adequate DNA to positively place you at the scene. And we have your fingerprints found in the red truck in multiple places. And thanks for the tag numbers. We're still working on those.

"Our last finding came as a total surprise. You didn't tell us you had driven to Pennsylvania. Once we focused on Phillips' red truck, the NSA satellite footage tracked his route after he left the Veteran's Center. Looking at the footage we realized the truck inadvertently crossed one of the roads to a warehouse we monitor, and there you are sitting in the front seat of Phillips' truck with your toes against the front glass. Our forensics crowd has created a special award for the most creative way to leave finger and toe prints!" Bonnie and Carrie could hear laugher in the room.

Frank summarized the call. "Forensics activities are tedious. We have Phillips in custody. We can hold him until we get answers." He covered the receiver with his hand and added for those in the room, "and kill him when it's convenient. We have significant evidence for a convincing case to convict Phillips for the murder of the three vets we photographed lying under a tarp in the parking lot."

She wanted to add the attempted murder of a certain student of mountain-climbing, but she knew her involvement would be withheld from the report. To testify under oath in a court of law would compromise her cover and the integrity of the team. She hoped her face wasn't too clear in the surveillance pictures in the truck.

"Thanks, guys," offered Carrie.

"Good luck with today's research. We need answers ASAP. Out."

CHAPTER TWENTY-FIVE

"Good day, ma'am," greeted the tour guide. "Who is the Misses Janice?"

"That's me. These are my folks, John and Eva Belle, and my friend Carrie. I hope you don't mind I invited them. They wanted to tag along."

"Everyone is welcomed. I'm Trevor Augustine. Our driver for today is Angus Butterwick. Righto. We're off to Featherlawn."

The names and British accents and phrases made her almost giggle. Maybe it was nervous energy anticipating important discoveries of the trip. She tried to maintain a gracious welcoming smile.

"The ride is two hours. The hamlet of Featherlawn is located in the historic county of Wiltshire. What's the 'urry, luv?" asked the driver.

"We're trying to locate our former neighbors, the Addisons," explained John. "They lived near us before WWI. My dad and uncle visited them when they took military training in England before being transferred to France."

"Ah, Miss Janice told me a few of the details. She said one of her great uncles was buried in France."

178

"Yes, my Uncle Anderson," added her dad. "We found his grave at the Meuse-Argonne American Cemetery during our trip to the Lorraine region. The cemetery was near the village Romagne-sous-Montfaucon in Meuse."

"The village was charming. What adorable old buildings with window boxes overflowing with summer flowers. EJ, the croissants served as part of the Continental breakfast at the historic hotel were absolutely heavenly. You would have loved the homemade marmalades and preserves," chimed Eva Belle. Carrie knew immediately where Janice had gotten her love of architecture and gardening.

"My uncle died when a trench or tunnel collapsed during a battle near the Argonne Forest sometime during 1918," redirected John. "The exact date is unknown. It was years after the war ended before the tunnels were discovered, excavated, and his body recovered."

"I'm sure you've seen the cemetery," added Eva Belle. "It was stunning. Such manicured landscape, formal, and symmetrical with rows of sharply trimmed hedges. A beautiful central pond had delicate water lilies and hedges of pink roses. The structured flower beds were such a contrast to bloody battles on the site. I was impressed Uncle Anderson fought alongside General Pershing."

"Eva Belle, there were 600,000 American troops besides Uncle Anderson," bantered John.

Eva Belle simply smiled.

"Did you drive through France?" asked Trevor.

"No, we flew to Paris and joined a tour of WWI battlefields and cemeteries. We had a letter addressed to my parents from President Warren G. Harding reporting Uncle Anderson's body had been found and identified by his dog tags."

"Yes, we flew, but once in France we walked and walked.

179

EJ, we must have walked twenty miles searching through the 130 acres row by row. There were many A. Browns listed in the cemetery directory. Your dad told me to wear my tennis shoes, but I couldn't bring myself to dress like a tacky tourist, especially to visit such a revered place."

"Mother, the concierge knows a few fantastic shoe stores in London. Maybe we'll have time to buy a pair of sexy walking shoes when we return to the hotel."

"Did I hear the mum needs walking shoes? There's a boutique in a nearby village. Quick as Bob's your uncle we can shop for comfortable shoes," said Trevor. "Our appointment with the church secretary isn't until two o'clock."

"We'll detour though Wiltshire's most famous Magic Roundabout at Swindon. Check your seat belts and hang on!" announced Angus, their driver, with a mischievous gleam in his eye.

EJ held her breath and wanted to close her eyes, but she wanted to watch the driver's finesse as they crossed eight lanes of traffic; four going to the right, crossing four lanes to the left to progress to a smaller roundabout, one of five intertwined mini-roundabouts. She had an epiphany and suddenly understood the name of the roundabout when magically they emerged from the chaos on the other side. The shoemaker's shop was down a seemingly peaceful narrow, winding side street lined with tranquil gray stone walls and gray block buildings. Window boxes were filled with shocking blue lobelia peeking between red and white trailing geraniums. When Angus stopped the van, there was a unison sigh of relief.

The shoemaker's shop was tiny and intimate. Mr. Wordsworth introduced himself as they entered his shop unannounced. He wore a stained leather apron covering his chest and suit trousers. Underneath there was a crisp white shirt and a dark blue patterned tie. The sales area resembled a cozy living room with European light wooden cabinets and a carved secretary desk with narrow legs. They explained their predicament. "Could I pour ye lasses a cuppa tea while the mum is fitted for walking shoes?" He placed a large silver tray on a gorgeous antique sideboard. On the tray was a flowered teapot with matching cups and saucers and a covered cake plate. He poured boiling water into the delicate teapot from a dented aluminum kettle brought from the kitchen. In minutes, the tea was ready to pour.

"EJ, you and Carrie pour me a cup—one sugar, please," asked Eva Belle.

"Mom, Mr. Wordsworth has Cadbury cakes," EJ exclaimed. "One Christmas these were included in a gift basket. They're scrumptious. We can't buy them at home."

"Where's ye be from?" he asked.

"Florida."

"Me and the Misses went to a wedding where the young serviceman was from Florida, we did. We were kids. It was during the war and the search went out for fabric for the bride's dress. My father regularly bought leather in London and helped the bride's family with the shopping on his trips. She left Featherlawn before the Spanish flu swept through in the fall. Killed more people than the Black Death, it did; wiped out whole families and entire villages."

"What was her name?" curiously asked Eva Belle.

"Let me ring my wife; she'd remember. She's probably watching the telly. She lives close by. Let's start with this selection of stylish shoes and I'll be back quick as Bob's your uncle!" EJ and Carrie wished they had time to try on shoes.

When Mrs. Wordsworth arrived the men conveniently disappeared.

*****

181

"Mr. Brown, it is a pleasure to meet you," said Trevor. "Can I buy you a cup of coffee? There's a coffee shop across the street."

"Real coffee? I've asked for a glass of tea and was brought a cup and a pot of water. Even in the summer I can't purchase a glass of sweet iced tea. Call me John."

"Can I pull ye a couple of beers?" asked the vivacious hostess as they walked through the door in a room of dark wood paneling and worn cobblestone floors. They sat at the stately wooden bar.

"Two cups of strong coffee please, ma'am."

"Thank you for looking out for my baby girl."

"You've been briefed. I wasn't sure. The details of this trip fell into place rather quickly."

"Frank's people have commandeered the ranch for a training center. It's been convenient; in fact, with their manpower, EJ's mom and I were able to make this trip. This mission is a challenge."

He wasn't at liberty to share details. "I've read your impressive dossier, sir. We were somewhat surprised when we organized security credentials for Janice and your name popped up. There are several classified commendation letters in your file for handling the placement of the Russian Lend-Lease pilots after WWII. You still have many friends at the State Department and overseas."

"I don't think she's aware Frank and I talk frequently. I haven't told her mother. It's probably safer for EJ and the team. She seems to be thriving, but I have to admit the bruises had me worried."

"She jumped out of a two-story hotel and escaped through a small hole when she kicked out the air conditioner. Her gutsy determination took us by surprise. You'd be proud of her resourcefulness, if I could tell you of her contributions in the investigation of the murder of three of our team. Keeping her busy has been our dilemma."

"She's high energy, but in a productive way."

"Agreed. She and the cat are favorites with the teams she's worked with. Her weaponry skills were unexpected. When she joined the unit, honestly, we'd underestimated her. At first the goal was to protect her, but she's rescued them on more than one occasion."

"She learns quickly and is skillful at slipping in and out of her Southern belle facade to the delight of her mother."

"But I have a question for you. With your background in military records, what's your opinion of our current problem?"

"Without knowing the full details beyond the little Frank told me last night, I can understand the logistics to create two identities with the current paper records system. Someone in a backwater field command could create two sets of records for one individual. During situations of war, personnel offices routinely reconstruct service records to replace personnel jackets lost in a fire or if field offices had been overrun by hostile forces. Hell, I specialized in record reconstruction. I'm told computerized records will expedite background checks. But even a modern system will only be as secure as the people typing in the data. With paper records we could control the physical area around them. But the computerized systems can be entered from a remote site, in total stealth. There was a sense of urgency from your team. I'm guessing the two identities must have high-level responsibilities."

He nodded.

"We probably should check on the ladies before they max out my credit cards." They laughed. "Well, after another cup of coffee."

"I'm going to pour a splash of Irish whisky in this second cup."

"I'll take a double," said her dad with sigh.

*****

Mrs. Wordsworth was delightful, charming, and plump. She wore a tailored blue wool skirt, tan sweater, and a coordinating patterned blouse with pearls, of course. Her hair was curly and short. "It is a pleasure to meet you," she said as she greeted Eva Belle, EJ, and Carrie. "Mr. Wordsworth said you wanted information on a wedding during WWI. It was an enchanting wedding. I wasn't even ten years old at the time. Miss Elizabeth taught Sunday school and invited the young girls in the church to be her flower girls. I remember the wedding well." She sighed. "She had dresses sewn for each of us and gave them to us along with leather shoes, slips, and stockings. Fabric was rationed during the war. I look back and realized the dresses featured groupings of tucks and wide hems allowing us to wear them for several years or pass them down to a younger sister or a neighbor. It was the first new dress I'd had since the war began."

"Thank you for meeting us. Sit here with me," invited Eva Belle as she patted the overstuffed pillows on the couch upholstered in a flowered print. "The wedding sounds lovely. You must tell us the details. What colors did she choose?"

"She held the wedding in the church garden in Featherlawn. Her dress had layers of white organza with a veil of lace and she wore hand-crocheted gloves. She was thin, barely a whisper. A pale orange ribbon was tied around stems of white roses, daisies, and garden ferns she carried. She requested the bouquets carried by the flower girls to be of single colors to match their dresses. The day of the wedding I remember we had orange lilies in our garden, but months before I'd picked a pink flowered fabric. A friend carried flowers from our yard. I carried pale pink roses from the church garden. I'm pleased to share my memories of Elizabeth's wedding. I remember her wedding almost as a fantasy from a fairy-tale, but I was young. What happened to

184

her was a mystery. She married Corporal Anderson Brown from somewhere in Florida in the early summer of 1918, and sometime in the fall she traveled to Florida to live with his family. We heard nothing of her or her husband. We hoped she wasn't traveling on one of the ships torpedoed when crossing the North Atlantic during the war. Mr. Anderson was in the Army; we'd hoped he would come back to the village when the Armistice was signed. Sadly, the Spanish flu arrived as the war ended, and most of the village was dead within a week. My lady, I didn't intend to upset you."

"Here's a tissue, Mom," EJ whispered. Janice wanted to share that Anderson Brown was her dad's uncle, and Elizabeth Addison Brown had safely arrived in New York. She hoped Frank's team would be able to find the missing pieces on "their side of the pond." She'd ask Frank to arrange for someone to return and share the delightful news of what had become of Elizabeth.

She hadn't noticed the return of her dad, Trevor, and Mr. Wordsworth.

"Did you find a pair of comfortable walking shoes?" asked her dad.

"Oh, of course. It was a difficult decision, though. I'm going to wear the navy-blue pumps to the church and carry the other shoes home. I saw EJ and Carrie secretly trying on a few pairs while we shared tea. Can you put those on my bill?"

"And here I assumed we were being so covert." They giggled.

"I hope you two don't give up your jobs at the hospital. Y'all would be terrible spies," said her mom giggling. Carrie and EJ joined in the laughter but for different reasons.

"Well, folks, we better go to keep to our schedule and appointments," rescued Trevor.

As their drove through the farmland continued, her dad commented, "EJ, look at the rosebushes planted with the grapevines. Early planters learned roses were the first to become infected with diseases deadly to the grapevines. Once the relationship was discovered, farmers planted a rosebush at the end of each row. The white fence posts may be indicators that farmers are using the famous Bordeaux Mix to spray the grapes, which leaves a white residue. Folklore indicates the formula was developed in France monasteries to control fungus and molds on grapes and roses. It's not a trade name or a marketing label, it was folk medicine or mix for plants, named after the Bordeaux region where it was formulated. Modern researchers confirmed the monks' hypothesis that the mix actually killed aphids believed to have spread the Great Wine Blight in the 1860s. The disease nearly wiped out wine production in the French countryside. The official recording of the chemical control was made by Millardit in 1885, twenty-something years later. The formula is a simple mixture of copper sulfate and slaked lime. Your grandmother mixed 10 teaspoons of copper sulfate, 10 Tablespoons hydrated lime which is calcium oxide with a gallon of water to spray her roses. At home we spray a variation of the Bordeaux Mix on citrus to control rust mites."

"Wasn't slaked lime used in buttermilk paint in the 1800s?" chimed EJ. "Grandmother said the paint prevented bugs in the house. I remember she painted a set of green chairs with buttermilk paint. It smelled awful while the bucket of milk, vinegar, and lime fermented on the back porch."

"John, you and EJ should accept teaching positions at the ag college. To me, the beautiful green agricultural areas resemble oversized gardens in rows parading across the distant hills. The scenic English countryside is pictographic," added Eva Belle. "The tree-lined streets are identical to the pictures in the gardening magazines. EJ, I'm glad you invited us to join you on this delightful trip."

"I was lucky to catch y'all before you headed home to Illahaw. Wouldn't it have been a hoot if we passed each other at the airport?" Everyone laughed.

"Time for sandwiches and sweets, or maybe a sip of tea?" offered Angus. "We've scheduled lunch at one of my favorite cottages."

A jolly hostess met them at the door of the country inn. She was dressed in a shift of blue tucking, with a starched white pinafore tied around her ample waist. The group was seated in a secluded dining room that stretched across the back of the building. EJ could imagine on a spring day the wall of French doors would open into the manicured English garden. "Good day, I'm Clementine. Welcome."

"EJ, I'll pass on trying another steak and kidney pie. I don't care how flaky the crust!" declared her dad.

"May I suggest the shepard's pie, Governor? It's served with grilled homegrown tomatoes and fresh garden peas," offered Trevor.

"Sounds wonderful to me," responded John.

"Me, too! Shepard's pie for everyone?" asked EJ.

Trevor stepped lively across the room to the kitchen to place their order while Eva Belle whispered, "Oh, this is charming. This is exactly how I'd dreamed an English country restaurant would appear, with a stacked rock fireplace, old, polished wood floors, dark wood panels on the walls, and lots and lots of pictures of hunting dogs and hunting parties in red blazers on magnificently powerful horses. Look at the dishes on the chair railings. Oh, I wish I'd brought my camera. My china painting class would adore the designs and colors." EJ made a mental note to share the information with Gustoff. She wished her mother could meet the elderly Russian women in Moscow who proudly displayed their mismatched silver and elegant china collected by Gustoff when she toured the kitchen at the Russian hotel. Charlie's construction company built a senior housing complex and the elderly Russian ladies loved Charlie and Gustoff.

"Mother, maybe I can find a book on English dinnerware for your birthday?"

"If we had time, wouldn't it be fun to visit English china factories? Maybe we could meet you here in the spring and we could also visit the tulip fields in Holland? The fall calf sales are in a couple of weeks. You remember how your dad likes to move the mother and calf pairs to lush pastures to increase their weight. He's won the top awards for the last three years for the highest price per pound for a single group of yearling calves. He says it's no big deal, but he and the ranch hands spend weeks selecting the entry representing the Ranch at Bay Branch."

"You're making me homesick, mom."

"EJ, you hated being at the ranch in the late summer when we sold the calves. At four years old you stood at the gate with the mama cows and cried for hours after the cattle trucks left the pasture. The following summer your grandmother took you and the cousins to the beach and y'all would work on inside projects to stay out of the sun during the middle of the day, and away from the cow pens. Remember the muumuus you sewed with rows and rows of gathers? I still have one of the Swedish embroidery tea towels you made. Another summer she taught the cousins to bake biscuits. Grandmother laughed when she told us of how you would eat one or two with butter and orange marmalade and feed the rest to the seagulls. One morning, she found you and the kitchen covered in flour while you were attempting to bake another batch."

Carrie desperately needed to redirect the conversation away from Janice's personal information and background. She had briefed the former military who filled the dining room, but a little information here and there compiled by a trained interrogator could put Janice's double identity in jeopardy. It was best to limit their information. She wished she was skillful at making subtle transitions. "Janice and Eva Belle, I wanted to ask you to identify the flowers that were so captivating in the landscaping in the gardens around the restaurant! The entrance was impressive with the manicured garden with a high-sided fish pond and the fountain in the middle of the circle drive," said Carrie.

EJ followed the change of topic immediately. "Did you notice the flowers were totally in shades of white at the portico? I get too distracted by all the flowers in the seed catalogs. I've never been able to be so dedicated to plant only one color. I may be able to duplicate their design of the white pallet but add a few subtle pale pinks and lavenders. The pale green hydrangeas against the fence harmonize the colors."

"We could plant wildflowers in raised beds under the hickory trees at the ranch," reflected Eva Belle. "The straggly blue hydrangeas planted by your grandmother along the east side of the barn could be the focus with a little pruning and a few shovels of cow manure. Maybe you can organize the project when you can spend some time at home? The flowers would be away from the fence, out of range of the cows where they couldn't eat them, unlike the fate of my climbing roses. Gone are my dreams that the roses would cover the run of the fence near the windmill. I would have loved to paint the scene in watercolors."

"EJ, what's the tiny yellow bird at the birdbath?" asked Carrie.

"I was looking at the cute fella. My best guess is he's a warbler with the sharp pointed bill, but the little ones move too quickly." The motto for most of her birding trips, she reflected. "Maybe a village bookstore would have a field guide for British birds." She could look, but Management would have a fit if she added one

189

to her luggage. It would document where she'd been. "I'm still learning British food patterns. Is lunch called lunch over here?" EJ pivoted the conversation to Clementine.

"If you had ordered sandwiches, soup, or a simple meal of cheese and biscuits, it would be called lunch. But if it's to be the major meal of the day, it's known as dinner."

"Where we live, we also call the heartiest meal 'dinner,' be it served at midday or sundown. It's remarkable we share similar food patterns," added EJ.

"EJ, you would be the one to look at food choices from an anthropological viewpoint!" teased Carrie. "I'm waiting for the journal article on your culinary critique of London foods."

"You should have lived through her college projects testing the premise of predicting cooking patterns based on family history and genealogy. One project was predicting the type of dumplins' made in Chicken-n-Dumplins'!" exclaimed Eva Belle. "She included a dumplin' survey in the family Christmas cards and asked if their dumplins' were round balls, flat, square, or long strips. She asked them to return instructions or recipes for her to categorize if baking powder was added to the dough or if yeast was used to make them fluffy. She also asked if the dumplins' were made in advance and air-dried similar to making homemade noodles. She even included a stamped, self-addressed envelope. She wrote her paper, and her dad and I enjoyed the personal notes included from our friends."

"The return rate was close to ninety percent," bragged EJ. "Far above the average return rate for mailed surveys of less than twenty percent."

"Her aunts still chuckle at her eccentric food projects."

"I liked the chicken project," added her dad coming to her defense. "She was quite scientific. I was impressed. Our freezers were filled with quarts of a standard chicken stock she used in each recipe. Of course, Chicken-n-Dumplins' is one of my favorites meals. It wasn't quite as exciting when she experimented with recipes to formulate tomato ice cream, although the one with buttermilk had a refreshing taste. The color was a problem, if I remember correctly."

The entire table and most of the dining room was in hysterics. She hoped the lunch was carefully orchestrated by Frank and Charlie's team and the room was filled with friendlies. She doubted they would let her forget the tomato ice cream fiasco. She trusted they would adhere to Frank's rule prohibiting divulging knowledge of other team members.

"Her dad and I are glad she's employed in something professional."

EJ avoided looking toward Carrie, or they would both break out in uncontrolled laughter. "What's on the dessert menu?" said EJ trying to stifle a giggle. She stoically ignored the chuckles from the room.

"My lady, I think you are referring to the dessert and sweets menu. Maybe we're a wee bit traditional, when we talk of desserts, we're meaning fruit. You probably desire our 'sweets' selections, ah, lass? The choices vary day to day. The offerings today are trifle based on a recipe from the 1500s. It's made with a puree of freshly picked raspberries, layered with sponge cake soaked in ginger syrup and a thickened cream flavored with a spicy mixture of sugar, mint, and thyme. We're also offering Gloucester tarts, a recipe borrowed from our neighboring Gloucester County. The tart filling is made from summer apricots thickened with ground sweet rice and seasoned with essence of almonds in a butter cookie crust. The tart recipe is ancient and is rarely shared. Everyone is sworn to secrecy," she whispered.

The room responded with a soft "Ohhh."

EJ knew the tart would be spectacular. It was perfectly logical rice flour would be used as a thickening agent before wheat was introduced to Europe. How could she have missed it in her food anthropology textbooks? What an opportunity to explore the superb food history libraries at USDA when she returned to DC.

"Also available are slices of Battenberg cake, also known as church window cake. Layers of delicate lemon cake and pink butter cake soaked in rose syrup are assembled to resemble panes in a window when the cake is sliced. Tart cherry marmalade is spread between the layers and frosted with multiple layers of a thin lemon sugar glaze as if it was a giant *petits fours*. Some cover the cake with a thin layer of marzipan, but we prefer a lemon glaze," she whispered. "The recipe dates back to 1884 when Princess Victoria married Prince Louis of Battenberg."

"We saw the Changing of the Guard on a tour of London yesterday. Buckingham Palace was lovely. The gardens across the street were spectacular, especially from the London Eye overlooking the gardens and the River Thames. We took a ride in a horse-drawn carriage through the park. The collection of cultivars was enormous; your dad pointed out many unusual plantings. I'm thinking of talking your dad into buying us a buggy to drive me around the ranch. The ride was romantic and such fun."

"Oh, yes, my lady. It is a joy to visit Buckingham Palace, but the trip is long and the traffic busy in London," interrupted Clementine. "Oh, I am so daft. I forgot to tell you we had warm treacle tarts."

"Mama," piped EJ. "The treacle tarts are to die for. They're similar to your buttermilk chess pie which is the base of your pecan pies."

"Your grandmother gave me her recipe when I joined the family."

"Maybe Thanksgiving we can research if Grandmother's

buttermilk chess pie is an Illahaw variation of the British treacle tart. I've thought her pie was a Southern classic passed down through her family, but no one else at reunions brings a similar dessert. Carrie, my mother's and grandmother's buttermilk chess pie is always served at Thanksgiving Dinner. Freshly cooked cane syrup is the key ingredient. Sugarcane grows at the Ranch at Bay Branch near the river in the rich muck dirt and is cut after the first frost, usually in late October or early November. The grinder was powered by a horse. Sometimes, when I was small they'd let me sit on the horse as it walked in a circle to turn giant wheels that crushed the cane stalks to extract the sugarcane juice. Last year, I heard Dad used a tractor to power the grinder at the community syrup 'boilin'. The juice is simmered outside over an open fire in a wide shallow kettle to reduce the water and concentrate the sugars. The finished dark glossy syrup was used to flavor Grandmother's chess pie."

"During the Great Depression cans of syrup were sold in town," added John.

"Really?" asked Carrie.

"At eighty cents to a dollar per can, it was first-class money in those days."

"I wonder if Grandfather obtained the recipe for the treacle tarts from the Addison family when he visited here during the war."

"Could be," responded Eva Belle with a ring in her voice. "Since you mentioned it, after you moved I rescued a shelf of Grandmother's cookbooks and found a collection of handwritten recipes on spattered file cards tied with an orange ribbon in the middle of one of her favorite cookbooks. I moved them to the big house for safekeeping. One of these days you're going to settle down and I knew you'd covet your grandmother's recipes. She would be delighted knowing you had them."

EJ looked at Carrie and raised her eyebrows out of view from her mom and whispered, "I can't wait to look through the recipe cards. Often cooks will write their name and date on the card when they share a recipe. It's possible her sons mailed recipe cards to their mother during their visits with the Addisons."

"Oh, there are too many 'sweets' choices," expressed Carrie diverting the conversation. "What if we order several of each? We can pass the plates around the table. Is everyone okay with a dessert buffet?" Carrie didn't mean to interrupt Eva Belle's and EJ's thoughts. She knew the fellow guests were retired military cleared by Frank, but inadvertently the conversation could reveal the real purpose of the trip.

EJ's pulse quickened. She had to focus to conceal her excitement. The evidence was mounting supporting the possibility the Brown or Browns in the scrapbook pictures could actually be the grandson or grandsons of her great-uncle. She was sure she felt her heart flutter realizing she may have had the answer hidden on the recipe cards carefully preserved in her grandmother's kitchen shelf of cookbooks. She wondered if Charlie had information he hadn't shared when he casually mentioned that the Browns may all be related. She couldn't say a word. She reached for the teapot to pour another round of tea.

"Ya don't be sayin' much, lass," inquired Trevor.

"Oh, I'm enjoying these delicious entrees. The lamb in the shepherd's pie was superb."

"You must have studied the history of English foods. You are correct, my dear lassie; true shepherd's pie has lamb because the shepherd herds lambs. If the pie had been made with beef it would have been referred to as 'cottage pie'."

"I can't wait to savor the desserts — I mean sweets — there are too many delectable combinations and cooking techniques. I love experimenting in the kitchen. It'll be fun to attempt to duplicate the English specialties when I return home."

She wanted to share her thoughts of the details which prompted the trip to Featherlawn, but she had to maintain her status as the daughter of John and Eva Belle Brown from Florida. Her head was spinning. There was the series of strange events which were swirling around her. She was still pondering what was behind thefts of medical supplies at the Veteran's Center. If someone was stealing supplies, they could steal other more important information. Was it smoke and mirrors? The focus was on thefts; were they missing their actual target? There was the security threat created by possibly two Brown military families. Despite all that, here she sat in a quaint restaurant in the English countryside discussing recipes for English pastries. It was part of her world with Charlie. If anyone could confirm the link between the Browns she identified in the scrapbook pictures and the Addison family, she could with the backing of Frank's crew, of course. The preliminary data was unbelievable. Even if Trevor was sent by the embassy, the situation with the Brown gentleman, or gentle*men* went beyond an exercise in family genealogy. The information could point to an imminent danger to national security. Trevor may or may not have been told the details. It certainly wasn't her responsibility to divulge the information. The conversation during the trip had to remain friendly and superficial, a true Southern art. She'd leave official updates to Frank.

"EJ, where is the ladies' room?" asked her mom.

The hostess, Clementine, pointed toward the entrance hall.

"I'll go with you."

"Me, too," said Carrie.

In the hall her mother whispered, "EJ, I don't mean to sound paranoid, but the couple sitting in the corner who came in after we did, I saw them on the tour bus yesterday."

EJ looked at Carrie with raised eyebrows. When Carrie's eyes grew large EJ recognized the couple wasn't part of the support Carrie had screened.

"What excellent observations, Mom."

"It's probably nothing, but I sensed I should tell you."

"It's no problem, Mrs. Brown, I'm glad you said something," added Clementine.

"I have a friend in the military police. I'll call her for a suggestion," said Carrie.

"Come on, Mom. Let's eat our dessert and act as if nothing is out of the ordinary while Carrie makes a call. And Mom, please don't tell other stories."

"Your dad loves to tease you. He tells everyone the chicken-n-dumplin' story."

"Oh, look at the yummy dessert tray!" she said.

Carrie dialed a long series of numbers. "Mom, a mangy dog has been following my mother again." Angus was emerging from the restroom. His pager was buzzing. He grabbed the phone.

"Here's a piece of paper to write a note," said Carrie when she handed him the list of invited retired military with an additional note concerning the couple in the corner. She disappeared to join the table.

Angus casually walked across the hall to talk to their local hostess, Clementine, who was hired for the day, a wife of a retired military.

"Eva Belle is sure the couple sitting in the corner was on their tour bus yesterday," contributed Clementine as she smiled.

"Were they on the list? Is there anyone else who wasn't on our list?"

"The couple told me they were extra security for the lunch. I didn't question. I'm glad you caught my oversight."

"We're fine. We'll revise our strategy. Do you have a

decorated cake? We'll gather the guests to join our group to sing 'Happy Birthday,' and with a room full of well-wishers we'll leave to continue our tour. We stationed guards in the parking lot to maintain security of the vehicles."

"Whose birthday are we going to celebrate?"

"Carrie!" He slipped EJ a note on the way back to the table.

Everyone relished in bites of the sweets selections when Clementine arrived with the birthday cake leading a procession of other guests. EJ stood, "Carrie, we're glad you could celebrate your birthday with us. You're family!" She began the 'Happy Birthday' song. Carrie didn't even blink and graciously bowed to thank the guests.

"Oh, blarmy!" cried the hostess. "I forgot the take-home cake. Ms. Eva Belle, could you assist me?"

"I'd be glad to assist." She followed Clementine as would any Southern lady, when asked to assist. In the hall Clementine whispered the exit arrangements. She nodded and returned to the party. EJ and Carrie had quickly sliced and distributed the cake, when Eva Belle said, "Would we have time to go by a pharmacy. I have a sudden headache!"

"Oh, of course, Mother."

Trevor and Angus quickly gathered belongings and the group rushed to the van. Meanwhile the other partygoers detained the uninvited couple seated at the corner table. Orders were to maintain the original team. Another crew was en route to seize the party crashers.

CHAPTER TWENTY-SIX

Featherlawn was a brief ride. Thankfully there were no roundabouts to navigate. "The church be on top of the hill," said Angus pointing to a white building on the horizon. The church could be seen in the distance long before arriving in town. It was the highest building on the highest hill in the green countryside. Crystals within the gray stone glistened against the blue skies. The sun reflected in rows of slender narrow windows. "Built in the 1700s, it was. The town was once known for the fabric trade, has recently taken a fancy to dairy products."

EJ knew her dad would be interested in the history of the rural agricultural English community. She loved her dad for his tolerance of her many changes in life's course. Whatever project she was working on she could count on her dad to be positive and supportive.

The countryside was dotted with scattered stone walls and abandoned fireplaces standing like watchmen guarding historic pasts. It reminded her of the Addison's house she adored as a young girl. She wondered if children played in these ruins as she had. They passed skeletal remains of an estate with seven fireplaces. A stately cemetery was perched on a hill with faded stone markers. She wondered if they were driving by the Addison's estate but she couldn't ask. With the church coming into view, she was mesmerized at the stately windows with the pointed arch. "Angus, what's the name of the architecture of the church? Is it Gothic architecture or Romanesque?"

"Aye, will ask the church secretary," he laughed. "There she is, waving for us."

She ran to the van before they were even at a proper stop. "Welcome. Welcome. Pleased to meet you. Come in, come in. I'm Angela Duncan."

"Thank you for taking time to assist our search to locate our relatives. I'm John Brown and this is my wife Eva Belle, daughter EJ, and her friend Carrie."

"Aye, Trevor and Angus rang the church and asked if I could look in ye records."

"We're trying to find information on my uncle, Anderson Brown. He came to visit the Addisons when he was stationed in England during WWI. He died in the war and is buried in the Meuse-Argonne American Cemetery in France. We visited the cemetery several days ago."

"Come inside. Let's sit down," said Mrs. Duncan. A tear rolled down her cheek.

She was petite and one whose height didn't support her weight, as they would say at home. Frenzied curly hair framed her porcelain skin with plump rosy cheeks, the same color echoed in the printed roses on her cotton apron worn over a pink striped blouse. She wore a long dark blue skirt with the hem below her knees, dark stockings, and clunky serviceable shoes. She sat with her hands in her lap and dabbed a tissue to her eyes.

"Oh, we didn't mean to upset you," said Eva Belle in her soft Southern voice. "Trevor, will you find us a glass of water?"

EJ and Carrie sat in the chairs by Mrs. Duncan's desk.

"Oh, the tears are joyful and sad tears. I a wee girl when my cousin, Elizabeth, married Anderson Brown. My mother and her mother were sisters. I was in her wedding. It was an enchanting wedding," she sighed. "Anderson would visit on the weekends and tell us stories of living on a ranch in Florida. We loved his stories of cows, cowboys, and the horses they rode. Mr. Brown was called to the war and we never heard from him again. We were heartbroken. Everyone liked him and his brother. According to my mother, soon Elizabeth was expecting a baby and Anderson encouraged her to travel to Florida to stay with his family. Elizabeth had the address of the Brown's family in Florida and sent a letter she was on the way. We wanted her to travel in the spring when the North Atlantic would be less stormy after the baby came. She left Featherlawn sometime in the fall. I don't remember the exact date; I remember how the leaves were bright yellow, orange, and red. The leaves were the only cheerful note on the day Elizabeth left. It was such a pretty fall until the flu came. The same colorful leaves silently covered the ground of quickly dug graves.

"When the flu arrived, at first we buried church members one by one, but in less than a week a single grave was used for those who died during the day. The Addisons along with most of the families in the area died. My grandmother had seen this death before. During the middle of the night she took my mother, me, my brothers, and sisters to an abandoned gardener's house far into the country. We hid for weeks. After two deep snows we returned; it was Christmas. The ones who survived have remained close. Mrs. Wordsworth called to tell me you were on the way. She was in the wedding too."

"She is a delightful lady," chatted Eva Belle, hoping to refocus the conversation to happier things. "She was so gracious to talk to us as if we were family. We happened to wander into their shoe store because my feet hurt. You were also in the wedding! How lovely! What color was your dress? You have to tell me every single detail of the whole wedding day; don't leave out a thing."

"My dress was a soft yellow with white swirls. Miss Elizabeth's wedding gave the entire village a brief sense of hope. Many soldiers from Featherlawn died. But the flu arrived and killed many more." She paused for a minute. Eva Belle moved closer and placed her arm around her shoulder. "After the wedding, I pressed yellow daisies from my bouquet, but my things were burned to rid the house of the flu sickness. I hid my beautiful dress under my clothing to protect it from the fire, I did. Everything we owned was burned to rid the house of the flu. In the dress I felt I was a princess." She sniffled. "I have a quilt constructed from the fabric when I outgrew the dress. It reminds me of such a blissful day."

"It must be a special quilt to have saved it these many years! Mrs. Duncan, are you aware if there were any written records of the wedding?" asked EJ.

"Bishop Roundtree had a meeting earlier this afternoon. He said he was going to have a snoop in the dusty marriage records. Oh, look. Our parish cat, Muckaleedun, is bringing her kittens to entertain while I check if the bishop has returned. Bishop Roundtree recently moved to our parish."

"Muckaleedun?" asked Mr. Brown. "It's the same term in Florida to describe the mixed brown, red, and cream color of our scrub cattle."

"Aye. Muckalee is the name of a traditional Irish village. Father Craig was raised in Ireland. He was the bishop here for forty years. Father took one of the kittens with him to the retirement community. It had the same coloring as the mother. Similar to your cows, you say, the unique colors of her fur we call muckalee."

"Can we hold the kittens?" asked EJ.

"Oh, yes, my lady. Ms. Muckalee brings the kittens to every church service. The church members spoil them. The kittens crawl into the children's laps. The children are quiet while the kittens sleep. At one service soon after he arrived, the bishop was deeply involved in his sermon and preaching well beyond his usual time. The ladies, we had pot roast cooking at home but we sat quietly hoping the angels would protect the roasts from burning. Muckalee let out a loud cry. We blamed Mr. Greenwich sitting on the back row for stepping on her tail, but whatever the cause, the bishop quickly bowed his head, lead a prayer, and the service happily ended," she said and laughed in a whisper.

"Look at this cutie," exclaimed EJ as she placed the kitten on her lap. "She is a tortoiseshell calico almost as cute as my Baby Kittie."

An orange marmalade jumped into Carrie's arms. "And the tuxedo kitty is patting my shoes. Look at her long fluffy tail; the kittens are too precious."

"Elsa Janine and Carrie," her dad stated their names sternly. EJ knew she was in hot water when he used her full legal name. "Remember, ladies, kittens are prohibited on the plane home." But in a jovial tone he added, "EJ, I'm amazed that regardless of the location cats will find you!"

"Oh, I'm feline-friendly, I guess."

"Mr. and Mrs. Brown, this is Bishop Roundtree. He joined our parish several weeks ago."

"Bishop, it is a pleasure to meet you. We appreciate your assistance," responded Mr. Brown. "I understand Mr. Trevor told you we're seeking information on my uncle, Anderson Brown, who died during WWI. We are proposing he possibly came to Featherlawn to visit our previous neighbors, the Addisons. The family built a house near us at Illahaw, Florida."

"Ah, Mr. Trevor called several days ago. I was having a difficult time believing you'd made a connection of a young woman named Elizabeth from England who arrived at the port of New York City and reported she was married to a soldier from Florida who was stationed in France. Subsequently to propose he was your uncle was unbelievable, especially based solely on a common last name."

"Ms. Elizabeth revealed to her sponsors, a New York family, she was from Featherlawn. The head of the house was an attorney and kept exceedingly detailed notes. It was a long shot that the same Elizabeth who lived in the Featherlawn village married my uncle during WWI. But we were in the area, and if nothing comes of the visit, it's been an informative trip and we've enjoyed the hospitality and the opportunity to see places tourists rarely visit. I tried the steak and kidney pie and the suicide roundabout and won't have to try those again. What was the name of the roundabout, EJ?"

"Magic Roundabout?"

"Yes, I am familiar with this roundabout," groaned the bishop as he sat back in his chair. "Too much traffic for my comfort. I am accustomed to less hectic driving in the Heather Lands of Ireland."

Janice held her breath. This wasn't going to work, but the clues optimistically pointed toward this connection and it looked so promising.

"Nevertheless, despite my doubts," continued the Bishop, "I found the parish records from 1917-1919 on a dusty shelf in the library. Perhaps it was divine intervention. The records from 1918 were on top. The book inadvertently slipped to the floor and opened to the page from August. Let me show you. On the first line is recorded a marriage between Elizabeth Addison to Anderson Augustus Brown on the afternoon of August 3, 1918 at two o'clock. The wedding was held in the church gardens according to the notes of the church secretary. The town council voted to approve the wedding since Mr. Brown was born in the US and was not an English citizen. Mr. Addison stood for Anderson Brown. The church secretary made a special note from Mr. Addison said Anderson had taught him to fly-fish. Ordinarily, Anderson would have had his brother stand for him, but his brother had already been assigned somewhere in France."

"Dad!" cried EJ. She couldn't contain the outburst. "We've found your uncle and have confirmed he married Elizabeth Addison from Featherlawn. This is marvelous!"

"Thank you, Bishop. I'm sure you are busy."

"You are certainly welcome. I wish I could visit longer, but my duties are required at the hospital."

"Yes; I'm sure our paths will cross again."

"I'll leave you in the capable hands of Mrs. Duncan." He grabbed his prayer robe from his office and left the chapel.

Mrs. Duncan was practically dancing on air. "Before you go, we must celebrate the happy news. The bishop wanted to host a tea for your travels."

"Is this a Foursies?" inquired EJ.

"Ah, my Lassie; a nibble of a meal for us working bloke served at four o'clock. I have a kettle on the burner and slices of fresh lardy cake."

"Lardy cake?"

"It was created in Wiltshire in the 1800s by my family, the Caswells. My ancestors were one of the first grain farmers in the area to grow white wheat. Most farmers grew rye which made the bread dark and heavy. The family had a mill, they did. To sell their flour they started baking light breads and cakes. People came from miles around to buy a slice of my grandfather's lardy cake. I had to watch my mother many times before I had the recipe correct. My grandfather forbid anyone to record the recipe for fear another bakery would steal his secret. The Caswell family did share a copy of the recipe only once to be served at summer garden parties at Buckingham Palace. At the palace the recipe is stored in a safe," she whispered.

"What an honor for your family," said Eva Belle.

"Lardy cake resembles a rich horizontal cinnamon roll," EJ said and chuckled. "There must be special techniques to create such delicate layers reaching for the ceiling." She leaned close to hear the detail, hinting she wanted her to reveal the recipe sequestered for centuries.

"I save a pinch-back and store it in the stone well house overnight to add to the dough the following morning."

EJ wondered if wild yeast in the atmosphere inside the stone well house was what made the dough delicate and airy. In college one summer she'd enrolled in Dr. Reynolds' food microbiology class to study European food preservation and processing. She and a group of students crawled around caves and basements of famous monasteries to collect wild yeast samples. They grew the specimens in petri dishes to identify wild yeasts which flavored classic French and Italian breads and cheeses. She could only speculate if wild yeast from the well house was the secret to the light and fluffy pastry.

"Only the freshest pork lard, fluffy and white, harvested from around the kidneys is used. To the batter I add sugared crimson raisins and homemade candied lemon and orange peel from fruit shipped from Valencia, Spain," willingly contributed Mrs. Duncan. "The dough is rolled flat and folded many times before the rolls are allowed to rise."

EJ smiled knowing many of the famous Florida citrus varieties originated in Valencia, Spain, brought by early Spanish and Portuguese explorers to the New World. One of the most

205

famous was the Valencia orange, named from the city of origin. Valencia juice is known the world over for its characteristic succulent aromatic juice and deep rich orange color.

"But before ye put the sweet dough into the oven ye sprinkle the top of the dough with brown sugar," she whispered with a wink.

"Oh, of course," added EJ. "The brown sugar would create a brown crust and preserve a soft moist top."

"For the gentlemen, I made for ye a proper syllabub. We ladies can sample." She giggled.

"I love this punch. Our Southern milk punch is similar; it is a regional specialty in New Orleans, Savannah, and Charleston, old coastal cities settled by British, French, and Spanish. It is a Southern custom to serve milk punch on Christmas Eve or at a holiday brunch, when the cooler weather preserves the delicate flavor of the milk," shared EJ. "We sprinkle nutmeg in the bottom of the punch bowl before adding the milk and bourbon."

"I serve shortbread cookies on a tea plate with a cup of punch," added Eva Belle. What is traditionally served with the punch in Wiltshire?"

"The same, my lady. I added a glass of sherry to the pitcher to warm you nicely for a cool summer evening on the drive home," she whispered. "The bishop would fuss a wee bit if he was here, but we rarely have visitors from Florida. And visitors who are my distant relatives, to boot! This has been a wonderful day."

Chapter Twenty-Seven

Carrie and EJ shared a cab to the airport with her folks, John and Eva Bell, to catch their early morning flights.

"Bye, dear! Thanks for inviting us on your vacation. Glad you were successful in tracking our family genealogy. Your dad is delighted you were able to complete missing family history. Don't forget where we live," teased her mother. "Carrie, you're welcome to visit with or without EJ."

"Thanks, Mrs. B."

"When are y'all flying home?" asked her dad.

"Our flight is out at noon. We'll have time to finish our paperwork and reports. Y'all have a pleasant flight. I promise I'll be home for Thanksgiving! Promise!" EJ hugged her parents and watched while they safely proceeded through the initial security checkpoint.

"We have reservations to fly home on a military transport," said Carrie once the folks were out of hearing and visual range. "Note the guy at the coffee counter with two coffees: a café latte for me and iced coffee for you. He's our ride to the air base." EJ was returning to Washington, DC as Bonnie Watkins.

Once onboard, the pilot handed her a headset and microphone.

It was Frank. "Kid. Another great performance. You connected the dots with optimal results. The couple who followed you to the restaurant worked for Timmerman."

"But..."

"Someone's using his authorization. We're working on it. JoAnne is seeing what she can do through their computer systems at the State Department travel office if she can track the two at the restaurant. We've increased the security at the ranch. Apparently, Timmerman's people cross-referenced 'Brown from Florida' and found your folks. It was simply by chance you were with them. We updated your dad and put the fisherman on their flight home. Your dad's gonna invite him out to the ranch. Actually, he was raised in Wyoming. He'll ask the right questions and his interest in your dad's cattle and the invitation to the ranch will appear fairly genuine. He's going to ride home with the ranch crew who are meeting your folks at the airport. We put the ranch on alert. They'll be okay."

"Thanks. Meanwhile, I'm settling in to watch the in-flight movie lounging in the custom leather seats. I wonder what's on the dining menu for first class today."

"Kid, what tour guide are you using? You'll be lucky if you get a bottle of water and a bag of peanuts. Be aware of events around you. Be careful. Out."

"How's Mother Hen?" asked Carrie with a grin.

Bonnie whispered, "What a perfect call sign for him! He told me someone used Timmerman's authority to send the couple to follow my folks." She should have let Frank brief Carrie on the updated information. "Who has the air-sickness pills?" She pulled the harness tight against her body. It was one thing to risk her safety, but now her folks had been targeted. A doubting thought questioned if it was worth being in Charlie's world to have placed her folks in danger. She rested her head in her hands and braced for takeoff.

CHAPTER TWENTY-EIGHT

Commander Brown, Major Brown, Colonel Land will see you now."

"Yes, sir," they said in unison, and looked at each other. They walked briskly into Colonel Land's office. Bonnie was watching the meeting on a closed-circuit television. She couldn't risk giving away her identity as Janice Brown, when she was supposed to be Bonnie Watkins. She'd done the genealogy research in England but with such rapid turnarounds, she didn't hear the findings from the other research teams. Her dad was seated at a long polished table with Sargent Major Dobbs. Her dad looked powerful dressed in Levis, a sharply pressed long-sleeved chambray shirt, and a blue blazer. His Stetson hat sat on the table. In a private moment, Sargent Dobbs said he would say hello, and promised he wouldn't share details of her project in DC, although she imagined her folks would be pleased with her contribution to the establishment of the outpatient clinic for military families.

"Gentlemen, I wanted you to meet Mr. Edward John Brown. He has a remarkable story to share." They were polite, turned to face him, and listened attentively.

"My father Stephen Brown, and my uncle, Anderson Brown, were drafted during WWI and sent to England for training preparing to join the war effort in France. First, I should probably tell you where I'm from. I'm a rancher in Florida. The adjoining land to the Ranch at Bay Branch was owned by a British family, the Addisons. During training in England, the two brothers visited the Addison family to discuss buying their land. Their brick house in Florida had been hit by lightning several years earlier and the fire destroyed the roof and most of the interior. They agreed on the sale and my father sent word to my mother to send the money.

Meanwhile, my father's unit was transferred to France. He worked with mule-drawn caisson bringing ammo to the 12-inch howitzers. My dad said the guns thundered twenty-four hours a day without a pause. My uncle Anderson stayed in England for additional training. After the Armistice we were notified Anderson was missing in action. Years later we received confirmation of his death."

The colonel continued, "Sargent Major Dobbs told me Commander Brown and Major Brown never met, am I correct?

"Yes, sir."

The colonel added his perspective. "When Sargent Major Dobbs' people noticed the similarities of the pictures at the scrapbook workshops presented by your wives, he asked friends at the Pentagon to quietly investigate. First, we had to confirm there were two separate individuals, especially with the compelling similarities of your appearance, as well as parallels of your blood DNA characteristics and the likenesses of your families. Your personnel jacket indicated both of you were outstanding students at the military academies at West Point and Annapolis. You both served in Vietnam and have received numerous awards and outstanding ratings. We moved quickly and quietly. The sergeant major's goal was not to tarnish your outstanding years of service and your careers."

The men looked stunned. "Sir, other than the same name, why are we here?"

The colonel ignored their question and proceeded. "It took time to go through the military records from WWI," said Colonel Land. "Sargent Anderson Brown was killed at Verdun when a direct hit collapsed the tunnel he was in. He was listed as missing in action in the day report, but before the records could be transported to the rear echelon, HQ was captured and the files were destroyed in the battle. His body was found several years after the war and his remains interred in France. We were able to confirm the attack from interviews of the few limited WWI survivors. We even found a man from his unit at a VA hospital. He had vivid memories of the battle, but had no idea the family wasn't notified immediately of their comrade's death."

"Sir, this is interesting, but are we being charged with something?"

"Gentlemen, I suggest you sit and listen. That's an order!" harshly demanded the colonel. His tone was soft when he addressed her dad, "Mr. Brown, would you please continue?"

"Of course. My father passed away ten years ago. He'd talked for years about how he wanted to visit the French cemetery where his brother was buried. Recently, my wife and I traveled to France in his honor. I tried to contact the Addison family to visit them during the trip. My father talked fondly of the family and how he enjoyed seeing them when he was in England for training. As WWI ended, swine flu stormed the community and we discovered the Addison family died along with most families living in Featherlawn at the time, except a daughter, Elizabeth. Church records indicated Anderson Brown, my uncle, married Elizabeth Addison in the summer of 1918 in a family service held in the church's rose garden. Shortly thereafter Anderson was transferred to Argonne Forest. In November, Elizabeth boarded a boat to cross the dangerous North Atlantic with a baby on the way. She said something was driving her to be close to her husband's family in Florida. Winter was approaching and everyone in the village warned her of the stormy weather, but she was determined. Military men seem to fall in love with strong women, don't they?"

The men smiled and nodded in agreement.

"Rough seas tossed her belongings throughout the cabin and in the turmoil, her luggage and papers were lost during a storm. Once at Ellis Island, she told the immigration officials she was going to Florida to a place no one could find on a map, to live with her husband's family, a family named Brown. The captain of the boat testified to the immigration agents her papers were in order when she boarded. She had a first-class ticket and the necessary papers when the boat left the port of Liverpool. Obviously pregnant and stranded on Ellis Island, an immigration agent took pity on the traveler and called a friend, an influential New York attorney. The attorney's family gave her an invitation to stay with them while he began a search to locate the Brown family in Florida."

Mr. Brown could tell his audience was getting restless, but he continued at a slightly faster pace.

"In May, Elizabeth delivered a son and with the attorney's connections, the birth was registered under her married name of Brown. Sargent Major Dobbs' investigative team verified the birth certificate. She named the baby Anderson Florida Brown after his father. According to the attorney's personal notes, Elizabeth tried multiple times to contact her family and found the flu had ravished the hamlet, and survivors had been moved to medical facilities throughout England. The attorney continued to search

212

for her family."

"Well, couldn't the attorney help? It sounded as if he had connections, couldn't he have gone deeper into the records?" asked Lt. Commander Benjamin Brown.

"He tried. With his friends at the immigration office, the attorney checked the rosters of troop ships returning to the US when the war ended. Often, he discovered the men were unfortunately listed as transferees from their training bases, rather than by their home city or state. In addition, many Browns were listed solely by first initial. Despite his efforts the attorney was unable to locate Anderson Brown, her husband, who was my uncle. Records of my father's return were lost in the joyful chaos at the end of the war, the war to end all wars. He survived and returned home to Illahaw, Florida, to the Ranch at Bay Branch.

"Where?"

"Illahaw used to have a thriving timber mill with its own railroad station in the 1870s. Once the timber was cut, the railroad tracks were removed and most of the town followed. It's hard to find on most maps even today. Illahaw is located an hour south of the Orlando theme parks."

"Gentlemen," continued the colonel, "Sargent Major Dobbs' people completed the tedious research to examine military and immigration records. He sent a group to New York and they manually searched the immigration reports at Ellis Island to verify Elizabeth's arrival in the US. They were lucky the attorney had also emigrated from Europe around the turn of the century, and recognized the importance of leaving a legal trail. Much of this information came from an *amicus curiae* (Latin for 'a friend of the court') document he filed on behalf of Elizabeth Addison Brown and her son in 1919."

"You are probably wondering how these details concern you," added John Brown. He could sense their muddled

213

confusion. "I have to admit, parts of the story are certainly unbelievable. The war ended and my father was discharged and boarded a troop ship home, unaware of the death of his brother," added Mr. Brown. "Months later, the family received notification of his brother's status as missing in action. They were optimistic he would return, but were busy protecting the ranch from cattle-rustlers as families struggled to survive the Great Depression."

"The child, Anderson Florida Brown, attended a prestigious college thanks to his benefactor," continued Colonel Land. "In 1940 Anderson married Carrabelle Meadows at a summer wedding. Carrabelle was the daughter of Major General Meadows. He had followed in the family footsteps of a long history of West Point graduates. General Meadows was home on Christmas leave in 1941 when the attack on Pearl Harbor occurred. Anderson volunteered for the Army within hours and transferred out immediately as an aide de camp to General Meadows. From Carrabelle's diary found in the attorney's personal papers, she hoped with the rank of her father, he and her husband would remain safe in a rear area. She hadn't mentioned the pregnancy. Raised in a military family, sharing knowledge of the pregnancy would have triggered unnecessary friction, and her husband would leave with her father, regardless. She and Mrs. Meadows put on a stiff upper lip, being dutiful Army wives. Months passed, and the twins arrived early. Delivered at home, which was common during the war years, Carrabelle died from complications."

"How horrible," simultaneously voiced the two men, Benjamin and Bradley.

"This portion of the Brown family history came from military death benefit records," added Colonel Land. "Within a week of the death of Carrabelle, Mrs. Meadows received word of the disappearance of the plane carrying General Meadows and Lt.

Anderson Florida Brown, lost in stormy weather en route to Dutch Harbor shortly after the Japanese attack in June 1942. With the deep frigid water of the Bering Sea, the plane and survivors were never found. Mrs. Meadows was overwhelmed with grief, refused to eat, and died soon after Carrabelle. The housekeepers buried Mrs. Meadow's body in the garden next to Carrabelle, and did their best to continue to care for the two boys trying to maintain their routine as before.

"Soon their deception was uncovered by the family banker and the twins were placed by private adoptions among wealthy families. The banker self-appointed himself to oversee the twin's investments and insisted the boys keep their names which maintained the general's estate and military benefits supposedly for the benefits of two sons, but especially for the financial benefit of the banker. The housekeepers disappeared under mysterious circumstances. Years later their bodies were found buried in the garden with the other two women. The young twins were never told their family history."

"Men, does any of this sound familiar?" asked Colonel Land in a gentle fatherly tone.

They both shook their heads.

"Gentlemen, this is your family history. We've tested your DNA which was on file at the Department of Defense. Our data confirms you are brothers. You haven't had time to talk, but your birthdays are the same. Further DNA testing substantiated the familial relationship to Mr. John Brown."

"We've talked with your adopted families who under pressure ultimately admitted the banker arranged the adoptions for a generous contribution and their silence," flatly stated Sargent Major Dobbs.

"Now since you mention it, when I applied to West Point, I was awarded the Major General Meadow's Endowed Chair."

"Me too, but at the Naval Academy. It seemed odd at the time. I read what was available in our library on General Meadows, but being he was Army, there wasn't much. I was unaware his aide de camp was Brown. It wasn't in the background materials."

"Brown was appointed as a second lieutenant in the field, without formal military training. Originally, he was probably listed as a member of the general's staff, but after a few years, a shortened summary of his command may have deleted his name. But back to the twins, you both are well aware there are few secrets between service wives." Everyone moved their heads and rolled their eyes confirming this truth. "Brown's fellow officers received news of the birth of the twins, but when they tried to contact his wife, they were unable to locate her, unaware she had died in childbirth. They were able to discover General Meadow's wife had died and the general's personal affairs were managed by the banker, who unfortunately denied knowledge of the status of the boys, and their inquiries unfortunately went nowhere.

"The war continued. Brown's men pooled their monies and funded the Chairs at West Point and Annapolis under the general's name to ensure two boys named Brown with birthdays of May 30, 1942 would be accepted into the service academies. It was a long shot, but it was a way they could honor their friend's death and would preserve access to the boy's family history."

"Wow. This is surprising. I didn't have a clue about my background." Benjamin pushed his chair away from the table.

"Me either," said Bradley looking at the other.

"Grab some coffee, men; there's further details which may be of interest to you," signaled Sargent Major Dobbs.

Bonnie glanced at her watch and knew she had to return quickly to the Veteran's Center. The evening diet classes had been rescheduled to accommodate the quilters. She giggled thinking of how the dorm crew hijacked the counting and cutting of the quilt pieces as if they were planning a major invasion. At odd hours they were at the worktables cutting red, white, and blue squares, strips or corners in solids, strips and fabrics in patterned calicos according to their calculations and chart on the blackboard. The quilts were destined for patients in residence at the VA hospital and recovery facilities. It was a community service project suggested by her good friend Susan Fisher when she served on the First Lady's ad hoc committee for military families. The impressive official name of the committee escaped her at the moment. She wanted to ask Dobbs how to send Susan an invitation to make an inspection tour of the Center and show off the quilting workshops. Dobbs was just crafty enough to devise an essential reason for her to visit. It was so fun catching up on gossip when they met in Moscow during her husband's promotion ceremony. It was hard to believe that was only several weeks ago.

When the quilting ladies arrived, they were armed with sewing machines to chain-sew the pieces together. She wished she had known the technique when she and her grandmother made a crazy quilt from scrap fabric sewed on newspaper squares as a pattern. It was fun working Grandmother's treadle machine, but the technique would have saved a lot of time by simply back-stitching the end of each seam. They could immediately start a second section without pulling and cutting the threads. She loved sewing, and would have liked to retreat into quilt-making, but her primary responsibility was unclogging the bobbins and rethreading machines. She chuckled about how the same military trained personnel who could disassemble and reassemble a weapon, a truck or tank in minutes, blindfolded, under fire and behind their backs in the dark, had such trouble with the bobbins and couldn't follow the threading guide painted in plain view on the front of the sewing machine. Given enough time, they'd catch on to the maintenance of less complicated equipment. She snickered when a broom appeared with embedded magnets to retrieve straight pins hiding on the floor. She'd heard rumors that a committee of barefooted midnight moochers prompted the sudden purchase.

On the way back to the Veteran's Center her driver was trapped in the roundabout at the Iwo Jima Monument and circled the statute three or four times. Afternoon traffic was horrible even for DC standards but the last rays of sunset lit the determined Marine faces and highlighted the red stripes in the flag of the memorial statue. She didn't mind the delay of several loops around the monument; the statue represented the cost of a strong-willed nation to obtain freedom for all. She was deep in thought and had no idea where they were traveling after exiting the roundabout. How fitting; her life since meeting Charlie was like living in a roundabout. She couldn't predict which direction her life was heading.

"Bonnie! We're glad you're back," rushed three leaders of the quilting ladies when she walked in the door. The Red, White, and Blue Veteran's Center was covered with connected strings of linked quilt pieces similar to signal flags on a carrier. A committee of men armed with irons and ironing boards were pressing the seams to ensure when the sections were joined the resulting seams would be flat. She guessed she had a puzzled took because one of them told her, "Ma'am, military men are experts at ironing our uniforms. This is a no-brainer."

"I am so proud of how the Red, White and Blue crew have volunteered," whispered Bonnie.

"Bonnie, we appreciate their skills. The Center's volunteers are wonderful. Thank you again for giving us a permanent space for the mechanical quilting machine. It allows us to keep it fully assembled. We only needed a space of fifteen by fifteen feet. At the church library, we spent most of our quilting time assembling and disassembling the machine. It's convenient to drop by the Veteran's Center to work on the quilting machine whenever our sewing guild members have time. The security teams at the center are comforting for older members of our sewing guild. I saw on the schedule you are working late tonight. Can I pour you an iced coffee?"

"Oh, how wonderful!" She suddenly felt guilty at the times she'd tried to slither quietly by the sewing area without disturbing the gray-headed speakers, which was usually a wasted effort. Yes, she was the official closer at the clinic tonight. She hated to leave the colonel's meeting and not hear the other details. At least the two Browns were aware they were twins. She could talk with Dobbs in the morning. She'd sleuthed the genealogy of their grandparents, but was dying to hear what else Dobbs' crew had uncovered.

"Bonnie, Bonnie? Can you show me how to fix this…damn… bobbin whatever?" hollered a loud, deep, demanding voice.

"Here's your coffee, dear. Thank goodness you're here."

CHAPTER TWENTY-NINE

It was Tuesday. Sue Li wore the same pale blue silk suit with her white blouse. Today she added a cheerful scarf scattered with hand-painted cherry blossoms, a gift from Timmerman. She couldn't wait for him to return home and to her bed.

As per the routine, she purchased two pink bags of chocolates at her uncle's favorite candy store in Alexandria, and her driver dropped her and her bodyguard at the Freer Gallery, at the entrance on Independence Street to view the Chinese porcelain collection. Sixty minutes passed slowly. Her bodyguard's American girlfriend had passed a message from Timmerman to proceed with their plan. After today, things would be different. She was thrilled at the possibilities of freedom from her uncle's control, but she had to guard her optimism. Week after week she'd performed the same routine. Her bodyguard disappeared through the tunnel, but today when they left the museum, the two boxes of chocolate truffles in bright pink bags held explosives and their freedom. As rehearsed week after week, the driver was waiting for her at the Jefferson Street exit.

At the restaurant her uncle was in the corner booth as she expected. "Sue Li, my niece, join me."

She smiled but tried to remain calm. "Uncle, I saw Ms. Brown on the plane in Seattle several weeks ago. Your friends at China Airlines tracked her ticket," contributed Sue Li. "We've watched her come and go to the Veteran's Center since she arrived. The team is ready to eliminate her and everyone who works for her."

He uncle nodded and sipped his tea.

"I am excited, my uncle, tonight I will kill Ms. Brown. I left message the custom chairs we ordered have arrived to compliment the antique Chinese cabinet. She be traveling, but be back in Washington. I deliver last of the chairs for the apartment when she be back at apartment tonight. Our spies called and she be at the Veteran's Center. Tonight, she go to meeting," stated Sue Li. "When I call, I will tell them the chairs will make her house perfect."

"Yes, very good. Very good, Sue Li."

"Uncle, I must go to meet the furniture delivery truck," said Sue Li, anxious to leave. Usually Ms. Brown be home by nine o'clock." After her earlier mistakes, Sue Li was anticipating killing both Ms. Brown and eliminating her uncle. "I brought you a box of chocolate truffles from the candy shop in Alexandria, your favorites." Once Mr. Tao was out of the way, she, Brian, and Ron could live together without manipulation from her uncle.

She motioned to the bodyguard to hand her the pink bag. The top layer of candies was inviting, hand-decorated in contrasting chocolate drizzles, but the bottom layer held explosives carefully crafted in the shape and appearance of chocolate truffles.

"Yes, thank you, my niece. I look forward to seeing you on my plane later tonight after you successful. You leave DC after the murder. You be happy in San Francisco." Mr. Tao had given instructions to the delivery crew once they killed Ms. Brown, they were to transport Sue Li to the freighter, enjoy her body, and dump her at sea. Mr. Tao's men had killed Ron Jones earlier keeping his body in the ship's freezer, another body to dispose of in deep waters. "Ron and Brian meet us in San Francisco in few days. They both very helpful. I meet you in Baltimore at hanger for my private jet."

Sue Li walked her uncle to his car and carefully placed the pretty pink bags of candy deep in the trunk on top of the gas tank and headed for the warehouse to prepare the chairs for delivery to Bonnie's condo. In a few hours she'd be her own person.

Once in the car Mr. Tao directed his driver to head toward downtown Washington, DC to talk with his friends on the Hill. His people would notify him when Sue Li headed to Virginia to deliver the furniture. He patted his briefcase containing his radio.

CHAPTER THIRTY

The excitement at the annual Multi-Regional Military Scrapbook Competition was electric. Bonnie and a group from the Red, White, and Blue Center arrived at the base high school auditorium after they closed the Veteran's Center early to attend the event. Bonnie waved at Mrs. Nelson and the DC team seated in the first row as the center's entourage found seats in the stands. Patriotic bunting hung from the ceiling. Bags of red, white, and blue balloons were suspended from the rafters. In the grandstands were unit flags and banners representing bases, forts, and commands from around the United States. Bonnie felt giddy watching cheerleaders in full performance mode as they jumped, cartwheeled, and tumbled across the floor. A military band stood at attention waiting to begin the festivities.

Several ladies from the scrapbooking workshops sneaked into the stands to deliver Bonnie and crew the printed competition protocols, and a box top filled with sodas and popcorn. "There are two stages of the contest. The first level is the known topics we completed at the Veteran's Center and an overall display. The known topics are displayed on the presentation tables prepared by the regions. Each group is required to display five entries in each of the four categories: Way Out, Once Upon a Time, Thru the Years, and All for One. The table with the Washington monuments is our overall display!"

"What creativity! I'm voting for the DC team!" cheered Bonnie. She suspected the coffee cups awarded at the evening workshops were the inspiration. She admired Mrs. Nelson's subversive leadership style.

"The second round of the competition is the creation of five original pieces of an unknown topic. It's the same timed format that we practiced at the Veteran's Center."

Mrs. Nelson looked their way, and the DC ladies quickly scampered back to the gymnasium floor. She was the mistress of ceremonies and Sargent Major Dobbs stood in dress uniform at her side. Bonnie would never tell him, but he looked sexy in his dress blues. Precisely at 1900, Mrs. Nelson removed a whistle from the pocket of her blazer thus signaling the opening of the festivities. Dobbs shouted, "Attention." The crowd rose and the men removed their hats. The color guard marched smartly to present the waving flags of United States and a flag representing each service—Army, Navy, Marines, Air Force, Coast Guard, and the Merchant Marines. Mrs. Nelson began the Pledge of Allegiance. As the pledge ended with "liberty and justice for all," the band started playing the *Star Spangled Banner*. Everyone stood silently, but when the band began *God Bless America*, the crowd sang with thunderous voices.

"Welcome," began Mrs. Nelson. "Tonight is the final competition of the United States Armed Forces Scrapbook Contest. Winners from the display competition will be going to Florida courtesy of the US Air Force at Patrick Air Force Base. The first-place winner from the timed competition will be representing us at the International Armed Forces Scrapbooking Contest to be held in British Columbia, Canada, as guests of the

Royal Canadian Air Force. During the timed competition, judges will be scoring the table displays."

The competing teams assembled in a single line across the auditorium. The DC Regional team wore matching blue golf shirts, a red, white, and blue scarf, and khaki slacks. Each rolled matching suitcases with their supplies.

"As in regional competitions," explained Mrs. Nelson, "there will be a one-hour work session and a ten-minute mandatory rest break before the concluding one hour to complete the projects. Only one entry from each team may be submitted. Teams may choose to work individually or as a group. A refreshment table has been prepared for participants. Snacks for the crowd are available at the concession stand at no charge courtesy of the Red, White, and Blue Veteran's Center," she said glancing toward Dobbs. "Visiting with your teams during the mandatory break will result in your team being disqualified."

Dobbs nodded and Marine guards holding rifles took positions by the contestants' refreshment area.

"Before the beginning whistle is blown, it is my pleasure to introduce each team to enable the crowd an opportunity to express their well wishes. When the DC Regional Team was announced, Bonnie and crew yelled and cheered, and waved banners made from torn sheets. If the sudden decrease in the linen inventory came into question, she was prepared to deny total-knowledge.

"The judge's spokesperson will announce the theme for competition."

"Thank you, Mrs. Nelson and the DC region for sponsoring this year's competition. The competition theme is 'Home Everywhere'."

Mrs. Nelson held the whistle to her mouth and the crowd shouted three, two, and at one she blew the whistle and the ladies rushed to the assigned tables to begin. The timing of the event was predictable. At fifty-five minutes, Mrs. Nelson announced, "Five minutes." Once the five minutes passed, she announced, "Mandatory ten-minute rest break."

The cheerleaders and cheering squads took advantage of the interlude to support their teams. The room was pure chaos. Eight minutes later Mrs. Nelson's voice rang throughout the room, "Two-minute warning." At the one-minute warning the ladies stood by their tables ready to grab their tools stored in their suitcases of paper, ribbons, and photographs. The crowd called again, "Three, two, one" as the whistle sounded. The room went silent. During the last hour, Mrs. Nelson announced, "Thirty-minute warning," and she gave two other warnings at ten-minute intervals. Exactly at eight o'clock, she blew the whistle with the order, "Stop. Tools down." The auditorium stood and cheered, including Bonnie and her veteran's retinue who waved their custom banners.

"Without further delay, the judges are going to announce the winners of the table displays and the preliminary competitions, while entries submitted from tonight's competition are being evaluated."

"On behalf of the judges, thank you again, Mrs. Nelson, and the volunteers from the DC region. The extraordinary entries made our task quite difficult. As I read the winners, will the teams please assemble near the podium? The first award is for the overall table display. The winner is the DC Regional Team for their three-D construction of the Washington, DC skyline created from family pictures." The crowd applauded and whistled.

"For the theme, Way Out, the winner is the Alaska Military District. The breathtaking pictures of military training in the remote areas of Alaska were awe-inspiring. Included were photos of the Coast Guard Icebreakers lunging thru ice flows, US Army repelling team traversing the mountaintops in the Aleutian

Islands, and Armored cold weather drills in the shadows of Mount Denali."

"For the theme, Once Upon a Time, the winner is Jefferson Barracks at Lemay, Missouri, with a display of historical pictures of the cavalry from 1826 through present day showing pictures starting with the Horse Cav to the modern Air Cav. We also thank the Air Cav for flying the teams from the Midwest region as a component of a training mission."

"For the theme, Thru the Years, the winner is the Southeast Regional Command who featured stages of military life from recruitment to retirement. Theirs was a moving display, no pun intended, but the motorized display has set a high bar for future competitions, I'm sure."

"And for the theme, All for One, the winner is the DC Regional Team for their entry featuring a reunion of twins separated at birth. Both men are in the service, and their wives met at a preliminary scrapbooking competition and realized their husbands looked similar.

The crowd erupted with wild screams and cheers. Everyone was on their feet. The wooden retractable bleachers shook.

"Thank you, judges. This year, commanders of the regional teams have offered to sponsor a trip for one of the competing teams. Sargent Major, would you do us the honor of drawing the names?"

"Yes, ma'am!" Spontaneously, the band started a drumroll as he reached into the two bowls. Cymbals sounded as the names were read teasing the sargent major. He turned to look at the band behind him and they responded with quirky mischievous grins. "Team Alaska Region, grab your suntan oil, you'll be traveling to the Southwest as guests of Fort Sill, Oklahoma."

Ka-boom, rang the cymbals.

"Team Midwest has won a trip to the Northwest as guests

227

of the US Coast Guard Base Seattle." Drums ta-ta-ta-ta! The cheers and laughs of the crowd nearly drowned the dominating voice of the sergeant major. He prevailed and gestured toward the band as he announced each of the winning teams, "The DC region will be traveling to Fairbanks, Alaska, as guests of Fort Wainwright; Northeast Team, pack your bags for the Midwest as guests of National Guard at Camp Dodge; Team Northwest will be traveling to the Southeast as guests of Fort Benning, Georgia; Team Southwest will be hosted by the DC region, the Pentagon, and bases in the Capital area; and Team Southeast will be going to the Northeast Region as guests of Naval Submarine Base New London at Groton, Connecticut.

The band played a rapid flourish.

"The sponsoring commander will coordinate travel and accommodations to the other commanders," added Mrs. Nelson. "I'm sure the sponsoring teams will arrange your visit with superb sites of interest.

The judges have signaled they have a decision. I'll relinquish the program to the chief judge to announce the winner of the trip to Patrick Air Force Base in Florida. The announcement will conclude the program for tonight. Enjoy the refreshments. Thank you for coming and supporting our military families."

"And be careful driving home," reminded Dobbs as the chief judge walked toward the microphone.

"Thank you, again, Mrs. Nelson and Sargent Major Dobbs. On behalf of the judges, it is my pleasure to announce the grand winner for their depiction of the theme, Home Everywhere. The winner is Team Midwest featuring a collage of Iowa National Guard families at worldwide duty stations. They will be representing us at the international competition. Congratulations to everyone."

The crowd rushed to the floor. Teams hugged. The band

started playing favorite military marches. Overhead the balloons were released filling the room with patriotic red, white, and blue. Once the celebration started, the team moved through the balloons toward the door and to home for soft-serve ice cream at the Veteran's Center.

Chapter Thirty-One

Randy met her and her escort on the patio. "Where's my ice cream? How was the contest?"

"DC won the All for One theme competition featuring the Brown families, and the team drew a trip to Alaska on the commander's drawing. The Midwest Region took the grand prize featuring photos of the Iowa National Guard deployed around the globe and will be going to the international competition in Canada."

"Fantastic!" He couldn't wait to call friends in Iowa to hear the details. "Let me pour you a bourbon and water?"

"Sounds wonderful." She scooted back into the overstuffed couch and put her feet up. Baby Kitty found her hands to get her ears scratched. While she was waiting she looked around and in horror she saw it. Why hadn't she seen it before?

"Randy. When was my apartment decorated? Who knows of the escape routes?" Her voice was getting louder, her frenzied tone was increasing. Suddenly her stomach felt queasy and a wave of nausea engulfed her. She didn't usually react viscerally to events. Southern women were supposed to be calm and gentile, well-mannered, and gracious.

Randy seemed overtaken by her abrupt questions and surprised by her rapid transformation of demeanor. "We decorated your apartment, the apartment next door, and the office several weeks ago, two or three days before you arrived in DC. Until you moved in, Charlie was in the building by himself. In fact, the other three apartments were unfurnished. Why do you ask?"

"Randy, was Charlie in his apartments while the workers were here?"

"No, he's been traveling," replied Randy. "What's wrong?"

"Randy, the fabrics used in this apartment are the same décor I saw at the spa. The same Chippendale chairs with the same upholstery, the same tables. I saw the same patio design in one of the guest wings." She could tell he wasn't making the connection. "You remember when I secured the contract at the Georgia spa at the last minute and they wanted me there immediately, and where Miller brought Charlie when he was shot because I suggested it? Randy, I have to sit down. I'm going to be sick."

Quickly Randy pointed her toward the bathroom door under the stairs.

When she emerged, Bonnie was wiping her face with a wet cloth. Her hair was wet at the temples.

Randy asked, "Are you okay?"

"Yeah. Too much scrapbooking, I guess."

"Talked to Frank; he said to give you a few minutes. He's running a background check on the decorator. Carrie's commander is sending her to Fort Myers in Virginia tonight under armed escort, and will orchestrate the paperwork for her official transfer in the morning. There's too much public access at the strip mall. While you washed your face, Frank had a chopper from Fort Benning fly to the spa and deploy an invasion team on the grounds. It's still deserted. They had looked at the property after Charlie was there. This trip the buildings are empty; even the power has been cut and the furniture is gone. Wainwright from the FBI is bringing in a forensics team in the morning. I doubt they'll even find a fingerprint or a stray hair. Damn! Grab Baby Kittie, Frank's invited us for coffee."

"What? I have to find Baby Kittie's carrier. It's here somewhere," she said as her tortoiseshell calico weaved in and around her feet. She could hear the panic in her voice.

"No!" Randy yelled. "No, no," he restated his command is a slower, even tone. "Leave everything, except for Baby Kittie, of course. She's a seasoned traveler. Leave everything in case someone planted another tracking device. Depending on what Frank recommends, we can purchase things along the way."

Her uneasiness continued.

Armed community members were arriving as Bonnie and Randy retreated to a dented Chrysler at the side office entrance. "We have to wait until the decoy team leaves in your Jeep." She, Randy, and the driver said nothing, Baby Kittie as well. No headlights were used. The driver drove down dark roads with a mask of bug-eye goggles. At the junkyard, Randy retrieved a key from his wallet to unlock the metal gate leading to a dark lot of rows of eviscerated vehicles. She recognized Frank's profile holding a chunky cup in the open doorway.

"Ma'am, glad you're home." Frank was calm, but he was always calm. "Welcome to our Virginia field office."

Inside the building she felt she was in the mechanic's shop at the Ranch at Bay Branch: oil pits, shelves of parts, overhead chains and pulleys—whatever was needed to fix, repair, or fabricate parts for the tractors and farm equipment. "I'm charmed with the decorating. Anything planned for those oil cans thrown in the corner? I was thinking chandeliers."

Frank smiled but ignored her comments and motioned them

to follow down a narrow hall past dirty walls, past the smelly men's room. The aroma was foul with paper towels on the floor; it was the kind of place her mother told her to avoid. They walked into the ladies' room, which looked equally deplorable. Frank closed the door. Even Baby Kittie objected to the smell and jumped into her arms. Randy didn't seem surprised. She and Baby Kittie followed his lead. He moved a tattered framed picture of a cat, and the wall slid behind a panel. They walked into an elevator. He pushed the button marked "3" but she felt the elevator was moving slowly downward into the basement. Suddenly, there was jolt and the elevator door slowly revealed a clean, spotless room. Behind a glass partition a man in a headset sat at an elevated station with multiple phones. He gave a friendly wave. She'd seen his face before. He activated buttons on a computer keyboard and another panel opened into a living room decorated like a set in a Western movie. She expected John Wayne to swagger from the kitchen carrying a bottle of bourbon. Frank motioned for them to sit at a round wooden table near the river rock fireplace. "Coffee? I can prepare you an iced coffee with cream," he said and paused.

"You wouldn't have any Wild Turkey, would you?" Baby Kittie jumped off her lap and curled in the corner of the deep leather couch.

"I hear you came to lodge a complaint concerning the décor in your apartment?" he teased.

"The decorating is the same I saw at the spa in Georgia where they brought Charlie after he was shot."

"Our people are running the film from the hidden cameras we used when the decorators were in the apartment. We ran faces against the AFIS computerized software, but found nothing from facial recognition; same for fingerprints. Many agencies lack the technology to log fingerprints in the US system, especially international police agencies. Randy inspected for bugs before and after the crews left. We even ran drug-sniffing dogs and a team of dogs trained in locating ammunition each morning and after the workmen left. After the possum episode, we ran the routine again. Everything seemed okay."

She wasn't sure Frank was making the connection with the decorating and the spa. "I adore the decorating, honest I do. Thanks for featuring my grandmother's French provincial bedroom suite and her baby grand piano. The pieces reminded me of home as soon as I saw them. Things have been busy lately. Truthfully, you've had me jetting here and there and I hadn't had time to sit in the living room and enjoy the décor until tonight. It took me by surprise when I realized I'd seen the combination of fabrics and furniture before at the spa in Georgia. How many Asian chests could resemble the one in the piano room? It is an old, old, enormously expensive imported antique."

"Tell me again the details of your trip to China. You told me when we were traveling somewhere between Yellowstone and Bellingham as we were rushing to transport Charlie to Russia, but refresh my memory and it may provide missing information for Randy."

"You suspect this is somehow related to my investigation of the *Ceratitis capitata*, the Mediterranean fruit flies? But I went to China months ago. It would be a real long shot to link my trip to China with the Chinese décor, wouldn't it? Was the decorator Chinese?"

"Well, her name was Sue something, I'll check my notes. She was thin with long dark hair. She had a generic look, but I guess she could have been Asian," added Randy.

"Back to the fruit flies," urged Frank.

"The request for me to go came as a complete surprise. There were many entomology experts at the Citrus Research Station who could have gone, but USDA wouldn't approve the change when I called. Nevertheless, in collegiate camaraderie the researchers gave me a detailed orientation on the flies and I caught the evening flight. It was a hasty trip with a combination of commercial and private flights. The Chinese port quarantined the rusty freighter when a cloud of fruit flies covered the docks. I wanted to quickly record the observations so fruit from other shippers could be released for sale. Every day the fruit quality declines. I was there within twenty-four hours to collect samples and take pictures. When I gathered the evidence USDA had requested, I grabbed a cab and returned to the airport. I was waiting for the afternoon flight but received a page from the embassy to catch a chartered flight. I wrote the report on the plane home. I was on the ground in China for only a couple of hours."

"JoAnne was looking into Sun'Luk Produce Company. They have offices in the same Chinese port. Do you recognize the name?"

"No, but I wondered why I was chosen to go. I assumed maybe JoAnne had pitched me to USDA. Earlier in the week we had talked on the phone and I'd mentioned I was between contracts. The consulting fee was delightful. But when I told her of the trip, she wasn't aware of my travel out of the country."

"You traveled on your own passport?"

"Yeah? It lists the post office box address at Illahaw. It was before I started hanging out with your crew and your creative resources."

Frank smiled. But his lips were tight as if he wanted to tell her something. He closed his eyes and lowered his head. He massaged his temples and twirled his finger urging her to continue.

"The USDA inspection seals were intact, but I discovered a shiny welded repair on the starboard side of the boat which was in the same area as the fruit-fly larva, and the same area I found the flimsy poor-quality packing boxes. No grower would have ever utilized such substandard cardboard containers to ship fruit over such a long distance and risk damage to the fruit. If the fruit was squished or bruised, the poor arrival quality would lower the price."

"Yes. I remember you'd sent your report to Mr. Stone at USDA, days before he died in a car accident."

"On our road trip, I was uncomfortable when you told me Stone died under mysterious circumstances. I think I mentioned it before, after I arrived home from China, I made a few phone calls to track down the boxes. I can't positively say they were the exact boxes I saw in China on the ship, but I was able to track a huge order of fruit-packing cartons delivered by air freight to a teeny island in the Philippines days after the boat left the port at Tampa. Coincidentally the island was located on the shipping route from the Panama Canal to China. On the island there was one warehouse for an import/exporter produce shipper and a two-mile runway, which seemed unusually long for an insignificant fishing village. Someone could land a jumbo jet on such a huge runway. I wasn't able to find the corporate name."

"We have the resources to track down those details." A staff member handed him a note.

"Did they issue an 'All Clear'?" asked Bonnie.

"Yep. You thinking of returning to the condo?"

"Of course, if everything is safe. I'm supposed to do the grocery store teaching lab tomorrow. Besides, I didn't bring Baby Kittie's cat nibble." As if on cue, Baby Kittie ran and pushed her paw against the bottom kitchen cabinet and a door opened with a bowl of nibbles on the bottom shelf. "Well, there goes my excuse to go home. But I'm fine. The decorating rattled me. Thanks for inviting me for coffee, Frank."

"My pleasure." He handed her an envelope and winked. "To open later." She tucked it in the back pocket of her black jeans with zippered pockets.

"Bonnie, we're going to leave by another exit," motioned Randy. Baby Kitty scampered toward the door. "Follow the cat."

Randy and Bonnie laughed nervously during the entire ride to the condo. Baby Kittie snuggled on to her lap and licked her hand.

*****

"Randy, you don't have to walk me into the house. I'm fine. Honest!

"Oh, come on. Management wouldn't forgive me if zombies had invaded while we were gone."

Chirp, chirp. Bonnie heard Randy's radio. He motioned for her to stand still. "Did you approve the delivery of some chairs?"

"What chairs?" she answered.

"The decorator is at the gate to deliver the remaining furniture. The guard told her he needed to check if you were home. This doesn't seem right, the furniture being delivered this late in the evening, and within minutes after we arrived. The guards are escorting the truck on foot, giving us some time."

"Randy, can't we go? Can't we sneak out through one of the tunnels? This is unnerving. I'm sorry I insisted we come back. Please, let's leave."

"If we can secure prisoners, we can figure out why they're following you. An emergency team is coming through the tunnels. We're staging a party. You have the apartment championship volleyball team coming to protect your honor, madam. Come on. We'll be fine," he cajoled. "They're simply furniture movers. We have the element of surprise." He slowed his voice, "Seriously, put Baby Kittie in the carrier and go upstairs. The floors are reinforced. You should be safe unless…"

237

Bonnie interrupted, "No details. Baby Kittie and I should be fine." Randy was planning events in his head. She hoped his crystal ball was working.

"Where are your guns hidden? Can't be caught cold if one of movers reaches behind a pillow and grabs a weapon during our discussion?"

"None in the piano room. I took one of the guns hidden in the kitchen; there's another in the bread box by the refrigerator. There's one in the back of a pot of begonias in the front courtyard and behind the white orchids, one on each side of the patio. There's one in each section of the bookcases behind the antique baskets. There's loaded ammo magazines in practically every drawer. Upstairs, there's…"

"Okay, we could defend off an attack by Attila the Hun. It's probably nothing, but until we assess the situation, can you and Baby Kittie hide upstairs? Please don't place me in a position to explain why something happened to you on my watch."

"Baby Kittie wouldn't let her best friend be in trouble. Come on, Baby Kittie." She found the carrier in the hall closet and nearly bumped heads with the first guy emerging from the basement. He wore a pair of sweatpants torn off above the knees and a stained blue T-shirt, long enough to hide a gun. He carried a six-pack of beers. She grabbed her backpack and headed upstairs. Out of habit she stuffed a few things in her bag and looked around the bedroom to determine the best position away from the stairs and doorways. She decided to sit on the shower floor behind the tiled half-wall. Baby Kittie was ready to pounce on the attacker if Bonnie opened the carrier door. She gave a demure hiss, as if confirming Randy's instructions. She mumbled, "Baby Kittie, we're playing hide-and-seek." She felt ready; scared as hell, but ready. It was different waiting for events to unfurl than reacting to spontaneous events occurring around her. She checked the

Glock and moved a shell into the chamber.

The smell of popcorn in the microwave drifted to the second floor. Randy arrived upstairs making one last inspection. "When the furniture movers arrive, I'll holler for you. Answer back you'll be down in a few minutes. Tell me to have the movers put the chairs somewhere in the front room near the piano. It has the best tactical position. We can come at the movers from two doors. I'm gonna turn on the stereo to set the stage, but I'll turn it off once the movers enter the house. Hopefully, with the beer cans sitting around, they'll assume they've caught us off guard, but we'll have the advantage."

"Sounds like a plan!" She tried to sound enthusiastic. What else could she say? She was increasingly uneasy with the events. She wished they had stayed at the junkyard.

"Are you okay using your gun? We didn't get you scheduled at the target range," he whispered. But before she could answer, she heard the music. His radio chirped. "Security's telling us there are two men in the cab of the truck, and in the SUV are a lady and a man. The guards didn't observe other passengers, but we're prepared. We have ten people downstairs," he said quietly. "We've locked down the compound and activated the passive door locks in case the movers are a diversion." His spider legs rapidly propelled him down the stairs.

"Baby Kittie, did you get the orientation tour of the passive security system? It wasn't on my tour," she grumbled.

"Meow!" expressed the cat with one sharp mew.

Three men, each carrying an upholstered chair, followed the woman into the condo. They had to skirt the partiers dancing with beers in their hands. Bonnie tiptoed to the front bedroom and looked out the window toward the parking lot. Several security cars had surrounded the delivery truck eliminating their escape. Her eyes were wide. The logo on the truck read, "Sun'Luk

Transport." That's the company Frank had asked her about at the field office. Why would a fruit company be delivering furniture? She'd hurried to return to her bath location when Randy hollered announcing the arrival of the furniture, and according to the script, she loudly called down to "leave the chairs in the front room." There was a shrill shout from a female voice, gunfire, and a shuffle followed by "All Clear." She leaned against the banister and saw two of the movers on the floor. Their fixed glazes told her they were dead. The third mover and the decorator were being searched in the hall. Bonnie felt the floor shake beneath her feet. She lost her balance when hit with an explosive force of hot air. She landed against the rigid corners of the carpeted stairs. Splinters of wood, springs, and clumps of cotton from the overstuffed furniture showered the room through the gaping hole beside the fireplace where the thick double doors used to be. In the dust and confusion, a giant hand grabbed the cat carrier and scooped her off the steps. Seconds later, a second blast propelled them to the first floor. She landed on her shoulder, covered with dust and shreds of wallpaper. Baby Kittie yowled.

Bonnie was stunned. She heard Randy talking on a radio in slow-motion as he shoved her toward the sliding glass paneled doors. "Yeah, Simmons has a broken arm, maybe a shoulder. Lewis has a nasty head wound, but she's lucid; blood is everywhere. Allen is breathing, but isn't moving. Three movers and the decorator are dead. Damage on the building? The blast cracked the bulletproof windows between the dining room and patio. Yeah, send the bomb-sniffing dogs in case we've missed something. She's okay. I'll check if she's okay with the travel plans. You're right. She can't stay here tonight."

She felt dizzy. "Randy. Randy. I saw the Asian lady in Seattle! She departed the plane in Seattle." Bonnie fixated on the piercing eyes of the young Asian girl dead at her feet, blood oozing from

240

her nose and mouth. They were the same dark almond eyes that haunted her from the plane. "Randy, the truck in the parking lot is from Sun'Luk Transport."

Randy nodded his head, listening to somebody on his radio. "Do you and Baby Kittie mind catching the sunrise at the beach?"

"The beach? We love the beach." Her focus was returning. Overall, she was fine — no obvious broken bones, no blood — but she felt light-headed. "I'm supposed to do the grocery store lab in the morning at the diet clinic."

"It's a go!" Randy told the person on the radio. He turned to Bonnie. "Wheels up in ten. We'll send a message to Dobbs. Official story is you've been sent to another assignment. But grab Baby Kittie. I have to find you another holster. I can't have you waving the Glock around willy-nilly."

She'd forgotten she still held the gun in her hand.

*****

Bonnie took a deep breath to gather her thoughts. She was still woozy and unsteady. She blinked her eyes hoping to clear her vision. Randy pushed her and Baby Kittie through the ramshackle apartment, across the living room, and at the same time told her to step gingerly through debris from the explosions. He grabbed her arm now pulling her faster and faster toward the patio doors. A sudden stream of air rushed past her face. She caught the motion of a blur as if it was in slow-motion. The bullet shattered the glass doors beside her, cutting Randy's hand, spattering her face and clothes with his blood. Flashes of gunfire lit the tree line on the remote side of the cow pasture. Shots were returned from behind her, from the open patio door. Randy's grasp on her arm tightened and dragged her to the dark shadows around the building's corner. He shoved her against the wall as faces from the party moved past them slinging rifles under their arms.

241

A dark minivan skidded to a stop seconds later. There were no lights. The side doors were open. The seats were gone. A young woman in crisp fatigues was at the wheel. Her chestnut hair was pulled into a bun. A headset covered her ears. A microphone floated in the air near her mouth resembling those used by rock stars at outside concerts. Randy and Bonnie leaped inside carrying Baby Kittie's carrier. Men dressed in black with hands on stubby guns hung on the door openings. The driver spun the tires between two buildings. A third explosion lit the sky.

"Randy, did you see the truck? Sun'Luk Transport was painted on the side of the truck. It seems odd the bombs exploded minutes after the movers were in the house. Were the bombs on timers or were they detonated by someone onsite? Why would anyone attempt to kill us, the movers, and the decorator?"

Randy's glare seemed to focus beyond her.

In minutes they were in the field behind the condo. Red Hereford cattle with furry white faces watched the commotion, pausing briefly as they browsed dew-covered grass as if the frantic events were routine. The van pulled into a fenced area in the middle of the pasture. Lights on top of the fence-posts briefly flashed once marking the landing pad as a green military helicopter landed. Randy nudged her. She grabbed the cat carrier. Bonnie rushed behind him into the chopper. The door slid closed as it lifted off. Ground time had been a handful of seconds. Darkness and cows reclaimed the pasture.

Someone threw her a green bag of first aid supplies to wrap Randy's hand. She had him bend his arm and lift his hand near his ear to slow the bleeding. She wrapped the bandages loosely to capture the steady drops of blood. She suspected glass remained in the wound, or at minimum the wound needed stitches. Seeing the blood sharpened her focus. She mentally prepared herself to suture his cut, if no medical personnel were available when they landed. Minutes later, they offloaded at a rusty corrugated aluminum maintenance building. Above the weathered wooden door, a lopsided hand-painted sign read, "Welcome to Quantico US Marine Base."

She looked a sight toting a cat carrier and dressed in a blood-splattered shirt. She probably wasn't the usual traveler who disembarked from a military helicopter, but she smiled politely, as if they were expecting exactly her. She followed Randy into a small office, crowded with three. Randy gave her a signal as he introduced her to the transportation coordinator reminding her of their situation in case the blast had caused momentary confusion. "*Bonnie*, meet Captain Reeves. We have a few hours to wait before departure. Captain, you care if we sit by the pallets of cargo?"

"Go ahead. First aid supplies are in the cabinet. If you're hungry, I have crackers in a box on the bottom shelf of the bookcase. The vending machines have been empty since the hospital started a 'Be Healthy, Be Strong' campaign on base. Surely, if they're going to pull the sodas, they'd at least replace them with apple juice or diet drinks, water, or something. Maybe I should count the number of people through here when the base café is closed and offer a few suggestions."

She made a mental note. She could send a note to the base commander. She realized, of course, she couldn't send a note; she was never there. There were different rules in her new life with Charlie. Baby Kittie purred when Bonnie unzipped the hand slots. She could hold the cat and the kitty remained confined in the carrier. She jerked when she felt Randy shaking her shoulder.

"*Bonnie? Bonnie?*" Randy repeated. "Captain Reeves is getting us a flight medic. Best to stay awake until we ensure you don't have a concussion. You took a nasty fall down the stairs."

It took a minute to realize Randy was calling her "Bonnie," her cover name, Captain Bonnie Watkins issued at the US Embassy in Moscow. She had to respond appropriately. "Oh, I'm sorry, I guess I dozed off," she replied. "I hadn't considered having a concussion."

"They're fueling our aircraft. We'll be leaving soon," said Randy. "If you want to wash your face, the ladies room is on the far wall. They found you a thigh holster. I'll sit with Baby Kittie, if it's okay."

Bonnie threw some water on her face and washed her shirt in the sink to remove the splattered blood. She stood in her bra while the blow-dryer dried her blouse. The mirror wasn't sympathetic. Bruises were starting to appear where she had hit the stairs. Her chest was tender, but nothing seemed broken. She hated to admit her mother maybe was right. She needed to act like a lady and avoid the tomboy activities. The ladies room offered toothbrush kits and collapsible hairbrushes along with lip moisturizer, cosmetic samples, first aid supplies, and other assorted personal items. She grabbed a few things and stuffed them into the zippered pockets on her slacks. She'd lost her backpack in the explosion. She wondered where the women were going who had been in the room before. She wondered if they had also looked at their bruises. There was a wall of private showers and dressing rooms, which were tempting. Once she returned to her clothing, she wished her reflection was as vibrant as the blue no-iron, drip-dry travel shirt she'd changed into during the staged midnight celebration when the furniture arrived.

She remembered the envelope she'd stuck in her back pocket of her dark slacks. She unfolded the gray-lined notepaper.

Sweets, I wish I could be there to hold you, kiss you, and wake with you in my arms. Soon we will be together, I promise. Be patient, it won't be long. I love you and always have. C.

244

CHAPTER THIRTY-TWO

"What? You're sure she's okay?" asked Charlie.

"Maybe a minor concussion. We'll have her checked when they arrive at Quantico. Randy said she was asking if the explosion was remotely detonated. She gave us a clue indicating the logo on the side of the furniture delivery truck was Sun'Luk Transport. JoAnne found a file on Sun'Luk Produce in the office of the agent you found dead in Mexico. You may be right—the attacks on Montana may relate to her China trip.

Charlie chuckled out of range of the phone receiver. He was proud of her.

"My guess is she's okay except for the notion of being in another explosion. We'll give her a busy schedule with little time by herself to contemplate recent events."

"Frank, keep working on the China angle. Transfer the mall property to the national veteran's group immediately to provide distance. Bring the other three locations on line as soon as possible. Put signs on the buildings if nothing else. Send some of our crew to sit at tables with nutrition brochures. Someone is bound to investigate the explosion, and Bonnie's identity could lead them to the outpatient clinic. Use the accounts in Nevada. We have a solid cover story on where the money came from. Who's listed as signers on the account? They can transfer the deeds to the veteran's organization. Their corporate office is in Kansas City, Missouri. Backdate the paperwork, but have the guys deliver the papers today."

"From the get-go, Dobbs buried Bonnie's assignment at the clinic during preparation for the move at Walter Reed," responded Frank. "We have her listed as personnel at the State Department, which doesn't know her from Adam's house cat. She signed in and out on the official visitor's log which will leave a record. We arranged for her to visit friends during her tour at the State Department. They should curtail interest if anyone tries to track her through them. She's been out of the country, which is helpful, and flew on military aircraft to support an anonymous mission through the State Department. They'll give their standard reply regarding overseas personnel: they'll neither confirm nor deny.

"Catch you in South Carolina. Out."

CHAPTER THIRTY-THREE

Randy was on his radio when she returned. The flight medic was wrapping his hand with white bandages. Her triage was correct: there was glass and the wound needed stitches. The medic motioned for her to sit, and in two seconds, he shined lights in her eyes, gave her a brief thumbs-up, and was gone. Randy's other arm was in Baby Kittie's carrier rubbing the feline's ears. "Curious news on the furniture movers and sniper. The death from the explosion at the entrance has been confirmed to be a Chinese gentleman. He was waiting outside the gate in a black limousine with diplomatic plates. The boys from Alcohol, Tobacco & Firearms are all over this. Shots fired at a State Department employee and the death of a diplomat is taken pretty seriously. We wounded the sniper who was in the tree line; he's apparently the sole survivor. The redecorating project is more complicated than predicted." He lightly chuckled. In a whisper, "We're wondering what we've stumbled onto."

Bonnie responded in a quiet voice. "Randy, you said the man who died at the gate was Chinese? Frank keeps asking me for details of my trip to China and seems convinced the recent events has something to do with the fruit fly trip, but why would someone target me?"

Before she could complete her sentence, Randy responded. "We moved your things to a storage area. Don't be surprised when your nutrition consulting company has a new address at another office/apartment complex. Carrie can live there and there's room for the company files. To repair the damage to your condo, we'll have to order additional bulletproof windows from a glass factory in Fostoria, Ohio. After the possum attack I'm on a first-name basis with their sales office. Carrie went with me last trip. You would've loved the glass museum there. You've probably realized you can't go back to the condo," quietly added Randy. He had an apologetic tone.

"I know, but I liked the condo. I was fond of seeing cows in the backyard. It reminded me of home at the Ranch at Bay Branch."

"Note to file—next place for you and Charlie has to have cows!" he teased.

"Randy, the design of the DC apartment was ingenious. The space was completely defendable if attacked. Your design saved my life. In the repairs, are you proposing modifications for your designs?" she asked trying to move to a big picture perspective.

"I've been evaluating the design and will probably increase the reinforcement in the ceilings and around the windows. For the openings around the fireplace, I'd planned for an assault from outside and hadn't planned for an explosion from inside the house. The explosion was relatively minor as explosions go, but it shredded the metal doorframe into gigantic projectiles and gutted the upstairs bedrooms. You were lucky you were on the stairs. I'm going to dust off my Bethlehem Steel tables to recalculate building materials to improve our defenses. I can guarantee it'll be totally possum-proof." He tried to lighten the conversation.

"Randy, you amaze me. Do you miss being an engineer?"

"Well, it's nearly as much fun destroying things as building them. Frank wants me to be your assistant, if you approve. You'll have to teach me a few key words to blend in."

"Baby Kittie thinks you'll do fine; she isn't this friendly to everybody. You should probably talk to Carrie. She's the best assistant I've worked with."

Randy blushed but before he could say anything he was rescued by Captain Reeves, who signaled preflight was complete. She was the last person to board. Captain Reeves handed her a dark long-sleeved sweater with padding on the right shoulder. "Miss, pull the collar of your blouse under the sweater. This flight is going in under blackout conditions." He handed her a handful of loaded clips for her Glock. "Bonnie, Frank asked me to remind you to check the weapon. Come back and visit if you are in the area. We have a local museum on base and the O' Club makes a grilled rib eye which will melt in your mouth. Sorry, the vending machines were empty. Glad you're okay. And, ma'am, Marines call helicopters helos; the Army calls them choppers."

"Which am I flying on today?"

"Helos."

"Thank you, Captain. You've been extremely gracious," replied Bonnie. She remembered the note from Charlie. She wondered if Charlie had given her a subtle warning.

CHAPTER THIRTY-FOUR

From his office in the West Wing of the White House, he dialed a series of numbers. "I read the report. Congratulations to your team. How is Timmerman's replacement working out? Is he getting settled in? Do what you can to be helpful; not too obvious, of course. In the big picture, it will give you cover that Timmerman didn't have as the section chief. Once he was given the promotion, he was too visible; too many people within the system are assigned to support the position. You'll have more freedom. Give it time. Working with Sue Li's driver was a stroke of genius. We not only eliminated her, but Tao as well. Tao was starting to boast a little too much. He was getting to be too high-maintenance. Too many meetings, too many phone calls."

"Yes, of course, I can kill the investigation. We have to eliminate possible loose ends, but with the others who unfortunately died in the explosion, we have to tread carefully; be patient, my friend."

"Janice Brown and the crew at the Virginia condo simply vanished? Shift the focus to locate Smith. He was with her in Russia."

"Have you heard from your man who infiltrated the diet

office run by the new veteran's group? No word? ATF and the FBI are still working on identifying the bodies found at the hotel site in Luray. Any other time I would push to expedite the investigation. Preliminary findings are supporting the meth lab angle, which is good for us. Delays in the crime scene analysis could work to our advantage. In a couple of weeks, I'll push the Veteran's Affairs committee to provide funding for drug rehab programs for military service members. I'll let them connect the dots."

Speaking of the new veteran's group in Virginia, what Intel do we have on them? The surge of radical militant groups is an increasing threat to America's security. Run your theory by the new section chief, but take a closer look at them."

CHAPTER THIRTY-FIVE

The helo made a sharp turn to the left. Bonnie bit her lip to maintain her composure and cinched her seat belt tighter. The aircraft suddenly dropped. She had flown with crazy pilots when working in Alaska, but landing without lights was terrifying. For an instant the sudden descent had the sensation of an impending crash, but the helicopter landed firmly and in one piece.

Someone was yelling. Her hearing was muffled from the slow drum of the helicopter rotors above her. The other passengers quickly stood and pulled night goggles to cover their eyes and rushed through the aircraft door. Randy spoke briefly to the pilot as Bonnie and Baby Kittie climbed out, the last ones off. She scanned the horizon searching for clues as to their location. The sky was black. There were no lights, no landmarks, even the guiding stars were dark. The rotor blade whipped sand in her face. She could hear the fading of the rotors, but in the dark the helo vanished. Even the red and green running lights were off. She heard a whistle. Randy nudged her forward.

They walked briskly through scrubby plants brushing against her legs. The ground was shifting as her feet followed the path of the crew. The route changed. The trail became flat and moist under her feet. Seeing lighter skies in the east, she found her bearings. The air held a faint smell of fish. She could hear the softened roar of waves. She guessed they were traveling away from the sand dunes and were following a stream or walking on a sandbar. A few stars appeared on the horizon as the clouds cleared.

Silhouettes holding guns at waist height were visible against the pale skies of sunrise ahead of her. Baby Kittie perched at the mesh panel of her carrier to watch the path in front of them. If they were going to do this again, Bonnie was determined to find a cat carrier designed similar to an infant tote. She wanted one that had straps she could wear over her shoulders and would enable the kitty to view the path in front of them and leave her with both hands free. Periodically Baby Kittie gave a questioning mew. Bonnie answered back in a low, reassuring hum. The silhouettes helped her into a Zodiac inflatable skiff and gave her two flotation vests—one for her, the other for the cat carrier. She apprehensively kept her hand on the zipper ready to unzip the escape panel of the carrier if the boat capsized. She rubbed the side of Baby Kittie's face through the mesh. There were no hisses from the cat; she seemed to be informed of their covert mission.

A red flashlight was used to check a map in the twilight. Water lapped along the sides of the boat as they silently motored toward the sunrise. Ahead, a narrow strip of land emerged in the distance, perhaps an island. With day breaking, the sunlit determined faces streaked with camouflage paint. One of the squad looked at his watch and focused on a handheld device. The helmsman deftly guided the raft into a stream. The passengers ducked to avoid low limbs of cypress trees and cabbage palms. A clearing appeared behind a curtain of foliage. The young woman at the back of the skiff guided the boat skillfully to a narrow boardwalk. Others quickly tied the boat to the cleats on the dock's edge. She was pleased she was able to offload without falling into the swamp and at the same time cling to Baby Kittie's carrier.

The Marine at the helm remained with the boat and the life vests. The leader started down the narrow boardwalk above the tidal hammock. Bonnie and Baby Kittie kept close to the group. Morning fog was lifting off puddled water surrounding crusty cypress knees. Beams of light pierced the palm fronds creating dappled patterns on the wet ground below. Crabs scattered on their ten legs into round holes in the mud as the group of six trotted above them.

In the swampy terrain she felt at home. She mechanically followed the team feeling graceful and at ease in the familiar landscape. As a kid, she'd spent summers tromping around the cypress swamps along the Kissimmee River on her parent's Ranch at Bay Branch. There were flowers to pick, or berries to gather. In the fall there were armfuls of colorful maple leaves to create a centerpiece in a crock pitcher on the rough planked table in her grandmother's kitchen. She wanted to catalog the bromeliads hanging from the low limbs of the cypress and maple trees. She remembered the graphite drawings on vellum she saw in the European museums on a college trip. Making drawings of swamp foliage using the same technique would be an appealing project to fill her time during her visit. She remembered cypress trees grew in fresh water. Around a freshwater spring, she might even find wild orchids in a warm microclimate. She heard a Northern mockingbird announcing the sunrise, repeating the local bird calls in patterns of three.

The team worked off a predetermined course of action. She was enjoying the escape to the welcoming marshy countryside. She squinted as her eyes adjusted to the full morning sun when they emerged from the shady swamp. The team was moving toward a weathered two-story house with deep porches and a dull, rusty metal roof. Sand dunes buffered the house from a wide beach.

The leader raised a closed fist to signal for the group to stop. He motioned two of the troops forward, and crouched low to run across an exposed area to the cellar doors. One secured the doors and turned his body fanning the air with the tip of his rifle, gesturing the team down the steps. In seconds, he likewise waved for the rest to cross the yard to the basement. His feet were set a foot apart holding his rifle ready for possible hostile contingencies. He scanned the area around them. The Marines made wide swinging motions with their weapons, carefully overseeing the move toward the house. Somewhere Randy had acquired a slim gun slung under his shoulder. Oversized gloves hid the white bandages on his hand. With the armed security, she was apprehensive as they moved toward the house. For a few moments she'd felt safe in the swamp. She was comfortable with the threats lurking among the cypress trees at the Ranch at Bay Branch. Those were familiar dangers. What unknown risks were anticipated by her escorts as they approached the house? Randy nudged Bonnie holding Baby Kittie to proceed across the field. They paused and stood flat against the house until motioned down the basement steps.

The basement went dark when the Marines soundlessly closed the two wide metal doors behind them. A flashlight provided a thin pinprick of light. The leaders ascended the stairs on the opposite wall, squirted oil on the hinges, and quietly opened the door into a center hall. One motioned for Bonnie and Randy to advance. The others followed. A leader held a finger to his mouth for the team to maintain silence while they checked the doorways down the hall. They waved them to move ahead to a closed door.

As she walked into the room, someone yelled, "Happy Birthday!" There stood Charlie, Frank, Roger, and four Marines in green fatigues holding a birthday cake. On the top in pink frosting read, "Happy Birthday, Ms. *Bonnie.*"

Bonnie had completely forgotten her birthday. "I'm speechless! Y'all are so bad. I guess Baby Kittie was in on this whole clandestine charade. She didn't fuss, not once!"

"I fully briefed her on the mission last week," teased Charlie from the back of the room.

Bonnie grinned at him and began passing slices of cake to a crowd in black and green camouflage.

"Is this almond custard cake? It's my favorite," she said as she licked her fingers. "Y'all must be a bunch of spies to have uncovered my secrets?"

Everyone laughed. She'd given them a promotion. The recruit leader volunteered, "Ma'am, it was a training assignment to transport a civilian in blackout conditions. We didn't anticipate the cat."

"Or the gun," added another one of the recruits. "It caught us off guard. We'll anticipate unknowns on future missions. They probably won't serve birthday cake."

"Okay, Swamp Dogs," barked one of the officers. "Grab your cake and I'll meet you at the base for debriefing. Dismissed!"

"Semper Fi," responded the recruits.

As the recruits were leaving the room, the officer addressed Frank and Charlie, "Gentlemen, always a pleasure." Turning toward Bonnie, he continued, "It is a pleasure to meet you, Miss. Watch yourself with this crew. Holler if you or the cat requires a rescue!"

"Thank you, Colonel, for your hospitality," said Bonnie as she folded her hands together and bowed slightly.

Baby Kittie decided she had been confined long enough and began a meowing petition to join the party. "Baby Kittie, here's a bite of birthday cake?" Bonnie explained. "Baby Kittie and I have the same birthday. Isn't there some vanilla ice cream left?" The guys were moving toward the porch but Bonnie ran back to the kitchen and poured Baby Kittie a bowl of melted cream from the bottom of the carton. On the counter was a bag of kitty nibble, cans of kitty pate, and a box of butter, Baby Kittie's favorites. She grabbed one of the mismatched flowered bowls from the open shelves for water and saucers for the kitty's breakfast buffet. "Y'all want iced coffees?" she hollered from the kitchen.

"Yeah! Any bourbon in the kitchen?" drifted from the porch. She noticed long, metal coolers in popular Army green stacked against the wall near the back door. It seemed there were too many coolers for five people. The top one contained bags of ice, and right now, for iced coffee she only needed ice.

Looking at the layout of the house, she had time to examine the hallway leading from the kitchen across the back of the house. "Baby Kittie, no offense, but this space resembles an enclosed dogtrot, a design which acted as a wind tunnel to cool the house before air-conditioning."

Baby Kittie answered with her soft, "Meowwtt," as if she understood each word.

Bonnie peeked in the door beside the kitchen with Baby Kittie standing between her shoes. "Yes, a bathroom!" It was simple, but a welcome discovery complete with a kitty box.

She put on a pot of coffee to perk. The refrigerator was hooked to a tank of propane on top of the rounded frame. It was similar to ones in Unalaska/Dutch Harbor. Many families used propane-powered refrigerators, washing machines, and ovens in the Aleutian Islands. The pitcher pump by the sink was working and simple to manage. Sometimes water this close to the beach smelled swampy, but the water gushing from the spout was cool and fresh. It confirmed her suspicions the cypress trees behind the house were in a freshwater spring. A survey of the yard from the kitchen window didn't reveal power lines. She didn't spot candles or lanterns. She shrugged her shoulders. "We'll worry tomorrow."

Randy had mentioned an upcoming consulting project. She wasn't sure what her assignment was going to be. She hadn't a clue as to her location except at a beach maybe near a Marine base. But at the moment being in this house, she enjoyed the feeling of having been transported back to the simpler life of the 1800s. After the excitement of the last few weeks, she would appreciate a simpler schedule.

"Sweets, the coffee's boiling," said Charlie, walking to the kitchen.

"Oh, dear..." She sighed. "I can't remember the last time I truly 'made' coffee. Usually I simply push a button on a coffee maker. Thank you for everything. Things were scary," she said in a whisper, but before she could say anything else, Charlie put a finger to his lips motioning for her to be quiet.

Charlie was slow to answer. His voice was quiet barely above a whisper. "It seems the investigation of the explosion in your apartment isn't going too well. Our investigative team was at your apartment within minutes after we loaded you on the chopper. We were aggressive to preserve the evidence. We controlled the scene to prevent the State Department from denying the existence of the explosions. Of course, there were the four dead bodies, each Asian without visas. Our people ran fingerprints to identify the bodies and the people in the car. Remember your dad's friend where you vacationed at his Russian chateau?"

She was learning how Charlie's world worked; maybe she should follow his lead in minimizing perceptions of danger. "Vacation" was the last word she'd select to describe her trip to Russia, especially after she killed Timmerman at the general's chateau.

"He used their embassy resources to assist us on the identifications. Thankfully, it's difficult to remove gunpowder residue. Our team used High Performance Liquid Chromatogram scientific techniques to determine the composition."

"You're referring to HPLC?"

"I forget you took chemistry courses. The team obtained an exact match of the gunpowder from the explosives in your apartment, hands of the workmen, the car at the gate, and in the cargo hold of a private plane owned by the dead man in the car, as well as the explosives recovered at the hotel in Luray, Virginia. We were shocked The State Department had taken the position since the perpetrators are dead. Why pursue it? It's been less than twenty-four hours. The Chinese government has since proclaimed the Chinese gentleman as having ambassador status, and thus his vehicle and plane are considered embassy property which is creating a legal nightmare and threatens the validity of the collected physical evidence in court. We're told the decision went directly to the vice president's office. Frank wants to ensure we aren't missing anything. He thinks there's a lot of commotion concerning something they're treating casually," he responded in a slow quiet voice. "We hope this will be the last we hear from the Chinese. In the meantime, we're going to keep you off the radar."

"But..." questioned Bonnie. She wanted to ask why Timmerman's people were tracking her, and if Timmerman's people were still working with the Chinese.

"Sweets, with the experimental directional microphones, people can hear conversations a mile away, further with the right equipment. Before, you were in secure areas. There will be time to talk later." She didn't have to read between the lines. Charlie was telling her she'd have to postpone her questions. She pulled off the heavy dark sweater.

259

He lost his focus watching her remove her clothing, even if it was simply a sweater. He longed for spending eternity with her. "Oh, are you interested in knowing the status of the young officers named Brown? DNA confirmed the men are your relatives."

"I listened to the beginning of Dobbs' briefing to the Browns but had to leave before I heard the information. Dobbs hinted there was more."

"The Brown twins are being given honorary status as Lords of the Village of Featherlawn, England. Their mother was from the community and they have inherited what is left of the Addison family estate, as well as the proceeds from the New York attorney estate who provided care for their mother when she arrived by boat without proper paperwork. The attorney had no children and outlived his wife. He left his investments to the twin's father, Anderson Florida Brown, and future heirs, which are Colonel and Commander Brown. Somehow in the confusion of the death of their father during WWII, complicated by the attorney's early dementia, there are many loose ends. Frank and Dobbs retained a team of international attorneys on behalf of the twins."

"This means a lot to my dad and would have been appreciated by my granddad if he was still living. I'm glad for both families. This isn't going to shut down the Veteran's Center?"

"Hell no! Dobbs is in the process of opening three clinics with funding from a national veteran's group. You were mountain-climbing or sampling crumpets, you stayed busy, when the potluck was held for the group to survey the first clinic."

"You're referring to the Friday potluck? I wondered why Dobbs was involved with planning the dinner."

"He was eager to show the success of the clinic. In hindsight, it was probably advantageous you weren't there which would have tied you to the clinic. It maintains Dobbs as the point person. His history is less complicated than yours. The diabetes squad, they called themselves, created a rap song to show off their knowledge and announced the winners on the team competitions for blood sugars, weight loss, and exercise. Everyone loved the fans. Oh, Dobbs solved the mystery of the missing medical supplies."

"What did he find?"

"The volunteers were taking medical supplies to provide medical support to fellow veterans who were too ill to leave home to go to appointments, or couldn't schedule an appointment. We've going to look at options. Thanks for being there to listen and for uncovering a problem area where veterans need assistance."

She reached for Charlie's hand and swung their clasped hand between them, "Charlie, I'm smitten with your beach house. How did you ever find such a delightfully antiquated cottage?"

"A high school friend told me of this place. The title search indicates the land was originally deeded from the British government to several New England families when the Crown claimed the territory from Spain in 1763. Sections of the land are in the Federal Coast/Shoreline Preserve. We're near Savannah Island Marine Training Center. This location could be a security nightmare if in the hands of the wrong people. With the environmental shift in politics, owning coastal land is falling out of vogue with liberal East Coast families. I bought the house at a bargain price. Plus, I can't anticipate when I or a friend would fancy an extended holiday." He reached to rub her back and the purple bruises emerging on her hands and arms. "This cottage had been abandoned for years when I bought it." He leaned to kiss her; she leaned in closer. It was a sensual kiss, a long and tender kiss. "Let me carry the coffees to the porch."

"Y'all take cream or sweetened condensed milk in your coffee?" she hollered. Roger liked his "plain," she remembered. Charlie took cream, as she did. Frank and Randy both liked sweetened condensed milk. Baby Kittie scooted by her feet out the screen door to the wooden porch in a blur. She watched in amazement as her kitty rolled around on Charlie's bare feet, hopped in his lap, and perched on the wide flat arm of his rocker, the one toward the beach. Baby Kittie purred and blinked her large black eyes. Baby Kittie and Charlie seemed to be getting along. Maybe too well — Baby Kittie didn't adore just anyone.

The view of the beach was gorgeous from the wide veranda. Frank, Roger, and Randy seemed absorbed in conversation at the west end of the broad, shady porch. Bonnie sat in the rocker beside Charlie. He reached to hold her hand. They rocked gently in tandem on the slightly uneven, weather-beaten boards.

"Do you have plans for sunrise?" he asked as he leaned toward her with another kiss.

About the Author

Sassy Sue Abbott lives in Florida with her housemates, stray and rescued kitties. She's lived in Georgia, Washington DC, Germany, Africa, and Alaska, places that flavor her saucy books and stage her character JANICE BROWN'S romantic mystery adventures. She likes to bird watch, hunt wildflowers, and eat her way across the US and around the world. Sassy loves to fall in love.

www.ingramcontent.com/pod-product-compliance
Lightning Source LLC
Chambersburg PA
CBHW030247200626
46816CB00002BA/537